JITI

TO
GREAT
DESERT

CAVE OF DEATH
(KURA)

SUNRISE

TO GREAT WATER

KURA

KURA STREAM

KIJITO RIVER

PANDAYA MTO

DAUGHTER
OF KURA

DEBRA AUSTIN

A TOUCHSTONE BOOK
PUBLISHED BY SIMON & SCHUSTER

NEW YORK LONDON TORONTO SYDNEY

Touchstone
A Division of Simon & Schuster, Inc.
1230 Avenue of the Americas
New York, NY 10020

First Touchstone hardcover edition August 2009

TOUCHSTONE and colophon are registered trademarks of Simon & Schuster, Inc.

For information about special discounts for bulk purchases, please contact Simon & Schuster Special Sales at 1-866-506-1949 or business@simonandschuster.com.

The Simon & Schuster Speakers Bureau can bring authors to your live event. For more information or to book an event contact the Simon & Schuster Speakers Bureau at 1-866-248-3049 or visit our website at www.simonspeakers.com.

Designed by Ruth Lee-Mui
Map by Elisa Pugliese

Manufactured in the United States of America

10 9 8 7 6 5 4 3 2 1

Library of Congress Cataloging-in-Publication Data
Austin, Debra
   Daughter of Kura / by Debra Austin.
      p.   cm.
   "A Touchstone book."
   1. Prehistoric peoples—Fiction.   2. Africa—Fiction.   3. Religion, Prehistoric—Fiction.   I. Title.
   PS3601.U856D38   2009
   813′ .6—dc22   2008042058

ISBN 978-1-4391-1266-3

TO DAYTON

DAUGHTER OF KURA

Southeast Africa, half a million years ago

CHAPTER 1

*S*omething obscured the horizon. Dark billows smudged the boundary between earth and sky; shreds of amber streaked up from the crumpled, scorched savanna through the colors of a healing bruise. She stood up and squinted over the rim of the dry wash, brow crinkled. Was a distant fire roaring through the parched grass, driving antelope and lions before it? These kinanas, the last yams of summer, must be dug before fire destroyed them or winter rains rotted them. As she stared at the muddled hybrid of sky and savanna, the roiling mass of colors coalesced into the blank, thin faces of her younger brother and sister as they had looked after the food ran out last winter. Just a few more, she

thought, and rammed her digging stick into the cracked, unyield-
ing earth. Thunder growled, low pitched and barely perceptible,
and her eyes returned to the disturbed horizon. Only a thunderhead. No need to run. These kinanas will feed us this winter.

Sweat soaked her neck, and several more small yams landed in
the basket. Thunder grumbled again. A dusty breeze lifted her hair
and cooled her sweaty back as she stood up to stretch her cramped
hamstrings and survey the sky. Where the thunderhead mush-
roomed above a ridge to the north, two tall figures reached the
crest and stood for a moment, silhouetted against the pall of the
storm cloud. One outline had hair in a familiar shape, most likely
that of one of the nearby ukoos. The other's head, however, seemed
much too small and strangely round, as if its owner were disfig-
ured. Unnerved, she froze, breath held, and watched the figures
move east along the ridge and disappear. When they were gone,
she drank from her antelope-stomach water bag and resumed digging, her nape hair still standing on end.

Rumbles punctuated the afternoon. Greens, yellows, and pur-
ples seethed from the gray cloud anvil into the blue expanse before it. Haphazard, dirt-caked kinanas filled the basket as shadows
lengthened disobligingly fast. Plenty of time, she told herself as
she jammed in a final kinana. Plenty of time to get home before
dark. As she grabbed the basket handle, a pebble skittered from
a stand of tall mavue grass, and she flinched. A cane rat, bigger
than a baby, teeth sharp as flint? A painted wolf, disemboweler of
buffaloes? A spear-wielding stranger? Eyes and ears fixed on the
mavue, she rose deliberately, balanced on the balls of her feet. Ten
heartbeats, an excruciating eternity, passed.

The mavue twitched. An ocher streak with curved claws and
enormous yellow fangs exploded at her. Panic jolted through her;

every fraught muscle erupted. She roared, heaved the basket at the leopard with her left hand, and swung her digging stick over her head with her right. The heavy basket slammed into the leopard and parried his attack, yams flying in all directions. His claws only just missed shredding her throat, but she felt them slash through her left arm as she splintered her heavy stick over his head. The leopard staggered and backed away, snarling and shaking his head as if troubled by multiple visions of his unexpectedly fierce prey.

She bellowed again and brandished a sharp fragment of her digging stick with a trembling hand. The savanna disappeared— she saw only the leopard, heard only the rasp of her breath and her heart pounding in her ears. Deliberately, the cat circled, eyes intent on her throat, nostrils flaring at the blood streaming down her arm. She blinked, and the leopard sprang again. As she dodged to her left, she thrust her improvised spear into his trajectory. The jagged stick tore into his shoulder, and she jerked it back before it could break again. He twisted away, snarled at the bloody lance, and slunk back into the mavue.

With one eye on the tall grass and a hand on her stick, she inspected the gash that split her arm from shoulder to elbow. Blood soaked the hair of her arm and splashed into the last hole she had dug. The smell was strong and earthy, like a damp stream bank with an overturned slab of moss, the unmistakable odor of injury. Hyenas will scent that, even a morning's run from here, she thought, and she examined the stand of mavue, the thickets, the horizons for a reflection of an eye, a movement unexplained by wind. Temporarily satisfied, she turned back to the problem of hiding the blood. Can't waste drinking water for washing, she thought. She took the zebra-hide carrying strap from her water bag, pulled the edges of the wound together, and bound her arm with the strip of hide, holding one end of the strap in her teeth as she tied the knot. As she worked, the sound of a branch rasping against another drew her attention, and a moment later, a soaring raptor distracted her. Finally, the bleeding slowed to an ooze from the ends of the slash. She kicked dirt over her spilled blood and cleaned her arm as best she could with her tongue. That will have to do, she thought, hyenas or not. With a last look for signs of the dazed leopard, she scooped up the scattered yams and started north along the dry wash at a fast lope. Her eyes swept the mavue on both sides of the wash, flicking back over her shoulder at intervals.

The edges of the wash blocked all but a rare breeze, and sweat soon soaked her back and dripped off her face onto her chest, though shadows in the deeper parts of the wash made her shiver. The banks of the wash limited her view as well, but she knew she could run twice as fast over the flat, hard-packed earth in the wash as she could through the dried grass of the savanna, where an unexpected sinkhole in the limestone karst might break a leg, or send her tumbling into a cave. Although she was familiar with the land within a day's run of Kura, a new sinkhole could appear overnight, and so she kept to the wash.

A distant moan of wind echoed the whoop of a hyena. A predatory shadow pursued her, and the rhythm of her pounding feet quickened until she recognized the shadow's source, a scudding cloud. Pain like a smoldering cinder kindled and grew under the improvised bandage, and each heartbeat throbbed against the strap. As a distraction, she began to tell herself the traditional Kura stories she would tell at festivals one day, when she became Mother of Kura like her mother and her mother's mother.

She started with her favorite, about the mother's-mother's-mother who first wove reeds into a basket so that she could carry food to an injured child. Her imagination always supplied the face of her own mother for the hero of this story, and her own face for the injured child. The next one had once frightened her badly on a particularly dark winter night: rock hotter than fire oozes from a mountain and destroys a village. In this story, her eight-year-old brother and four-year-old sister became the children saved by their older sibling who leads them up a high granite outcrop. By the time she got to the tale of the mother's-mother's-mother who left her mother's shelter at Panda Ya Mto and built the first shelter at Kura, her pain was worse, but her mood slightly better. As she ran, an idea hummed through her thoughts. These stories are all about change—big, long-ago change—but their purpose is the opposite: to preserve tradition, pass on memories, explain how things happen. Remember what worked before, they said. It will probably work again.

She kept watch on the flat-topped cloud as it ballooned south. By the time she climbed from the dry wash and turned east to clamber along the base of a jagged gray-white ridge, the thunderhead had boiled over most of the sky and occasional fat raindrops raised tiny puffs of dust in front of her feet. The distant rumbling seemed closer, and she whiffed a sharp, disconcerting odor that reminded her of crushed pine needles. The tall grass became distantly spaced shrubby trees, and the ground grew rougher, with stretches of scree slowing her pace. When she stopped for a drink of water, the shadows of the rocks on the uplands above her stretched eastward like giant upraised fists, and she saw something feline slip into a cleft near the top of the ridge and several stone's throws behind her.

In spite of her throbbing arm and stiff legs, alarm quickened her pace. Rested, unhurt, and over even ground she could chase a gazelle for the hunters until it was exhausted, but today, her pace was nothing like a gazelle's. As she sped up, the leopard emerged from the scrub and scrambled over the broken terrain far above her, but she had the advantage of more even ground and kept well ahead of her pursuer. At the end of the ridge, the karst smoothed out into savanna and stretched north toward Kura, and she reckoned she could reach shelter by dark if only she could discourage the leopard. A flash, followed by a rumble, startled her, and the sporadic raindrops coalesced into a steady drizzle that made the fine taupe dust slippery.

Each breath tore through her chest now. Her eyes sought the quickest route and surest footing. Her ears excluded all sounds except the soft scrapes of rock shifting on rock above and behind her. The back of her neck prickled. Finally, the ridge to her left tapered off into yellow-brown grass that brushed her thighs and she risked a backward glance as she turned north, just in time to see the leopard leap onto a low tree branch just above her. A few round stones under her foot sent her sprawling forward. The kinanas rolled in all directions, and the last of her water spilled. Air knocked from her lungs, she struggled to her hands and knees, unable to make a sound.

Over her shoulder, she saw the black spots of the leopard's ginger coat shimmer in the last horizontal ray of the setting sun as he shifted his weight back and forth from one set of rear claws to the other. A wild, terror-driven explosion of energy erupted in her chest and sparked through her body to her fingertips. A desperate gasp flooded her lungs with air and she tried to scramble up, but before she reached her feet, she was knocked back to the ground, blinded and deafened by a crash with the force of a volcanic eruption.

Sometime later, she felt rain falling on her closed eyelids and opened them. Nothing new hurt, the sun was still setting, and the air seemed cooler. Her injured arm looked about the same, and the fall had only bruised her knees and hands. Plastered against her skin by the rain, her hair was too wet to bristle against the cold. The tree from which the leopard had been preparing to attack smoldered in the rain and generated a cloud of steam and smoke. A blackened carcass hung over one of the larger remaining branches. With a shudder, she expressed relief with a sound like water pouring from an upturned jug, gathered her water bag and yams into the basket, and ran north into the gathering dusk as fast as pain and fear could drive her.

As the rain and the light faded, she struck a familiar, well-trodden path. Her legs became stronger and the basket lighter, and her pace quickened. Soon the white heights of Kura's limestone outcrop appeared, dotted across its southern face with saffron-colored watch fires. When she judged herself near enough, she announced her arrival with a low-pitched, reverberating sound, like a deep-voiced, peculiarly persistent owl. A tall, dark brown form ducked out from one of the highest shelters, climbed a rock, and looked in her direction. A moment later, it sprang from the rock and sprinted toward her. She recognized her brother Thump, even taller than he had been two years ago, and with his much longer beard and hair now twisted into the style of the Panda Ya Mto. She squealed greetings and sped up the slope, pain and exhaustion forgotten.

He stopped a few feet from her and began to make the respectful signs usually made by a man returning to a village after his summer journey. She laughed, dropped her basket and stick, and grabbed him around the middle with her uninjured arm, mixing sounds for relief and greeting as if she were a stream squealing with pleasure. They broke apart and both began to gesture simultaneously. Two sets of hands flew as they formed words with their fingers, with an occasional sound to convey emotion.

"Don't be silly!" she signed. "You needn't act like you're here for the Bonding—you can't take a mate in your birth village."

"Snap, what happened to your arm?" he signed at the same time. "Let's wash off that blood before a lion comes after you."

Eventually, the torrent of words slowed and they began to pay attention to each other's words. Thump picked up Snap's basket and broken stick, and they walked toward the Kura stream where she could clean her wound.

"You're as tall as a white rhinoceros. A trader thought you had gone to the Panda Ya Mto people. Half the men in that ukoo must have been born in Kura. Don't you need to be there for the Bonding? What are you doing here?"

"Tell me your story first," he signed one-handed, "and then I'll tell mine."

The story of the leopard attack fluttered from her hands in the fading light, and Thump rumbled in the back of his throat with amazement and disbelief. When she reached the lightning strike, he gave a bark of astonishment, and then a gurgle of relief. They passed the origin of Kura's stream where it issued from the limestone just below the village, and then followed its bubbling course down a tiny ravine. Snap reached up and tucked in one of the felted coils of her brother's beard. "Nice twists. You only had rabbit fur on your face when you left." Thump glanced at her sideways, as if he suspected sarcasm. Apparently reassured, he straightened up as they walked on. She took a long look at Thump in the dusk. He was bigger, she thought, and his beard was more impressive. She tried to avoid staring at his now adult-size genitals by reminding herself that this was still the same older brother who had taught her to drive gazelles toward the hunters, who had helped check snares when it was not his turn, who had even been known to share his food. After his two-year absence, she was disconcerted by how she felt: oddly maternal, with a hint of the feelings that the older men induced in her.

When the stream slowed and widened into a pool, Snap untied her arm and waded in to immerse it in the water. Blood blossomed into the slowly moving water like a huge pink amaryllis. Snap imagined the pink-stained water flowing downstream, faster past the white limestone below Kura, where hyenas denned in the banks, and slower through the flatter savanna, where crocodiles imitated floating logs, to the Kijito river, a morning's walk to the south, and she hoped nothing would come in search of the source of the blood.

While she cleaned up, Thump recounted his experiences since he had left Kura. Two winters ago, the arrival of his adult beard had compelled him to leave the village in the spring with the other men to spend the summer traveling, hunting, and trading. Not allowed to seek a mate in his mother's ukoo, he hoped to find a mate in one of the nearby ukoos at the fall Bonding festival, but unfortunately, the women of both Panda Ya Mto and Jiti found him young and poorly supplied with tools, meat, and hunting skills. He spent the winter in an uneasy truce with several other young bachelors in a makeshift shelter near the Kijito.

The following summer, Thump's trading and hunting were more successful. That fall, he offered better gifts to the appealing women, and interested one called Dew, of the Panda Ya Mto people. She was healthy, slightly older than Thump, of medium rank, and with no living children, and when the Bonding of the Panda Ya Mto was celebrated, she chose Thump. Dew had twisted his hair and beard into the style of her ukoo and taught him the hoots to identify himself as Panda Ya Mto. When her brother described Dew, Snap noticed he had a partial erection and looked distracted, pleased, and a bit foolish, something like the way he had looked after his first successful hunt.

"Aren't you going back there this fall?" She grimaced as she freed a blood clot from her arm, and the wound gushed again.

"Of course. But I met someone interesting this summer, and I've brought him here to visit. I'll get back to Panda Ya Mto in plenty of time for the Bonding."

She frowned, which made her brow ridge even more prominent. "Where is he from?"

"Far away sunset-ward. He is called Bapoto."

She snorted. "Didn't his mother give him a real name?" The Kura called all children "Baby" until their fourth spring, when they received a Kura name, a sign similar to those for common sounds. Bapoto's name, on the other hand, meant nothing; it was not like any sign she had ever seen.

"They have different kinds of names there."

She finished washing her arm and rinsed out the strap she had used to bind it, and he helped her tie up her wound again. Around them, sepia and beige had faded to black and gray, and both scrutinized the shadows as they walked back to the shelters. Snap signed, "I'm a woman now. I can choose a winter mate at the Bonding."

He nodded. "Good, it's about time. You certainly look like a woman now." Snap wondered if her brother had been trying to avoid staring at her as well. "Is anybody interested?"

"There are more than a dozen men staying at the men's shelter already, back from their summer journeys. They all bring gifts to Chirp, because she is the Mother of Kura, but she never takes a winter mate anymore. Whistle gets something from most of the men, but she always chooses Meerkat. Not much for me." She tried to look pleased about gifts for their grandmother and mother, but her brother knew her too well and patted her shoulder.

"There will be more next fall. Men don't like to be chosen by the lowest-ranked woman in a household." Snap thought he looked patronizing and gave him a small kick to remind him which of them would be Mother one day.

The nearly full moon was rising as they neared Chirp's shelter. High on the Kura ridge, it faced southwest toward the Kijito. Like the other shelters of Kura, its walls were white limestone, shaped partly by nature and partly by generations of occupants. Antelope hides laced together with leather strips formed the roof. Often repaired and rearranged, the shelter seemed to have grown from the ridge, an aboriginal refuge from winter storms and spring downpours.

Snap hooted softly outside the door to announce their arrival, and a woman emerged from the door flap carrying an infant on her hip in a sling. At thirty, Whistle was no longer beautiful, but she was nearly as tall and strong as Thump. Her large, calm eyes were unusually green and wide set, like a buffalo's, and she habitually slouched, as if to hide her high status by disguising her size. Perched alertly on her mother's hip, the baby crowed a sort of greeting and stretched an arm out to Snap, moving her fingers in a fair imitation of Snap's name.

Whistle squealed greetings, nuzzled Thump's ear, and waved him into the shelter with the basket of yams. As she turned to her elder daughter and leaned down to nuzzle her ear as well, Snap's makeshift bandage caught her attention. "Snap! What happened to your arm? And why are you out in the dark? We have been hearing hyenas nearby all day."

"I met a leopard on the way home, but don't worry. I didn't bring him along."

The older woman jerked her head upward in amusement. The baby squirmed as Whistle peeked under Snap's binding. "Does it need to be cleaned?"

Snap shook her head. "Thump and I went down to the stream already. The cut is deep but it's clean, and it's not bleeding anymore."

Satisfied with her inspection, Whistle straightened up. "Thump has brought a far-walker, and also two rabbits. Some of the meat is saved for you, if he hasn't eaten it already."

Snap followed her mother under the door flap into the shelter. A small fire burning in a stone ring struggled to illuminate an irregularly shaped room filled with smoke unable to find its way to the flap in the roof or out of the narrow gap that served as a window. Rolled sleeping hides in an alcove in the far wall cocooned her younger brother and sister and her grandmother Chirp. Her neck and back relaxed as her nostrils filled with familiar smells— unwashed women and children, smoke, recently cooked meat, the nearby midden. An unfamiliar male smell, however, made her nape hair bristle.

Thump was sitting near the fire with a man Snap didn't know. Both were signing rapidly, and Thump was laughing. The man was tall and broad shouldered, nearly as big as Thump. Instead of one of the usual elaborate hairstyles, the visitor appeared to have shorn his gray-streaked mane to the length of his body hair. Snap thought his eyes were too close together and his nostrils too narrow, like a shrewd cobra, and she wondered what this old man was doing so far from home.

Whistle greeted them with a soft squeal. The men jumped to their feet and greeted the two women with respectful gestures appropriate to their high standing—daughter and granddaughter of the Mother of Kura. Whistle went to a storage alcove in the left wall and began to rummage in it. The stranger placed his hands on each side of his face, palms outward. Snap did likewise and squealed a muffled greeting. "This is Bapoto, of the Kao," signed Thump. "This is my sister Snap, of the Kura." Formalities completed, she took from her mother a wooden bowl containing a portion of a roasted rabbit and several tiny sour baobab fruit. With profuse one-handed thanks, she squatted at the fire facing the men and began to eat with an occasional oblique glance at the visitor. Whistle waved the men back to their places at the fire, where they resettled themselves and resumed their conversation, unaware of Snap's surreptitious surveillance. Snap had met most of the men returning from summer journeys as they paid their respects to Chirp on their arrival, and most of them had at least transient erections when they met Snap, but this one, she noticed, did not. When Thump finished telling a story, Bapoto turned to Snap.

"Thump says you were injured by a leopard today," Bapoto gestured.

She nodded, chewing. Her arm hurt, she was tired and hungry, and she had told the story to Thump already. If the stranger had been one of the younger returning men, one of those with the fascinating scents, she might have told it again, but not to this graybeard.

"And the leopard was killed by lightning?"

She nodded again.

Bapoto made a low-pitched, quavering whistle, a sound that communicated nothing to Snap. "The spirit of the leopard may have entered your wound. You must be careful."

"What is 'spirit'?"

He made the odd sound again and signed, "The soul of the leopard. That which lives inside during life, and goes to the Great One after death."

"Soul" was not a sign Snap recognized either. "I have cleaned the wound, and there is no part of the leopard left inside." She caught her mother's eye and raised one eyebrow. Whistle gave her a *be polite* look. She turned her attention to sucking the last bit of meat from the rabbit bones.

"It's full dark," signed Whistle. "You two had better go to the men's shelter, or Meerkat will come around to collect you, and I don't think either of you would enjoy that." Meerkat, whom Whistle had chosen at the Bonding every fall for as long as Snap could remember, was a stickler for tradition in the matter of visiting members of the opposite sex after dark.

The two men took their leave with polite signs, picked up bundles near the door, and ducked under the flap. Through the window gap, Snap watched her brother and the shorn-headed stranger as they headed down the slope in the direction of the men's shelter in the bright moonlight.

"Why is he here?" Snap asked, still worrying at the rabbit bones.

"Bapoto? Or Thump?" Whistle squatted next to her daughter,

drew fibers from a basket, and began to braid them into a rope.

"Both. Thump should be hanging around Panda Ya Mto to make sure no one else pays too much attention to his woman, if he wants her to choose him this winter. And that pompous old man had better think about where he's going to spend the winter. I can't imagine any of the Kura women would be interested in someone so peculiar."

Whistle picked at a tangled strand of unanasi, eyes narrowed. "He's different, yes, but Thump says these odd ideas make Bapoto a better hunter. In fact, Thump seems to think one of the Kura women will chose Bapoto."

Snap watched Whistle's shadow as it flickered on the limestone behind her, one instant appearing solid and ordinary, the next twisted into a contorted, wildly unfamiliar shape. Dubiously, she began crunching up the rabbit bones. It didn't seem likely to her that weird warbles would make anyone a better hunter, and the idea that some part of a leopard had gotten inside her and would be dangerous was just loathsome, but surely that odd old man would be gone soon. Wouldn't he?

CHAPTER 2

S nap's gash throbbed, every pulse an explosion of agony, a drumbeat in the endless night. She wasn't due to watch until midnight, but with no hope of sleep, she arose and ducked out under the door flap. Her arm felt cooler in the night air, and it seemed to throb less when she was upright. A yellow-orange moon lit the uwanda, a level clearing containing a fire ring, a large flat rock, and several well-worn stumps. To the north, the shelter and a firewood storage recess burrowed into the sharply rising hillside. Whistle sat near the glowing embers of the uwanda fire.

"I'll watch," Snap signed.

With a concerned snuffle, Whistle untied Snap's bandage and inspected the wound. It had been oozing. Snap clenched her teeth while Whistle cleaned the arm with her tongue and rewrapped it in a soft antelope hide. The door flap fell shut behind Whistle, and Snap heard Whistle crooning to Baby as she nursed her back to sleep, a sound even more comforting than the new soft bandage.

Snap had no trouble staying awake. Firelight reflected from close-set, ground-level eyes several times, but their owners were easily discouraged by small pebbles. Once, when the moon was low in the sky and dawn had not yet hinted at its arrival, a larger pair of eyes at the height of Snap's waist reflected the yellow-orange firelight. Snap got to her feet and stirred up the fire. Guttering light showed intelligent brown eyes in a heavy-jawed head atop a cobby body, clad in chestnut spots on an ocher coat—a cave hyena of about Snap's weight. She pulled a flaming branch from the fire and took a step toward the hyena, a growl rising in her throat. For a moment, the hyena matched her threat with a low grunt, but then he turned and disappeared into the night. She threw a new log on the fire and held a brand for the rest of the night, but nothing ominous appeared. As the night wore on, the hide around her arm grew tighter, and she loosened it several times. When Chirp's turn to watch came, Snap still saw no hope of sleeping and didn't wake her.

The first streaks of gray light revealed an arm twice its normal size, with burned-looking skin around the wound. Something had soaked through the antelope hide, now stiff and brown. As soon as Snap heard the sounds of people arising inside, she started down to the stream to bathe her arm again. Her balance was slightly askew, and she shuffled to stay upright. The shelters she passed seemed out of focus, even unfamiliar, and twice she stopped to be sure of her route. At the stream, she rinsed the strip of hide and cleaned her wound, careful to watch the awakening savanna for signs of hyenas or another leopard. The breeze was cool and smelled like change, disquiet, and opportunity.

As she made her way back up the slope, the ashen colors of dawn resolved into the browns and greens of day, and she could hear people stirring in other shelters. By the time she reached Chirp's shelter, her odd feeling of unreality had abated. Skewered chunks of kinana were already hissing over the newly stoked uwanda fire, where Whistle sat nursing Baby. From the shelter echoed the sounds of her brother and sister squealing and howling with early morning laughter. Snap's peculiar confusion disappeared completely. She greeted Whistle with a soft squeal and started to lift the door flap but was nearly bowled over as eight-year-old Rustle and four-year-old Swish erupted from the shelter and darted off, hooting shrilly, apparently on urgent business of their own. As Snap entered the shelter, Chirp was storing the last of the sleeping hides in a corner of the alcove. The old woman straightened up and turned to her granddaughter as she entered.

"Whistle says your arm is hurt," she signed, her gnarled fingers morning stiff.

Snap greeted her with open palms and a purr of respect, and nodded. Chirp gestured for her to sit on one of the rolled sleeping hides. With a grunt, the old woman bent her ancient, misshapen knees and knelt next to her granddaughter. The calloused hands untied the bandage and probed the injury. Snap suppressed a low growl; Chirp's fingers hurt, but she wanted her grandmother's help. This tiny old woman with her sparse gray hair, many missing teeth, and permanently bent neck was the Fifteenth Mother of Kura, and her understanding of injuries far surpassed that of anyone Snap knew.

"The swelling might keep the edges from knitting. Keep it bound, not too tight. Today, rest and eat." Snap nodded again, and Chirp snorted in annoyance as she wrapped the arm securely. "Why does this happen right before the Bonding? The bachelors will not bring you any gifts when they see this."

Snap propped herself against the rolled hide, a water bag by her side and her arm held motionless against her body, while Chirp took her weaving basket outside. Sounds of people going about their business drifted in. A raven landed on the roof, looked through the smoke flap at her, and pecked at the edge of the roof hide. She hissed at it, and it responded with a scornful cackle. Its wings beat the roof as it flapped off, a welcome distraction from her pounding arm. Whistle came into the shelter and tucked a sound-asleep Baby into her basket. From outside, Snap heard Thump's Panda Ya Mto hoot, and squeals of greeting from Chirp and the children. In a moment, Thump and Bapoto ducked under the flap and greeted Whistle and then Snap. The old man had a loosely wrapped bundle under his arm, and Snap was slightly offended that he seemed more interested in surveying the shelter's contents than in its women. Her brother had an enormous bundle packed and tied around his shoulders, and he bounced on the balls of his feet as he signed.

"I'm going to Panda Ya Mto. I have some things for Dew, and the air is filled with fall today."

Whistle hummed with satisfaction. "Good luck for the Bonding, Thump. Dew sounds perfect for you."

"Thank you." Thump hummed as well, pleased at his mother's approbation. "Bapoto will stay here in the men's shelter until the Bonding. Chirp has given permission."

Whistle nodded. Snap noticed Bapoto studying Whistle now. What did he see? A mate, an ally, a victim?

Thump turned to his sister. "How is your arm this morning?"

"Worse. Chirp told me to rest."

Bapoto looked at Snap's enormous arm and addressed Thump. "A healer might be useful."

The sign he used for "healer" was unfamiliar to Snap, but Thump seemed to understand. "Maybe. Let's talk to Chirp." The two men saluted Whistle and ducked out again.

Snap unrolled a sleeping hide and stretched out next to the ashes of the previous night's fire. Soon, she heard Chirp make a hissing sound usually used to shoo away small animals or children, and then the old woman stomped into the shelter, lips pursed and eyes narrowed.

"Thump has gone to Panda Ya Mto. He sends you his respect," she signed to Whistle. "Bapoto will stay in the men's shelter until the Bonding. I asked if he would be returning to Kao before the rains come, but he showed me his teeth and told me the Kao were his mother's people. Well, it is traditional to accept all strangers at this time."

Snap raised her head on her right elbow. "What did they ask you?"

"Among Bapoto's people, there is some sort of ceremony for people who are ill or injured, and he asked if he could perform it for you. It is not our way, and I refused."

"What harm could it do?" Snap asked.

Chirp stirred up the fire and added another log, her thin lips puckered even more than usual. "Our festivals unite us and prevent discord. The Bonding celebrates the end of the harvest and the girls who have become women, and welcomes the men into the ukoo for the winter. The Naming celebrates the coming of spring, and the end of infancy and beginning of childhood for those who have four springs. Each person has his or her part, and each person is celebrated at the appropriate time. We have no ceremonies to glorify misfortune or death, and need none."

Snap made a purr of respect and lay her head back down on the sleeping hide. As she drifted into a state of half-wakefulness, she watched Whistle braid a rope, frowning at escaping strands that refused to blend in.

Each day Snap's wound grew redder, more swollen, and more painful. She ate little and declined even a taste of a perfectly ripe marula fruit Rustle found. Each day, Bapoto visited with polite greetings and a small gift for Whistle, complimented Chirp's care of her granddaughter's arm, and offered to perform the healing ceremony. Whistle accepted a bird, two lizards, a hyrax, and a small stone chopper, but Chirp, with her jaws set, continued to veto the healing.

On the sixth day, fall sunshine angled through the open door flap of Chirp's shelter but didn't warm Snap. Rolled in sleeping hides, she shivered and moaned in a netherworld between sleep and waking. Now and again, her hands waved restlessly but incomprehensibly. Her huge maroon arm stuck out from her bedroll like the corpse of a limb, the thick, black crust over the gash like a charred bone. Whistle, stiff faced and puffy eyed, sat nearby, helped her change position, and offered her water. Chirp made a show of weaving a patterned basket, but often she shook her head and seemed to lose her place. Rustle and Swish, uninterested in their usual earsplitting pursuits, played a game involving a pile of twigs and several round stones.

Around midday, Chirp stopped in the middle of a row, put away her partly finished basket, and sent Rustle to the stream to fill a large wooden bowl with water. A finely woven grass mat, soaked in fresh water and wrapped around a warm stone from the edge of the fire, became a poultice. When Chirp held it to the tense, shiny wound, Snap squawked and flailed her arms. Whistle's face looked brittle, as if it might shatter when the tears finally spilled from her eyes, but she put out her hands, palms up, to offer help.

"Hold her. This might help, but she must be still." Whistle and Rustle positioned themselves to hold Snap, while the Mother held the warm, wet mat to the encrusted wound. The day wore on, the mat was rinsed in fresh water again and again, a cooled stone was replaced by a warm one over and over. Snap keened and moaned and writhed and eventually, she slept.

She dreamt a leopard had entered her body through the opening in her arm. It slunk through her blood, up her bones, around her organs, and became part of her. At first she resisted its presence, fighting the leopard traits, but finally, she relented, allowed her hair to become spotted, her teeth to sharpen, her nails to curl into cruel claws. At last, she was completely transformed. Crouched in a tree, exhausted, she watched a thunderstorm approach.

When Snap awoke, slanting rays of late afternoon sunlight streamed into the shelter. Confused, she tried to remember how long she had been sleeping and wasn't sure why she had been asleep in the daytime. Her arm hurt, but in a strange, distant way, as if it were someone else's arm. She was aware of Chirp doing something to her but wasn't interested in finding out what. She lay limply, occasionally shivering, and did not use her free hand to communicate.

An odd sound drifted into the shelter, coming from uphill, from the top of the white outcrop that formed the rear wall of the shelter. It was a human sound, but not one she could identify, although it was vaguely familiar. Soon, she remembered the quavering whistle made by Bapoto on the night of his arrival, and realized a number of people must be making the same noise. Thumping sounds began to accompany the whistling, and then developed a regular pattern.

Snap opened her eyes. Chirp, on her left, was rearranging the poultice, and Whistle squatted on her right with her arms folded. Rustle knelt near the alcove, uncharacteristically still, with his hands open on his thighs, frowning. Swish clung to his back, her eyes just visible next to his ear. Snap blinked in surprise at her siblings' stillness. In a moment, she signed coherently for the first time since the previous day. "What is that sound?"

Whistle waved at the ridgetop. "There are about a dozen people up there, and they have brought a fire. Bapoto made a huge drum that doesn't look like one of ours, and they are dancing and making that odd sound." As Whistle signed, Snap heard Bapoto's voice raised in an ululating warble.

The crust over the wound opened, and yellow pus drained onto the mat under her arm. Snap gagged at the stench, and then shrieked as Chirp compressed her arm, expelling the evil with her hands. Whistle and Rustle pinned Snap's arms while Chirp poured water into the now gaping hole. To Snap, it seemed to take forever, but finally Chirp declared that the wound was clean, and told her not to bind it, but leave it open to the air. Compared to the agony of the previous six days, the pain was gone, and Snap cried for the first time, with relief. She pulled Whistle, Chirp, and Rustle, in turn, down to her with her unhurt arm, kissed them, and released them damp with her tears. As the dusk faded, Snap's shivers turned to sweat, and Whistle helped her crawl from her sleeping hides and into the cool air outside, where Chirp stood looking uphill.

The eerie whistling and Bapoto's warbling were much louder outside, and Snap could see the figures on the ridge flashing in the flickering light as they danced. Chirp made a sound of disgust, and Snap could just see her fuming in the dark. "It is full dark, and not yet Bonding. Those women should be in their shelters, and those men in theirs. Where is Meerkat?" In a moment, she had sent Whistle off in the direction of the men's shelter, and shortly thereafter, the drumming and whistling from the ridgetop turned into a scrabble of people climbing down in the dark, accompanied by what Snap recognized as Meerkat's roar.

Snap was fiercely thirsty and drank all the water at the shelter, but it was too dark to go to the stream for more. She slept for several long stretches, although still unable to find a comfortable position. By morning, she was feeling hungry. Whistle and Chirp were happy to allow her more than her share of the dried fruit. The rigid expression Whistle had worn during Snap's illness returned to normal, and the children became more boisterous than they had ever been. Meerkat brought a porcupine he had snared,

Whistle roasted it, and Snap ate the entire thing. In the afternoon, Whistle, with Baby in a sling, took Rustle and Swish on an expedition to collect egusi gourds. Snap was sitting at the edge of the uwanda crunching the last of the porcupine bones when Bapoto appeared, accompanied by several men and two women, one of whom was Whistle's cousin. Snap supposed she had heard them on the ridgetop the previous night. Chirp appeared at the flap of the shelter.

Bapoto squealed polite greetings, palms outward on each side of his face, and Snap replied in kind.

"How are you feeling today?" he asked.

Snap thought his smug expression deserved a pinecone between the eyes, but she replied politely, "Much better, thank you. Chirp put a poultice on my arm that made the pus drain, and now the fever is gone."

Bapoto made the quavering whistle Snap had heard from the ridgetop on the previous night, and the group behind him echoed it. "The Healing has succeeded. The spirit of the leopard has spared you," he signed. Chirp made a sound of disgust, and Bapoto turned to her with a purr of respect. "Mother of Kura, do you see the power of the Healing? Others who suffer could be helped as well."

Chirp straightened up as much as her bent back allowed and signed with steady hands. "Sometimes we have full stomachs, sometimes empty. We have pleasure in our mates; we have pain in our injuries. Life is as it is; whistles and drums and dancing bring us delight, not good fortune." She hissed at the group in front of her shelter, and they dispersed like termites from an overturned mound. Bapoto backed away making the same gesture he had used for greeting, apparently forgetting which was appropriate.

When he was out of Chirp's sight, but not quite out of Snap's, she saw him sign, apparently to himself, "The old one does not believe. There is no hope for her."

Snap sniggered into her hands until they were out of sight, and then laughed out loud, rocking back and forth. "What idiots!" she signed to Chirp.

Chirp shook her head and looked toward the ridgetop, wisps of gray hair flapping like feathers. "No, not idiots." She turned and hooted loudly as she walked toward the central uwanda, a large open square roughly in the midpoint of the village. Snap followed her. Soon, most of the Kura women, their children, and their potential mates had gathered in the uwanda, and stood looking at Chirp.

Chirp used the large, two-armed signs used for crowds or long distances. "Fall is coming. We will celebrate the Bonding in three days." The crowd whooped and hooted, and the sound echoed from the limestone ridge and rolled across the uneven savanna to the grove where Whistle heard it. She looked up from the egusi, eyes and ears focused on Kura. "Something's happening."

CHAPTER 3

The cool nights, the first rain, the men's return—everyone had already known that fall was near. Nevertheless, Chirp's announcement provoked a storm of activity. Snap watched a group of newly arrived men eye one another appraisingly and imagined what each was thinking. Should I join the main band of hunters? We'd probably make a kill, but it probably wouldn't be my spear. Should I hunt with my brother and my cousin, and maybe make the kill myself, or maybe come back with nothing? Or should I fish, nearly a sure thing, but not very impressive? Which will that woman over there admire most? In no time, all the men had departed with spears or fishing nets over their shoulders. Bapoto appeared to be leading the largest hunting party.

The women flew around like darting swallows. Whistle traded some dried zebra for a patterned basket from her sister Peep. Chirp forced Rustle to sit still long enough to hollow out a new wooden bowl. With her arm bound and a little help from Swish, Snap laboriously dug as many bambara nuts as she could carry. Women visited one another on the flimsiest pretense, surreptitiously comparing the lavishness of their feast preparations.

Over the next two days, Snap struggled to shell and roast her bambaras with her one useful arm. By midday of the day before the Bonding, she was on her knees just outside the shelter door, grinding them with a heavy stone mchi. Chirp plaited a mat in a sunny corner. At the back of the uwanda, Whistle split firewood with stone wedges and a hand axe and stacked it in its storage alcove near the shelter. Baby was propped in her basket at the best vantage point to see all the activity. Rustle and Swish had gone off with a group of other children, their chores finished. Snap's arm ached, and sweat matted her hair. She tested the meal with her fingertips. Nearly fine enough, she thought. This flatbread will be my best ever.

An unfamiliar hoot came from the direction of the central uwanda and Snap looked up. Climbing the path was a stranger, as tall as Whistle, with a huge bundle tied over his narrow shoulders and only the beginnings of a beard on his cheeks. Snap guessed he was a few springs older than she was, but exhaustion lined his face, and he picked his way carefully up the track as if he were much older. He greeted them respectfully, hands on each side of his face, and addressed Chirp, the oldest person present.

"I am Ash, of the Kilima people. You are Mother of the Kura?"

Chirp responded with the same polite greeting. "I am Chirp, Mother of Kura. This my daughter, Whistle, and her daughter, Snap."

Ash signed greetings to Whistle and Snap in turn. As he glanced at Snap, his surprised eyes widened briefly. At once, he dropped his gaze to avoid disrespect. Snap was gratified that this young man, unlike Bapoto, obviously found her attractive. He faced Chirp again. "I arrived here yesterday evening. I ask to use the men's shelter until the Bonding."

"You are welcome here."

"Some of the hunters have returned. I just saw them carrying an antelope to the large uwanda." The sign he used for *uwanda* was not the one used in Kura, but Snap understood what he meant when he waved in the direction from which he had come.

Whistle dropped her axe. "They will need help with the butchering. Thank you for the news." She dashed into the shelter and came out with two obsidian knives and a scraper. Teeth bared, Whistle scooped up Baby's basket and strode east, down the path to the central uwanda. Snap knew that Whistle wanted to be helpful, but she also suspected her mother wanted to be present when the hunter decided who would get what. I suppose I should go, too, she thought, but I won't be much help with a crippled arm. In any case, I want to know who this stranger is.

Chirp signed a farewell at Whistle and turned back to the young man. "Please come into my shelter and share my fire." With her partly finished mat tucked into her basket of grass fibers, the old woman shuffled into the shelter, followed by Ash. Snap hurriedly covered her partly ground bambaras with an upturned wooden bowl and did likewise. Inside, Chirp prodded the fire with a new log and forced her creaking knees to kneel at the flames. In the light of the blazing fire, Snap thought her grandmother looked strong and more erect than usual, the regal Mother of Kura.

The old woman stretched her gnarled fingers toward the smoky warmth, and Ash dropped his bundle and squatted opposite her, fatigue and age mirroring each other. Snap retrieved a basket of dried fruit from the storage alcove, offered it to her grandmother, and then to Ash. When Ash accepted a few marula slices and a gourd dipper of water, Chirp nodded gravely, as she always did when welcoming one of the returning men. Today, however, Snap thought her grandmother's eyes seemed more good-humored than solemn.

Ash drew a small leather packet from his bundle. "Please accept a gift. This tool is called a shazia among my people." Snap did not recognize the sign he used, so she moved closer to see better, squatting so her knee almost touched his. He glanced at her, and then opened the packet, which contained several sharpened slivers of bone, each with a hole bored in one end. With a purr of respect, he chose one and presented it to Chirp, who raised her eyebrows and accepted it graciously.

"What is this?" she asked.

Ash took a hank of grass fibers from his bundle and demonstrated how to pass a fiber through the small hole and use the shazia to repair a woven mat, or to join two together. The Mother looked amazed and delighted, to Snap's surprise. She thought her grandmother knew everything worth knowing.

"What an idea! Won't you excuse me? I want to show this to my daughters. Please entertain our guest, Snap." Chirp excused herself with a polite sound and scurried out carrying the shazia, the twisted fibers, and two old mats.

Snap moved around and took Chirp's place at the fire. Acutely aware of her sweaty body and obvious injury, she did her best to represent the Mother. With no higher-ranking women present, Snap no longer needed to keep her eyes down, and she knelt at the fireside with her head above Ash's.

"I am Snap, daughter of Whistle, daughter of Chirp."

Ash purred respect and looked at her with his mouth slightly open, which made his face look even younger and a little silly. He had an erection again. "I am Ash, of the Kilima people."

Ash's disarming expression made it hard for Snap to maintain her dignified gaze. "And where is Kilima?"

"Toward the dawn and the Great Desert, near the Great Water. It took longer than a moon to walk here from my mother's shelter."

"You arrived yesterday?"

"Yes, at nightfall. It was too late to pay my respects to the Mother then."

"How did you happen to come here?" Snap continued to kneel up, but her inquisitive expression and the way she leaned forward to see his words spoiled her attempt at aloof decorum.

"I began my journey in the spring with Tor, who was my mother's mate for many years. He has taken many long journeys, and has paid his respects to Chirp before, long ago. Half a moon ago, he was swept away when we were crossing a river. I searched far downstream for him, but didn't find any sign of him." Ash made a brief keening sound, to which she responded in kind, and then they sat in silence. This Ash, she thought, is a far-walker, and probably not so foolish as he looks. She prodded the fire, and added another log. He showed no sign of departing, and kept his eyes firmly on Snap.

Finally, he pointed at his own eyes and then at hers. "Your eyes—I've never seen anyone with green eyes."

Snap shrugged. "Nor have I, except for my mother. They work just like yours, I think."

Next, Ash indicated her bandage and asked, "Is your arm injured?"

She waved the question away with her uninjured hand. "Just a scratch."

"I understand the Kura will celebrate the Bonding tomorrow?"

"Yes."

"Among my people, all are welcome at the Bonding, and any man may be chosen by any woman of the ukoo. Is it so here?"

"Yes, but often women choose the same mates over and over. Didn't you have a mate last winter?"

"No, among the ukoos near my home, there is an excess of men. I spent the last two winters in a bachelors' shelter. Would it be rude to ask if you will choose a mate this fall?"

Snap briefly lifted her chin in a gesture of amusement. How unlike Thump he was, how improbably polite. She supposed it was the reason he didn't manage to find a mate. "I became a woman this year, but I'm not interested in any of the bachelors who have arrived."

Ash's eyes were intense but not unfriendly, and the rest of his face was solemn. With a discreet glance, she noticed his erection was gone again. He seemed to be thinking something over. Snap helped herself to a dried marula and chewed slowly as they considered each other. "There is a custom among your people I don't understand," he signed. "Last night, in the men's shelter, several of the men made a circle around the fire, beat a small drum, and whistled together, like this." Ash imitated the quavering whistle Snap had heard from the ridgetop two nights before. "They seemed to be asking for success in the hunt, but I couldn't understand whom they were asking. Can you explain this to me?"

Snap shook her head. "This is not our custom, and I don't really understand it. It's Bapoto, a far-walker from sunset-ward, who does it. He tried to heal my arm with something similar. He seems to think he's addressing someone called 'Great One' who can't be seen or touched but controls everything. I don't know how that works. Chirp isn't happy with him."

Ash nodded and once again sat in silence, his keen, concentrated gaze still focused on Snap. She dropped her eyes, discomfited, and then immediately raised them again, afraid she might appear deferent. Apparently embarrassed, Ash looked down and began rummaging in his bundle again. "I have something for you as well."

Snap raised her eyebrows in what she hoped was an imitation of Chirp. Ash took out a small packet tied up with a scrap of hide, walked around the fire, squatted in front of Snap, and handed her the packet with both hands, bowing his head between his arms.

"Thank you." Snap used the formal gesture of thanks Chirp always used in accepting gifts. She untied the thin strip of hide holding the packet closed and unwrapped a small, round box carved from a single piece of mungomu wood with a lid that fit closely inside the top, like a stopper. It contained salt. Snap's eyes opened wide, and her mouth became as round as the box. So perfectly shaped, such a precisely fitting lid, she thought. I've never seen such a thing. And salt, so far from the Great Water! At Kura, a man gave salt only to a woman with whom he had a long connection, not at first meeting. Snap was stunned.

She couldn't think of anything appropriate to say about the salt; possibly Ash simply didn't realize how valuable this gift was. "What a beautiful box! Who made it?" she asked.

"I did. Tor used to collect special bits of wood on his summer journey. He would bring them back to my mother's shelter and make beautiful and useful things during the winter rains. He taught me to shape wood, and was teaching me to make the special knives he used for shaping wood."

"You were lucky to know him."

Ash nodded, and his thoughts appeared to drift away to places Snap would never see. Just then, Whistle lifted the door flap and signed, "Snap! I need your help." Apparently, she failed to notice Ash's presence and dropped the flap abruptly. Snap and Ash jumped to their feet and signed polite good-byes. Snap followed him out of the shelter with her salt box in her hand and watched him head in the direction of the men's shelter, whistling like a canary and swinging his bundle as if it were filled with feathers.

As Snap turned back to the uwanda, she saw Chirp had returned to her sunny niche with a pile of old mats and baskets to be repaired with twisted unanasi fibers and her new shazia. Baby was tucked into her basket next to her grandmother, sound asleep. Whistle had returned with a share of the antelope meat; she was cutting it into thin slices with an obsidian knife while Rustle and Swish pounded the slices with a paste of crushed berries and herbs. Snap squatted by Chirp.

"Well, that young man took his time paying official respects,

I'd say, especially since I wasn't even there." Chirp seemed amused by the mat she was mending.

"He gave me this." Snap showed the box to the old woman, who put down her work and examined it carefully. When she opened it and looked inside, her ragged gray eyebrows disappeared into the hair above her brow ridge. She closed the box and handed it back to Snap.

"You had better keep that in a safe place. And you had better help Whistle. She is stewing about something."

Whistle was indeed slicing the meat with much more enthusiasm than the task warranted; the tree stump on which she was working was covered in deep crosshatching. Snap located a new obsidian knife, a gift to Chirp from one of the bachelors, and approached her mother cautiously.

"Swish and I can work over there." She waved at another stump. When Whistle looked up, Snap saw that tears threatened to leak from her eyes and her jaws were clenched tight as if to keep the tears contained. The older woman nodded and cut the meat in half. Snap took her piece and signed to Swish, "Bring some of that stuff over here. I'll make slices for you to pound."

With a handful of the paste, Swish moved with her sister to the other stump. As she sliced, Snap watched the small girl earnestly slam a rock the size of her four-year-old fist into her slice, doing an adequate, if not beautiful, job of introducing the preserving and tenderizing paste into the antelope flesh. After Baby was born, Snap had watched her placid, round-cheeked baby sister become a lively, wiry child, a gifted hunter of lizards with an almost unnatural ability to appear whenever anything edible might be shared. Whistle's first daughter snorted in amusement as her sibling neatened a jagged edge with her teeth and added the portion to their growing stack. As they worked, Snap stood so Swish could see her hands but their mother could not, and asked, "What's wrong with Whistle?"

"Don't know. She came back from the butchering like that. Rustle told me to look out, and I've been looking." Swish sneaked another morsel of meat into her mouth and chewed surreptitiously.

"Good job." Snap waved at Swish's stack of flattened slices.

The two sisters were nearly finished with their part of the meat when Whistle sliced her last strip and stood up. "Hang the meat on the drying rack, please, Rustle, and make sure no animals get it. I'm going to the stream." Whistle strode away, and Rustle rolled his eyes at his sisters. In no time, Snap and Swish were finished as well.

"Will you put these on the rack, too, please, Rustle? I'm going to talk to Whistle," Snap signed.

"Better you than me."

Snap walked south, around the periphery of the other shelters, and met the stream where it spilled from a small pool beyond the lowest shelter. The water had a late summer, grayish tinge, and she thought she smelled a hint of sulfur as she paralleled its gurgling, splashing course. As she reached a grove of stunted trees where the stream widened and slowed, she found her mother sitting on the bank with her hands and feet in the water, staring blankly into the distance. Snap hooted to signal her presence. When Whistle turned and waved an invitation, Snap thought she looked more like her usual self; her eyes were red, but dry, and she no longer looked like she might bite.

"Come over and sit with me," signed Whistle. "My hands are sore from cutting that meat; the water makes them feel better."

The young woman sat down on the bank as well and plopped her hands and feet into the water.

"What's happened?" Snap asked. The older woman looked away again, and then back at her daughter with her face expressionless and as smooth as if she were suspended by her hair.

"I'm sorry I didn't tell you at the uwanda—I didn't want to cry in front of the little ones. Meerkat was lost during the hunt this morning. He was a chaser. They had separated a young antelope from its herd, and were driving it toward the hunters' line. Bapoto says he saw him fall into a cleft in the ground with moving water at the bottom." Whistle's eyes looked empty now, as if her tears had washed out all emotions. "He saw Meerkat disappear under the water. After the antelope was taken, they all looked for him. They couldn't get into the hole where he fell—it was too deep. They looked in all the sinkholes and caves in the area, since they are sometimes connected, but. . . ."

Snap put her arms around her mother. Initially, she wanted to be comforted, for her mother to make everything all right, the way she could when Snap was a small child, but as her tears began to drip down Whistle's back, another emotion took form; she wanted to comfort her mother. Snap had known Meerkat her entire life; he had taught her how to make things from wood and bone and stone, how to find water when the dry washes all seemed truly dry, how to take advantage of her long legs and perseverance to excel at chasing game for the hunters. To Snap, he was a teacher. To Whistle, Meerkat was a mate, and now that Snap was a woman, she could begin to understand the difference. She recognized that the emptiness in Whistle's eyes was only a faint echo of Meerkat's absence.

They sat at the stream until Snap's tears were as exhausted as

Whistle's. As they walked back to Chirp's shelter, they told stories about Meerkat in turn: how he had rescued Thump from a hyena just a few days after the boy had received his name; how Whistle chose him for her first mate when she had twelve springs and he had twenty; how he helped Rustle make a beautiful wooden spear and learn to use it; and how he failed to appear for the Bonding five falls ago. On that occasion, Whistle refused to take a mate, which made Chirp furious. Six days after the Bonding, he appeared with a large bundle of especially wonderful gifts, a ragged, healing wound on the side of his head, and no explanation for either his wound or his lateness. Whistle beat him with a willow switch, which he suffered without protest, and then she took him into her shelter just as if he had shown up on time. Everyone else had ignored this irregularity.

When they reached the shelter, the last rays of sunshine were illuminating the ridgetop. The meat had been hung inside on the drying rack, safe from vermin. In the uwanda, Rustle and Swish shelled egusi seeds, both with swollen eyes, while Chirp turned an egusi over and over in her fingers. As Snap and Whistle approached, Swish hiccuped a sob and Chirp stood up and stretched out her arms. Her tall granddaughter and taller daughter dropped to their knees in front of her, and Chirp folded them in her knobby-elbowed, partly bald arms. Finally, she released them and signed, "Peep came by and told us. He was a good man."

There were no more tears. Snap and Whistle sat down next to Rustle and ate egusi seeds in silence. After she had eaten a handful, Whistle stood up and looked into the basket where Baby was sleeping. "Baby ought to be starving."

Chirp shook her head. "She woke up and was hungry when

Peep was here, so she fed her. If you need to, you could see if Peep's Baby is hungry."

Snap thought Whistle looked awfully full of milk, and wasn't at all surprised when Whistle took her sleeping Baby and went off to see if Peep's Baby was awake and hungry. Chirp and the children went into the shelter to prepare for night. Snap sat at the door and shelled the rest of the egusi seeds into a basket. In the far distance, she could see a line that might be the ridge where she had met the leopard, a dark wall behind which the sun had disappeared as if it never meant to return. Was the country of the Great One somewhere to the west, over the hills where the sun had set? She looked appraisingly into the dusk, swept the egusi hulls into the midden heap, and took the basket of shelled seeds into the shelter.

Chirp had stirred up the fire and was tucking Rustle and Swish into their sleeping hides. Snap put the seeds away in the storage alcove, made sure her salt box was safe, checked the drying rack, and started to unroll her sleeping hides. Chirp fastened the flaps over the door and window, left the roof flap open, and settled herself beside the fire to watch. Now that Snap was feeling better, she was able to take her usual turn watching at night, and she liked to watch last, in the cold time before dawn. Vigilance at night was always necessary, since hyenas and other predators knew quite well when small children slept, but when there was fresh meat in the shelter, the watcher needed to keep a burning stick handy as well.

"Chirp?" Snap finished arranging her hide and squatted next to the fire.

"My daughter's daughter."

"Will I choose a mate tomorrow?"

Chirp's old face cracked like the bed of a lake after its water disappears in the summer. "That nice young man would be pleasant to have around this winter. He's not very big, though. Do you think he can hunt?"

"Ash's people are over a moon's walk away. He walked part of the summer on his journey with his mother's mate, Tor, but he was killed, and Ash came the rest of the way alone. At least he doesn't seem likely to get lost, hmm?"

Chirp looked into the fire but seemed to see something other than burning wood. The old hands moved in her lap, as if signing only to themselves. "Tor? There was a far-walker." For an instant, Snap saw a young woman, a reflection of herself, who watched in the flames scenes from an unknown past, or maybe an unknown future, but then the aged countenance wrinkled again and became old, as old as the limestone walls around them. "Do as you will. We probably won't starve to death, whether you choose a hunter or a trader or no one at all." She winked, squeezed Snap around the shoulders, and added, "Having a mate is the best thing in the world, sometimes, and also the worst, some other times."

As Snap crawled into her sleeping hides, the Bonding crouched on the verge of her consciousness and formed the shadows flickering over her sleeping family. Like a late summer cloud, shapes flowed one into another: the feast, Ash's meager whiskers and long tapering fingers, Whistle's empty eyes. One of the shapes on the ceiling beckoned, luring her to morning, and she fell asleep.

CHAPTER 4

Despite the next day's looming possibilities, Snap slept as if hibernating. Whistle's gentle taps failed to rouse her, but a cold breeze from the open door flap had a salutary effect. Awareness arrived by stages, first of the cold, then of Whistle's persistent tapping, and finally of her duty to watch. Snap stretched, shook off her sleeping hides, and yawned. As Whistle arranged her hides in the sleeping alcove, Snap stirred up the fire, checked the drying rack, and squatted where she could see both the door and window and could grab a flaming branch if necessary.

Whistle returned to the fire with an expression like a

grandmother watching a baby's first steps. "Chirp told me about Ash's gifts."

Snap hid her annoyance under a blank face. "He's a far-walker, from near the Great Water. That shazia he gave Chirp will be useful. The salt . . ." Her hands momentarily wilted into her lap. "He's not big, but he's well traveled, and he's handy with wood."

Whistle nodded. "Ash would be a fine choice. A high-ranking woman like you must have a mate, or all sorts of disputes will trouble us this winter. Every man would look at his woman and imagine he could have done better."

Snap raised her eyebrows and examined her mother's profile as she looked into the fire. "I remember when you didn't choose a mate."

The older woman's face softened. "He was late, but I knew he would come. Completely different situation." She turned back to her daughter looking businesslike. "And people must see your mate is worthy of you. I will be sure to mention the salt to Warble tomorrow; everyone will know about it by evening."

Whistle rolled herself in her sleeping hides and began to snore almost immediately. After a short while, Snap went out to visit the latrine pits, Rustle's small spear in her hand. The path was well lit by the nearly full moon, and snores drifted from the distant men's shelter. On the way back, she saw a tall, thin figure standing on the ridge high above Chirp's shelter. His arms were folded, and he looked down the valley to the southwest. After a few moments, the figure turned and she recognized Ash, brow furrowed thoughtfully. He disappeared toward the path that led down from the ridgetop, and she returned to the shelter.

Occasional snufflings around the door and window flap kept Snap alert. When the sky began to lighten, she stirred up the fire and opened the door and window flaps to let in the sharp morning air. She could hear people all over Kura waking up. Excited children squealed, smoke poured into the sky from twenty fires, gravel crunched under the feet of people on every sort of important errand. Someone was starting an enormous fire in the central uwanda pit; Snap's mouth watered when she thought of the hog that would be roasted on the coals of that fire later.

Determined to make exemplary flatbread, Snap started heating a large flat cooking rock set over the outdoor fire in Chirp's uwanda. Whistle fed Baby and then hurried away to supervise the preparation of the hog, a job that Chirp had passed on to her five falls previously. Chirp detained Rustle and Swish before they could escape with their friends and sent them to the stream bank to dig up and clean huge white grubs for the feast, and then settled down herself to arrange fruit, nuts, vegetables, and insects in her best baskets and bowls.

The sun was high when Chirp lined up her family and started the procession. After Chirp was Whistle with Baby in a sling, and Snap, Rustle, and Swish followed in order. Chirp's croaking hoots drew everyone from the shelters of Kura, and her people gathered along the route to watch them pass, hooting in response. Snap looked at those standing among the shelters—there were her aunts and her cousins, there were the two other girls-who-had-become-women, there were some of the men who had visited Chirp on their arrivals. A number of the men had weapons and some struck bold, fierce-looking stances as Whistle passed. Bapoto stood on a rock with an exceptionally long, heavy spear and watched the procession as if reviewing preparations for a hunt. Snap finally located Ash watching from behind the rest of the men.

My people, she thought, and hooted with all her breath.

The first shelter they visited belonged to Peep, Chirp's second daughter, and ranked next after Whistle, Snap, and Swish. They tasted the delicacies displayed in Peep's best containers, pronounced them delicious, and then proceeded to the shelter of Chirp's third daughter, Warble. Peep and her children followed. At each shelter, each member of the parade tasted the food, admired the variety and the presentation, and proceeded to the next, and that household joined the end of the line. Snap noticed the amount and variety of food and the quality of the containers lessened at each shelter, and families became smaller. The last woman, Hum, had only a basket of dried fruit, a bowl of unshelled nuts, and no children at all. Her shelter needed repair. Chirp complimented her hospitality nevertheless. After visiting all the women's shelters, they passed the door of the men's shelter, where no food was offered, and the men joined the end of the parade, jostling, and in no particular order. Snap's family continued back to Chirp's shelter, where they left the procession and served their food to those who followed. Each subsequent family did the same, so that each person was received in every shelter in turn.

With the hog still to come, people merely nibbled politely during the morning procession, and there were leftovers to be stored or contributed to the later meal. As Snap and Rustle worked together to put away the uneaten nuts and dried fruit, he glanced around to make sure neither Chirp nor Whistle were watching, and then signed, "So much for trotting around parading our rank and comparing our pantries."

Snap jerked her head upward in agreement. "Bring on the stories and the food."

"You mean, bring on the dancing!" Rustle leapt around the shelter and pretended to mate with an invisible woman, and Snap laughed.

Soon, Whistle had fastened the shelter door and window flaps tightly, and they set off toward the large central uwanda. Snap carried the meat-drying rack, so as not to attract scavengers while the shelter was unoccupied, Chirp was nearly hidden by a pile of thick mats and soft hides, and Rustle and Swish balanced bowls of interestingly arrayed fruit, insects, and fish. Whistle brought up the rear with the wood and bone plates on which the family would eat, and a towering stack of Snap's bambara flatbread.

The large central uwanda, dominated by a flat-topped rock near the center, was already filling with people. Snap, Whistle, Rustle, and Swish arranged their mats near the rock, settled Baby in her basket, and watched the Kura gather and position themselves according to rank. The men, with no rank until after the Bonding, stood around the periphery of the square in ones and twos, feet apart and shoulders squared, as if to appear as large as possible. Some looked hopefully at the pit where the hog was roasting, but most were more interested in the women, especially in Whistle and Snap. When everyone was present, Whistle helped Chirp climb onto the flat-topped rock. She stood and looked slowly over her people, as if counting them, and then used large, slow, two-armed signs.

"People of Kura! It is fall again. Some of us are here for the first time, some of us have returned, and some of us have always been here. Some who were here last fall are not with us. Those who have a new ukoo, we wish full stomachs and mates with many children. Those who are dead, we mourn." Chirp made a brief, keening sound, and the crowd joined her. Snap noticed that Whistle, while she did not cry, keened a bit longer than the rest of the crowd.

"The summer has been good to us. We have eaten well, our pantries are full, our children are safe, and our men have come back." Chirp hooted as she signed, and the women joined her immediately, with the men a bit later, as some were just learning the Kura hoot. "Men! Thank you for your gifts, for your strength and skills, and for your company. Please join our feast and our Bonding. If you are not chosen at the Bonding, stay in the men's shelter tonight, but you must leave tomorrow. Women! Thank you for your children, your food, and for your company. Please welcome the men to our feast and our Bonding. Choose well!"

At this, the entire company hooted enthusiastically. Snap looked around the uwanda as she hooted and finally located Ash, alone at the far edge of the uwanda. He was watching the other men uncertainly, as if he weren't sure what to do next, but he hooted just as enthusiastically as the others. Bapoto stood not far away with two men who had wintered in Kura before. The three of them had folded arms and serious expressions, and did not seem to be hooting as much as the other men.

When the hooting died away, Chirp spread a thick mat on top of the rock, sat down, and continued to sign with both arms. She told stories of the Kura: how her many-times-great-grandmother, the First Mother of Kura, had come from Panda Ya Mto with her mate and children and built the first shelter at Kura; how, in the time of the Third Mother, the Kura had suffered a winter so cold the rains became white and hard; how, in the time of the Seventh Mother, strange men had attacked the Kura women and children harvesting in the summer and kidnapped several. She filled the afternoon with stories of pride and terror, bravery and disaster, and the children sat entranced at her feet. Snap thought she was too old to sit with children and make sounds of amazement, but she paid close attention nonetheless. One day, she hoped, she would have to tell these tales, and they must be told accurately. All the while, the smell of the cooking pig reminded everyone of what was still to come.

After Chirp's stories, the three girls who had become women in the last year were made to stand up on the flat rock. So she would not appear embarrassed, Snap stood as tall as she possibly could and looked over the men who lounged at the edges of the square as if she were choosing a tool from a trader. The other two on the rock with her were from families that had been in the second half of the parade, and both kept their eyes cast down. The men began hooting in the Kura manner, some of them obviously still learning, but all wholeheartedly. She hissed at them and they fell silent, although some still grinned in a way that made her uncomfortable.

Finally, as the afternoon shadows lengthened, the cooking pit was opened. Snap had only tasted the foods offered at the procession because she wanted to be hungry for the feast, and now the smell of the cooked pork, fruits, nuts, and vegetables made her ravenous. Four people lifted the rack from the pit, and the food was arranged on large wooden serving platters lined with Snap's flatbread. Chirp should have served the food, but this time, the job was delegated to Whistle. Everyone lined up again in ranking order, each with a plate or bowl of wood, bone, or gourd, to receive a portion.

The men jostled for position, rumbling and growling, but no blows were struck. After receiving their food, the men did not return to the periphery of the square but squatted with their plates and bowls among the women and children. Whistle's mat was unoccupied while she served the food. Bapoto planted himself on a corner of it with his food and showed his teeth to anyone else who seemed about to sit down nearby. Chirp, who was eating with her grandchildren, returned the gesture, but he ignored her. Ash, who had been close to the end of the line, approached Snap's mat and hovered several feet away as he tried to catch her eye. When she realized he was there, she jerked her head up in amusement, waved him over to her mat, and squealed greetings.

"This is spectacular," he signed as he squatted and began to eat.

She nodded. "It's been a good summer, but Whistle also knows just what foods to cook together." With both hands, they devoted themselves to their plates. Even the youngest children understood the need to eat as fast as possible to reduce the chance of unintentional sharing with those who might be out of food, still hungry, and bigger than oneself. As a result, the sounds of gustatory pleasure in the uwanda were as loud as the hooting had been earlier, and not many hands were available for conversation.

After Whistle had served the last person and filled her own plate, she returned to her mat and looked down at Bapoto, who had finished his food and was licking his bone bowl. He put down his bowl, stood up, and greeted Whistle formally. At close quarters, Snap thought he seemed larger than he had before, and Whistle had to look up into his face.

"I hope you have enjoyed the meat from my kill yesterday," he signed, and squatted again. His expression was polite, but Snap thought he occupied more of Whistle's mat than was proper.

Whistle sat down and began to eat rapidly with one hand as she signed with the other. "We are drying the meat for winter." She waved her hand at the rack near the edge of the square. She glanced at Chirp, who had licked her bowl clean and was looking over the square with an impassive expression.

"I've never eaten hog cooked this way," Bapoto went on. "I don't recognize those small round vegetables, or the big nuts, but they go well with the meat, don't they?"

Whistle was using both hands to eat now, but she responded with a polite nod. Bapoto gave her a self-assured smirk, stood up, and walked away. Snap finished her food and began to lick her bowl clean, which smeared her face with the remains of her dinner. Ash pointed at the splotches and laughed. "Your face looks delicious."

She leaned toward Ash and offered him her cheek. Like a mother with a messy child, he put down his plate and licked her face clean. A number of people were beginning to drift away from the square now, some going to the stream to drink, others doing errands, most looking sleepy. Some stretched out on their mats and fell asleep in the late afternoon sun without bothering to return to their shelters.

As Whistle was finishing her food, Chirp leaned over and patted her knee. "Bapoto is not like us, but he is big, and a good hunter. You will make a wise choice." Snap thought Chirp looked indecisive herself, not at all like the Mother of the Kura should look.

After he had finished eating, Ash fell asleep on Snap's mat. Chirp went back to her shelter to make sure no animals were visiting and to have a nap. Snap and a few other women cleared away the remnants of the feast and divided leftovers among the hungriest-looking children. By the time they had finished, several of the men had started a fire in the central fire ring of the uwanda, and were bringing all the wood from the men's shelter. "We won't need a fire there tonight," signed a stocky man who had been chosen by one of Whistle's distant cousins for the last two falls.

"I won't," replied another man, who was several springs older and much taller than the first, "but you might. Better keep a few sticks there, just in case." The men laughed and stirred up the fire.

Snap sat near the flat-topped rock and watched Ash sleeping. He is certainly polite, but what does that count for? Meerkat never signed the right thing at the right time, or made respectful noises when he ought, but he ran fast, threw hard, and we were never hungry, at least not for long. This one, though, is smart. He knows how to travel, and he knows how to make beautiful and useful things. A trader might be as good as a hunter at keeping his mate and her children fed. But he's so young, so small, and not so aggressive. How will he protect us? Can he bargain with a leopard?

The dusk was well established by the time people began returning from their naps. The fire was huge, with leaping flames taller than any of the men. Several of the men had brought from the men's shelter two drums as big around as a wildebeest's chest, and with tones as deep as the voice of a lion. The two oldest men settled themselves behind the drums and began to tap out a soft rhythm. Chirp, Whistle, and the children were among the last to return to the uwanda, and they found Snap still sitting near the center rock, with Ash still asleep next to her. Swish's squeal woke Ash with a start. He sat up in confusion, and then looked relieved when he saw Snap and realized where he was. He started to gesture to her, but she waved at the group of men collecting at one side of the uwanda and signed, "Over there. The dancing will begin soon, and you need to get in the line." Bemused, he wandered off as directed.

Chirp appointed several of the older children to be guardians of the younger ones, and established a nursery area near one side of the uwanda. Mats were spread on the ground close together, the smaller children were rolled in sleeping hides, and the older children were assigned to watch over them. The drums gradually became louder and more insistent, and the men started to hum, a low-pitched drone that came from their chests, as if their hearts were vibrating instead of their vocal cords. The men breathed asynchronously, which made the hum continuous and a bit eerie.

Snap felt her hair bristle; her arms and legs seemed twice as big as usual. She had watched the Bonding every fall of her life; she knew exactly what to expect, but this time it seemed different. Anything might happen; the men might all turn into elephants, the fire might multiply into a forest of flame.

The thirty or so men formed a line which began to snake around the periphery of the uwanda, creating a large, moving circle with the men separated from one another by more than the lengths of their outstretched arms. The women began to organize themselves as well, in order by rank as usual. They formed a circle around the fire, facing outward, with Chirp, the highest-status woman, beside Hum, the lowest. The women stood nearly shoulder to shoulder, so that, even though the women slightly outnumbered the men, their circle was smaller and much nearer the fire. The women began to move to the beat of the large drums, the circle rotating contrariwise to the men's, and the women started to make another sound, a trill unlike any bird. Snap had never made this sound herself, but found she joined in effortlessly and sang the strange tones as if she had practiced for her whole life.

Slowly, almost imperceptibly, the drums became louder, and the tempo increased. As the dancers moved faster, the inner circle steadily expanded and the outer circle gradually contracted. At first, Snap was aware of a few background noises—a baby cried, the fire crackled, one of the older children laughed. Eventually, the other sounds disappeared, and she heard only the ancient rhythm of the drums, the dancers' voices, and the sounds of her own feet as they beat a path to an unclear future. Time passed, and the sound of the women's song began to change. Lower in pitch, steadier, a chant emerged from the trilling sound, and at the same time, the men's hum altered as well, acquired a vibrato, and increased in pitch. Before long, the two songs merged into a single ecstatic sound, bursting from each pair of lungs, howling life into the night.

Chirp moved outward from the women's circle and stopped, although the drums and the dancing continued. She faced the men's circle as it passed in front of her, and the women continued to circle behind her. Most of the men were aroused by now, although Chirp seemed not to notice, and none seemed particularly interested in her. After each man had passed her once, she stepped between them and left the circle. She went to the mats where Rustle stood guard over his sisters with his small spear at the ready. Chirp collected her grandchildren, the mats, and the drying rack, and started off with them in the direction of her shelter.

Whistle left the women's circle next. She stood between the circles and considered each man as he passed. Finally, after the entire group had circled once and was beginning a second round she took Bapoto's hand and led him from the circle. The volume of the song increased briefly, and then returned to its previous level as Snap stepped out of the circle. She still felt her hair standing on end and her heart beating fast, but she tried to appear unperturbed and met the eyes of each man with as much dignity as she could. She didn't wait for the second round, but took Ash's hand as he passed the first time. He looked startled, as if still unclear about what was supposed to happen, but he allowed Snap to lead him out of the circle.

Away from the fire, their eyes quickly adjusted to the moonlight. When they were out of sight, he stopped, turned to her, and dropped her hand so he could sign. "Among my mother's people, choices made at the Bonding last until the next spring, until it is time for hunting and trading journeys. Is it so among the Kura?"

"Yes. Whistle chose Meerkat every fall, but she could have chosen someone else if she had wanted, and he could have gone to another ukoo in the fall had he wished. I don't remember Chirp ever choosing a mate at the Bonding, but Whistle told me when Chirp was younger, she chose the best hunter, who was usually someone different each fall."

"I'm not the best hunter, nor the second best."

"No. But you are the best traveler. An antelope is an excellent gift. It feeds one's children for a long time, keeps them warm, makes tools. But an antelope is not hard to come by; even a poor hunter will sometimes get the kill if he hunts with others who are better. On the other hand, we have had no real traders among our men for a long time. Sometimes far-walkers visit in the summer; we trade food and tools for things we can't make here, like special knives or supplies like salt, but none of our men ever come back to Kura in the fall with a trader's bundle."

Ash looked pleased, nuzzled her ear, and took her hand again. As they walked toward Chirp's shelter, the sounds of drumming and dancing were gradually muffled by the intervening shelters and irregular terrain, and they began to hear other sounds— growls, squeals, hisses, and an occasional spitting noise—which became progressively louder as they approached Chirp's shelter. Cautiously, they looked down into Chirp's uwanda from behind a natural hedge that grew on the ridge. There, Whistle and Bapoto faced each other from opposite sides of the open space and slowly circled the uwanda, while they made the threatening noises Snap and Ash had heard as they neared Chirp's shelter.

Snap watched, confused and fascinated. Whistle and Meerkat had mated as if it were a game, hooting and laughing, playing chase or pretending to hide from each other, always with cheerful goodwill. She had seen a variety of other courtships, some long and complicated, some extremely brief, but invariably affectionate. Tonight, Whistle seemed engrossed and determined, but not at all amused. When Bapoto tried to approach Whistle on his elbows and knees with a conciliatory hum, she flared her nostrils and hissed, and when he stood upright and beat his chest with his fists, she showed her teeth and growled at him. However, something about Bapoto riveted her, and she made no effort to drive him away.

Pulling Snap down with him, Ash squatted so they couldn't be seen from the uwanda. "Is this how your people mate?" he asked, waving at the other pair. "I would think these noises might attract hyenas."

"No! Sometimes people make a lot of noise, but not like this.

They sound like they're fighting over a kill. How do people usu
ally mate in your mother's ukoo?"

Ash did not respond with words.

Snap had seen adults mating often, since privacy was onl
necessary for keeping secrets, and as a child, she had often playe
at mating with other children. A girl pretending to be a woma
squatted with her back to a boy pretending to be a man and the
bounced on the balls of their feet, figured out what goes where
pretended to keep watch for predators, and made mating noise
which they found hysterically funny. Pretend mating had becom
more interesting to Snap as she got older, and she found severa
of the older boys were equally interested in watching adults mat
and willing to play at mating with her. She had yet to mate witl
an adult male, and was a little nervous about the size of an adult'
erection compared to those of the children with whom she ha
practiced, but her nerves didn't dim her enthusiasm.

The hesitancy Ash had demonstrated since their first meetin
was gone. His back steadied against a boulder, he squatted witl
his knees and arms spread wide, and invited Snap to come to him
She looked at his face, examining his intentions. Ash's moutl
was a bit open, and she saw his hands tremble momentaril
Reassured, she backed into his arms, turned her head to nuzzle
his face, and soon forgot whatever fears she might have had. He
awareness of the night and the sounds around them shrank, unti
only her body and his existed; she forgot to breathe, she forgo
how to balance herself, and she clutched his knees desperately
Peculiar snorts at the back of her neck distracted her and almost
made her giggle, and then he sat down, panting. Flushed and
shaky, she knelt and turned to face him.

"That was good," she signed. "Can you do it again?"

Ash leaned back, breathing a little faster than usual. "In a little bit, all right?"

"Yes."

The sounds from Chirp's uwanda had decreased to low growls, somewhere between a respectful purr and a threatening snarl, and Snap and Ash peeked through the bushes. They were curious about the ongoing drama but didn't want to be involved in an altercation. Whistle and Bapoto still faced each other, but now they were squatting and much closer together. His show of supplication had apparently succeeded. Gradually, with many hisses and looks over her shoulder, she turned her back and allowed him to approach her. Still in the fog of her own excitement, Snap expected the curious courtship to conclude with additional uproar, but the reality was brief, almost perfunctory.

Quiet at last, the pair in the uwanda settled themselves near the fire. Whistle peered into the shadows like a serval on the hunt, while Bapoto concentrated on the fire with such a hopeful look he seemed much younger. "A fine ceremony," he signed. "One of the best I've ever seen."

Snap thought Whistle's thanks a bit cynical, but Bapoto didn't notice.

"The Great One smiles down on our people tonight. Will you join me in giving thanks to her?" Bapoto stood and raised his arms, looking expectantly at Whistle, but she shook her head.

"You can tell her thanks from me," she signed agreeably. Snap ground her teeth at Bapoto's words. *Our* people?

He lowered his arms. "Please? You are so important to . . ." He broke off. "I only want to help. How could it do any harm?"

"No harm at all. You go right ahead. I'm going to check on the children." With a good-natured wave, Whistle went into the

shelter. Snap heard the children's sleepy murmurs and watched Bapoto climb onto a stump and raise his arms again. By that time, Ash indicated he was sufficiently rested, and she backed up to him again enthusiastically.

This time, Ash was in no hurry and devoted himself to finding the best way to provoke squeals and other amusing noises from her. Once again, the rest of the world disappeared. Everything seemed new, a chance to experiment. Her imagination vaulted from notion to notion; some ideas seemed to please Ash, others Snap found more interesting. How does this feel? How about this? Breathing fast, she ignored a cramp in her leg, too focused, too intent for pain, until something unexpected and monumental happened and she lost her balance. Her last squeal was heard by several households, where a few older women nodded to themselves and discovered that they'd like to back up to their own new mates one more time.

It was quite some time later when Snap noticed that the sounds of singing and the cadence of drums had faded and disappeared. The two of them made their way down to the now empty uwanda and ducked under the door flap. Whistle sat by the fire, watching. Her expression was uninterpretable as she greeted them with a soft squeal. Everyone else appeared to be asleep. "I'm not at all tired," Snap signed to Whistle in the dim light of the banked fire. "Go to sleep. I'll watch first." Whistle nodded, rose, and moved into the sleeping alcove.

"I can watch first," signed Ash, and he stifled a yawn. Snap rolled her eyes, found her sleeping hides, and spread them out next to the fire.

"Just lie here next to me. I'll wake you when I'm tired, and you can watch next."

He yawned genially and lay down on Snap's hides, curled up on his side with room in front of him for Snap. She sat with her back against Ash's warm chest and watched the door and window flaps, wide awake, listening to his breathing become slower and deeper. The shelter was warm with two extra bodies in it, but more than that; their male smells were exciting and frightening, reassuring and threatening. She felt a profusion of possibilities, wonderful and horrible, had come into the shelter with the men, and she was both eager and anxious to discover them.

When Snap could no longer hold her eyelids up, she woke Ash and swapped places with him. She awoke when Bapoto opened the flaps and let in the morning sunshine, cool fall air, and waking sounds of birds. She curled against Ash's back, then jumped up and hurried out into the uwanda. Bapoto stood on one of the flat-topped stumps with his arms stretched over his head and made the eerie quavering wail Snap had heard on the night her wound had drained.

When he turned and jumped down, she asked, "What is that?"

"I am greeting the Great One, and giving thanks for the morning and for all the blessings of life. Would you like to join me? I see you have something for which to be thankful as well." Bapoto glanced at Ash as he came out of the shelter.

"I have chosen Ash myself. He was not a gift." While she recognized that Bapoto did have Whistle's rank now, and that peace in the shelter would require a certain amount of courtesy, she still didn't plan to spend the winter watching Bapoto spout nonsense. Ash greeted them with a sleepy sign and headed toward the latrine pits.

"There is a spirit in everything, every person, every animal, every plant, every stone, every river." Bapoto used large, two-handed signs, as if from far away. "All blessings come from the Great One, every successful hunt, every infant, every tree full of ripe fruit. We send her our thanks and our entreaties, and she rewards us for our attention."

"How do you know this?" she asked.

"I see the work of the Great One all around me. I ask the spirit of the leopard to leave your injured arm, and it is done. I ask the spirit of the antelope to come to me during the hunt, and it comes. The world fills me with wonder; how can it be so? The Great One has made it thus." Bapoto raised his arms and made the warbling sound again.

She was impressed with his sincerity but unconvinced of his sanity. He seemed to believe the world was filled with invisible monsters that controlled everything. As she turned toward the latrine pits, she hissed skeptically but very softly, so Bapoto wouldn't hear, but apparently he did. Snap heard a low growl behind her and looked back to see Bapoto eyeing her with his teeth bared, as if she were a gazelle, or a viper.

CHAPTER 5

I t *seemed* to Snap that Chirp's shelter had shrunk noticeably. In the winters of her memory, Meerkat had filled the shelter with his fervent, musky odor, his genial roughhousing with the children, his frequently successful hunting. She missed the smell of his damp hair drying before the fire, the comforting sound of Meerkat and Whistle mating in the night, the fresh meat for breakfast when Meerkat had spent his night watch with spear in hand. But even Meerkat's size and boisterousness had not made the shelter seem as small as could the two new males, with their unfamiliar routines and foreign smells.

By the end of a moon, Snap no longer felt awkward around Ash. His habits of bachelor living endeared him to Whistle and Chirp; no task was unfamiliar or somebody else's responsibility. His availability and interest in mating pleased Snap, and often distracted her from her work. She imagined they had invented several new ways in which to enjoy themselves, until one day when Chirp made several additional suggestions that revealed an expertise previously unsuspected by her granddaughter.

After several days of cold rain, a clear morning dawned, and Bapoto set out to hunt with a group of men. Ash declined Bapoto's invitation to join the group and went in another direction with his two best spears and a determined expression. By late afternoon, the midday warmth was gone. Rustle and Swish found a sunny corner to play a game that involved rolling small stones into a circle scratched into the earth, interrupted by Baby's attempts to crawl after the stones. Whistle and Chirp squeezed into a niche out of the chilly breeze with their basket weaving, and Snap sat in the smoke of the uwanda fire and scraped a hipparion hide.

Bapoto's hoot drifted into the uwanda from the west, followed by its maker, gnawing on the end of a bone. With a grunt of greeting, he dropped a nearly stripped gazelle bone in the children's circle and crossed the uwanda to the fire, where he stirred up a blaze and held his hands to the warmth. Whistle squealed a greeting, and Bapoto flared his nostrils in her direction. Before long, Snap heard hissing and angry yelping in the direction of the central uwanda, followed shortly by the appearance of two women, Whistle's sister Warble and Hum, the last woman of Kura. Both were spitting in indignation and signing incoherently at each other.

Warble had round, well-fed hips, healthy, symmetric features, and a sociable laugh. Snap liked her, but she had noticed that Whistle was careful never to trust her youngest sister with anything important. It was clear that most of the women thought her silly, and didn't understand why she had received a gift from nearly every one of the men returning for the Bonding. Warble's mate, Jackal, a powerfully built man at the peak of his abilities, followed her uncertainly.

Hum was around Whistle's age, with gray-streaked hair, crinkled skin the color of a mungomu nut, and a back bent as if burdened by one of her many children, all of whom had died before they were named. Her size, health, shelter, and possessions were the worst in Kura. Hum held something bloody clamped under one arm. Her mate, Wart, was a well-muscled man barely taller than Chirp with an asymmetric beard and a limp due to mismatched legs. The last man chosen at the Bonding, he followed her now with an uncomfortable look remarkably like Jackal's.

Whistle dropped her weaving and stood up. "Warble! Hum! Calm yourselves. Can Chirp settle this disagreement for you?"

Chirp gave a *chht* sound, and waved at Whistle. "You can handle this."

Whistle turned back to the two angry women. Snap carefully noted her mother's judicial bearing and expression, and thought, I need to learn how to do that.

"Warble, tell me what has happened," Whistle signed.

"Bapoto distributed the kill fairly—you know he did. He *gave* Jackal that forequarter, and it belongs to me." Warble's hands flapped like trapped ducks, and Snap could barely understand her words. She knew Bapoto, now having Whistle's rank, was in charge of the hunt and responsible for distributing the meat, but she didn't understand what Warble was complaining about.

Whistle frowned. "Hum, you tell me."

"Jackal received a forequarter after the hunt today—Wart got nothing." Hum appeared composed, but Snap noticed she curled her toes as if to make fists with her feet. "When Jackal passed my shelter, he stopped and cut off part of the meat for me. Warble saw him do it. She came down to my shelter and insisted I give it back."

Whistle looked at her sister as if Warble had failed to take her turn properly in a children's game. "Your storeroom is so full, I had to help you make it bigger. Hum's is half empty." Warble set her jaw and looked away.

Bapoto, who had not moved since the arrival of the others, stepped away from the fire and attracted Whistle's attention. She looked at him, and he turned so she could see his words, but Hum and Warble could not. "I gave that meat to Jackal. Wart was nowhere near the kill today, and didn't deserve a share." His expression challenged her to override his judgment.

Whistle's judicial expression faltered. Uncertainly, she looked into the faces of the two women and their mates. Only Hum met her eyes, but looked quickly downward. Finally, Whistle made her decision. "Warble, you have the right to the whole forequarter, although you don't deserve it. Hum, give it to Warble."

Hum, still curling her toes furiously and looking anywhere but at Warble, held out the bloody fragment. Warble looked at the meat and then at Whistle. She stamped her foot, spat at Hum but missed, and marched out of the uwanda. Jackal shrugged in a conciliatory way and followed her. Bapoto turned to the fire again, a hint of satisfaction at the corners of his mouth.

Ash hunted as often as the weather permitted. When he was successful, he brought Snap the carcass drawn, but otherwise whole, which allowed her to distribute or to use the meat, organs, bones, and pelt, just as Meerkat had done for Whistle. Although Ash returned empty-handed more often than not, Snap was satisfied; neither of them was hungry. On days not occupied with hunting, Ash made tools and containers from wood and bone, repaired the roof hides, and invented a more waterproof way of connecting them to the rock walls. Rustle soon developed an interest in learning to make tools like Ash's, and Swish developed an interest in Ash himself. A rainy day would often find Ash, with Swish in his lap, sitting with Rustle near the shelter window where the light was best, experimenting with pieces of wood and bone, all of them getting damp from the rain coming in the window.

Bapoto, on the other hand, was an uncommonly successful hunter. Each evening before a hunt was planned, Bapoto orchestrated a hunting ritual. He led a group of hunters to the top of the ridge, or to the men's shelter if it was raining or bitter cold, where they made a fire and accompanied quavering whistles with exotic drum cadences. Each time, Bapoto invited Ash to join them, and Ash politely declined. When Bapoto returned long after dark, he smelled of sweat and smoke, and Snap sometimes caught a pitying look from him. During the hunt the following day, Bapoto decided who should chase the game, who should lie in wait, and who should attack, and as a result, he himself often made the kill. He then distributed shares to those he felt deserving and kept the choicest pieces, which he often started to eat before he reached home.

Eventually, it seemed that Snap had meat for Rustle and Swish more often than their mother did, and Whistle's gratitude began to embarrass all of them. Quietly, Whistle began to join Bapoto for his morning rituals. Snap suspected that her mother hoped Bapoto would share his meat more readily with those who shared his beliefs, but she didn't think there was much change in his hunting habits after Whistle became proficient at the vibrating warble.

※

"Now that square. Roll it into *that* square." Snap was trying to distract Rustle and Swish from their rumbling bellies by teaching them a game she had invented involving squares scratched into the floor of the shelter, small round stones, and carefully chosen forked sticks. Cold, dark days had shrunk into midwinter. The feeble light was nearly gone, but Snap was determined to put off the moment when Whistle would dole out a slice of moldy dried fruit and a few nuts to the lethargic children so they would have something in their stomachs as they tried to sleep.

"I can't." Swish wrapped her arms around her knees and rested her head on her arms. "It's too cold."

The men were out, taking advantage of a break in the never-ending rain to hunt, but Snap knew there was little game left near Kura. Whistle lay curled on a sleeping hide, nursing Baby, while her other offspring sat as near the fire as they could without singeing themselves. Chirp sat in front of the storage alcove as she had all day, wordlessly watching for pests that might be interested in their food. Occasionally she rumbled unhappily to herself and sucked on her teeth, and Snap suspected she was about to lose another of the few remaining.

With a resigned nod, Snap swept the game paraphernalia into a basket and put it away in the storage alcove. Whistle got up, leaving Baby asleep in her warm hides, and chose some of the stored food for their meal. Chirp accepted only a single slice of marula fruit, which she sucked on and worried at until it was soft enough for her loose teeth to handle. The last light faded, and the men hadn't yet returned.

While they ate their pitiful meal, Whistle turned her body to hide her hands from Chirp and spoke to Snap. "You watch first, and wake me around midnight."

Snap nodded and took another tiny bite of her marula. The two younger women unrolled the sleeping hides and tucked in Swish and Rustle. Snap took a burning stick to start the uwanda fire and an extra hide to wrap herself in as she watched and ducked under the door. Chirp shot an indignant look after her granddaughter and shuffled out after her.

As Snap was lighting the fire, Chirp tapped her arm. "I always watch first."

"There's no need for you to watch during the winter. The men will be back soon, and we four are plenty of watchers."

"I watch first." Chirp set her jaw and pressed her lips into a thin line.

Snap nodded and ducked back into the shelter, but she stayed at the door flap, watching through the gap. Chirp got the fire blazing, wrapped herself in the extra hide, and squatted at the fire with her back to the shelter. In a few minutes, Snap saw her grandmother's head nodding, and she heard a soft snore. Chirp's hair, now almost completely white, was escaping its Kura twists and flapped in the light breeze. Snap shook her head affectionately and settled down to watch from the door.

The crescent moon had moved from the zenith halfway down the western sky when Snap heard a grunt and soft snuffle from the downhill side of the uwanda. The fire had burned low and no eyes reflected its light, but something was there, something with feet that carelessly disturbed medium-size rocks, something large enough to make a very low-pitched grunt.

Snap did not want to embarrass her grandmother by finding her asleep on watch. She tried a soft *chht*, and then a twig tossed at Chirp's back, but the old woman slept on, and the grunts came closer. Snap rose to her feet and began feeling in the dark for the spear that she was sure was leaning against the wall somewhere nearby. Scrabbling footsteps and another grunt came from outside, and she looked out to see an enormous bushpig trotting into the dying uwanda firelight. Long coarse hair swung between short tusks as the bushpig's snout foraged from side to side. It sniffed at Chirp's gnarled foot protruding from under the hide and took an experimental bite.

Snap and Chirp yowled simultaneously. The pig leapt straight up to nearly its own height and shot into the darkness with a long, resonant growl. The sound ended in a loud crunch and a brief, almost human-sounding scream. Snap finally located the spear and fell out of the door, Whistle on her heels. Now silent, Chirp lay curled on her side, her foot in both hands. Something dark oozed from between her fingers. She looked at Snap and raised one bloody hand to speak.

"Maybe it would be best if I left watching to you younger ones."

As they helped Chirp into the shelter, they heard Kura hoots from the direction the pig had departed. Snap left Whistle to help Chirp clean up her bitten foot and returned to the uwanda. As she built up the fire, Ash dragged the dead bushpig into the light, a bloody spear in his other hand. As they dressed the carcass, Ash told Snap how he had followed a small herd of gazelles most of the day but had started back to Kura at dusk without getting near enough for a shot. The bushpig had startled him just as he was about to hoot on his return to Kura, and luckily he still had his best spear in hand.

It turned out that the other Kura men had followed the same gazelle herd and had stayed near them through the night to hunt again in the morning. When Bapoto returned to Chirp's shelter around midday with part of a hindquarter, he found the others with greasy fingers and faces, sucking the marrow from bones of roast pork. He had no interest in joining the well-fed joking and teasing, but he was willing to finish the gazelle meat when Whistle kindly roasted it for him.

Winter grew old. Cold rain and wind battered the shelters and forced everyone into one another's company. Chirp's foot healed slowly, and she now required a sturdy stick to lean on when she walked. The kinanas, fruit, and nuts were nearly gone, the dried meat was moldy, and the scarce greens brought by the rain were not very filling and unsettled their stomachs. Late one afternoon, Ash had gone out into a downpour to check his snares, while the others crammed into Chirp's shelter tried to distract their attention from their rumbling bellies. Near the fire, Chirp helped Rustle and Swish sort reeds for baskets; both children kept glancing nervously at the adults as if waiting for an explosion, and were careful to stay out of everyone's way. Whistle and Snap were struggling to stretch a zebra hide over a wooden frame for curing, but seemed to be working at cross-purposes. The hide kept springing free from the frame, and they were forced to begin again. Baby was exploring, and her mother and siblings kept her from crawling into the fire over and over. Bapoto was asleep in the alcove.

Ash lifted the door flap and came into the shelter, spraying raindrops over everyone and making the fire hiss. Swish shrieked, and Bapoto awoke to find Baby's face looming over his and her finger just about to poke him in the eye. He awoke with a snarl and swept her away with his arm, rolling her across the floor. She squealed with pleasure and started to crawl back to be rolled again, but Whistle jumped to her feet and whisked Baby into her sling.

"You are a warthog!" she signed at Bapoto and grabbed a scraping blade from the floor where she had been working. Bapoto bared his teeth and crouched as if preparing to spring, but Whistle stood her ground.

A tense moment later, he turned to Ash. "What did you get?"

Ash spread his empty hands in answer.

"You should have joined the hunting ritual with us six nights ago. We took a zebra, as you know."

"Fifteen men are more likely to be successful than one, yes."

"The Great One favors us because we give her the respect she deserves."

"I have yet to meet this Great One," signed Ash as he squatted by the fire and stretched his wet arms to it. There was no threat in either his expression or his words, but Bapoto stood up with a queer grimace.

"Unless you are wise enough to join us, you will join those who must discover the power of the Great One another way."

Snap stood up as well. "Rustle and Swish are not my children, yet I am able to feed them better than their mother can this winter. Why do you think that is?" Rustle and Swish clearly did not want to get involved in this conversation, and both seemed to be trying to crawl into Chirp's lap.

Bapoto snarled again. Whistle stepped between Bapoto and Snap and faced her daughter. "You will respect the rank of my mate. If you and Ash would join us in greeting the Great One every morning, we would all benefit from her blessings and avoid angry words over nothing in our shelter."

Snap stared at her mother in disbelief but dropped her eyes without responding. Can this be my mother? She squatted next to Ash, looked at her clenched fingers, and forced them to open and lie relaxed on her thighs.

Bapoto sidled out from behind Whistle and picked up his short spear, which had been leaning against the wall near the door. "Checking for hyenas," he signed at Whistle and was gone, a mist of raindrops flying from the edge of the door flap as it fell behind him.

Snap suppressed the urge to spit after him.

Whistle settled down to nurse Baby. After a few moments, Snap gathered her courage and attracted her mother's attention with a *chht*. "Bapoto is disrespectful to you."

Whistle looked cold. "What do you mean? He is trying to help Ash—to teach a younger man what he should know."

"I mean about the hunting. He never brings you your share of the game."

"Bapoto knows well who is deserving. It is not how our men have hunted in the past, true, but it is how things were done in his mother's ukoo. He doesn't mean disrespect. You, on the other hand, ought to know better."

"This is *not* his mother's ukoo! He should respect *our* ways!" Snap's hands shook with indignation, and without thinking, she rose to her feet and stood looking down at her mother, eyes flashing. Chirp's sudden intake of breath brought her back to her senses, and before Whistle could respond to her daughter's insolence, Snap threw herself out into the rain and ran blindly downhill, away from the other shelters.

Gasping sobs shook her as she stumbled on and on, filled with visions of possible punishments that might await her on her return. As Snap's angry tremors became shivers, she became aware of fading light, wet hair, and a grove of stunted evergreen annona trees, with broad branches that swept the ground around each. In search of a drier spot to rest, she crawled under the bottommost branches of one of the larger trees and found a space big enough for her curled body, lined with ancient, musty leaves, and quite dry. Rain whispered around her, and a gust of wind sent a shower of cold drops over her face. At last, her shivering subsided and she fell asleep.

A thumping sound entered her dreams, and she was at the Bonding, flushed with anticipation as she danced around the women's circle, but then she awoke. Darkness, unfamiliar smells, an uncomfortable stick in her back, peculiar thuds—brief confusion became alarm as Snap remembered the argument, her flight, the annona tree. Silently, she moved a branch and peered out between the branches.

The rain had stopped. The full moon illuminated a small clearing and three figures. Bapoto beat an unfamiliar rhythm on a small, high-pitched drum while two other men tended a fire. When one of them turned, she recognized Jackal, her aunt Warble's mate. The other was vaguely familiar; he had been at the previous Bonding but hadn't been chosen. She suspected he had ended up at the bachelors' shelter near the Kijito with the other young or unsuitable men not chosen in any ukoo. The drumming seemed more interesting to Bapoto than to the other two;

soon they began to yawn and looked as if they might curl up and go to sleep. Bapoto stopped drumming and began to speak with ordinary small signs. In order to see his words without revealing herself, she twisted herself into an uncomfortable crouched position, one eye peeping through the branches.

"Thank you for joining me for the hunting ritual. The Great One is with us, and I hope she will send us a sign of her presence. We are humble worshippers of the Great One. We thank her for her attention tonight." Bapoto warbled as he signed, and the two other men joined him. Their voices seemed deeper than usual, and the vibrations of the warble slower, as if a parliament of owls filled the clearing with their debate. "The long rains have kept us from hunting, and our people are hungry. Thank you, Great One, for the clear sky tonight. Please give us sun to hunt by in the morning, and help us to find game before the storms return."

The two men snapped their fingers and stamped their feet in response, and sparks flew up from the fire as one log collapsed onto another. Bapoto joined the foot stamping, and soon, the three were dancing around the fire, making a gray stew of fallen leaves and muddy earth with their feet. At last, Snap heard a real owl call, and Bapoto jerked to a stop, listening. While the other two watched him with eyes wide and mouths slightly open, he closed his eyes and raised his arms slowly and stiffly, palms upward. Finally, he seemed to awake and fell onto his knees, gasping for breath as if he had been running.

"The Great One will bless our hunt tomorrow," Bapoto signed. "She will send us gazelles fat with new grass, too lazy to run far. In return for her blessings, she asks us to demonstrate our devotion to her by living together in peace, men and women. We should no longer cast out the men who are not chosen, nor force old men to take summer journeys."

Jackal shook his head and offered Bapoto a hand up. "I think the dancing has made you a bit dizzy, my friend. I will be happy to hunt with you in the morning, if the storms haven't returned, but now, it's bedtime." Jackal clapped Bapoto on the back and clumped off.

Bapoto turned to the other man, who stood uncertainly on the other side of the fire. "Surely you see the brilliance of the Great One, Burrow?"

Burrow knit his brow. He kicked at the edge of the fire and avoided Bapoto's gaze. "Do you mean I should live in Kura, even without a mate?"

"Yes, clearly. The ukoo needs us men. They need us to hunt, need us to trade. We are essential, Burrow, just as much as they are."

It seemed Burrow wanted to believe Bapoto but couldn't reconcile these ideas with his understanding of the world. Finally, he nodded. "Sure, sure. Maybe next winter, I'll do that. Let's get to sleep now, if we're going to hunt in the morning." Burrow departed in the other direction, not following Jackal toward Kura, but heading toward the bachelors' shelter near the Kijito. When he was gone, Bapoto stood staring into the fire, teeth clenched, and then kicked the embers into the mud, extinguishing all but a few sparks.

CHAPTER 6

By the time Snap was alone, the rain had started again. Whistle is usually more agreeable early in the morning than late at night, she thought. I'll stay here until it gets light. When she awakened in the predawn chill, she was convinced she could smooth over her clash with Whistle with a humble, carefully worded apology. A carroty glow crept up the clear sky as she made her way back to Kura and found Ash sitting at the uwanda fire, apparently the last watcher of the night, the others still asleep.

"Perfect day for an expedition," she signed as he rose to

greet her. "Maybe there are new onions down where the stream runs into the Kijito. Maybe it's time to try out my new fishing basket." She nuzzled Ash and climbed onto the flat rock. Her gaze followed the stream, and she imagined in the distance a flash of sun on water. "The Kijito is probably full of fish."

Ash climbed up after her and looked in the same direction, eyes wide and hungry. "Do you feel like hunting? It's a great day to run. You chase, I'll try out my new spears, and we'll have fresh meat for dinner."

No hunting parties had asked her to chase since the previous spring, and Ash's proposal galvanized her into action. She jumped off the rock and began to gather hunting gear with a loud hum of approval. Before the bundles were ready, Bapoto and Whistle emerged from the shelter, climbed onto the large rock, and began their usual morning ritual. When their last vibrating echoes had died away, Whistle descended from the rock and scrutinized the heap of objects at her daughter's feet—several wooden spears, hides, good stone knives and scrapers, two empty water bags, a quantity of twine. Bapoto, still on the rock, folded his arms and watched the two women.

Snap squatted before her mother, eyes downcast. "I am sorry for my lack of respect yesterday."

Whistle gave a satisfied nod. "You will be a good Mother, one day."

"Ash will hunt today," Snap signed. "I will chase. Don't expect us until nightfall."

Bapoto addressed Ash. "I will be happy to show you the proper way to ask the Great One's help."

Ash made a polite gesture of refusal. Bapoto bared his teeth.

Snap and Ash tied their bundles around their shoulders and set off toward the stream at a rapid trot. When they were nearly out of her sight, Whistle gave a single booming, reverberating hoot. Snap did not turn, but raised one arm in acknowledgment and ran on.

No game remained near Kura—no need to search for spoor yet—so they ran like untroubled giraffes chasing each other for pleasure. The clouds were gone. A huge sky-blue sapphire, pierced by the most dazzling of diamonds, stretched over an equally huge grass-green emerald. New shoots punctured the hard earth and cushioned their pounding feet.

Snap studied Ash as they ran. He seemed as pleased to be free from the stuffy shelter as she was, and she noticed his hair was finally starting to acquire the proper Kura shape. The last three moons had aged him; his beard was bushier, his shoulders seemed wider, and sun creases had started at the corners of his eyes. She thought about the distances Ash had run that winter, great spans of danger and exhaustion, hunting for her and her family. I chose him for his talents, she thought, because he is a good traveler, a good trader, and a good craftsman, but there is a more important reason. He is a good man. Even her growling stomach couldn't dispel her pleasure and hope.

At the place where the Kura stream joined the Kijito river, Ash spotted a few chenga in the water and pulled out a spear. "Hungry?" The hand-size silver-and-black fish darted from shade to sun, glinting like shining aquatic birds.

Snap gave the fish a doubtful look. "We don't eat those."

"No? Chenga only make you sick when it's hot. They're perfectly fine in the winter."

With a skeptical grunt, Snap speared one of the small fish, cleaned it with a few quick strokes of her obsidian knife, and handed it to Ash. "You first."

With a ridiculous formal gesture of thanks, he took the fish and bit off a large chunk. He finished the chenga in two more bites and then speared and cleaned a second for Snap. Dubiously, she accepted the fish. Her stomach rumbled, and she ate the second chenga as rapidly as Ash had eaten his.

"I guess I'll find out whether you're right."

They ran on. A long way from Kura, they slowed down and began to swing their gazes from side to side like pendulums as they searched for signs of game. Near a small seasonal stream, Ash stopped abruptly to examine a patch of recently trodden grass, and then looked south. Snap climbed a boulder as tall as Ash and shaded her eyes with her hand. "I see them. Just beyond that wash." She pointed southwest, toward a stand of starved-looking fig trees. "Wait in those trees. The wind is from dawn-ward. I'll circle around that way and drive them toward you. The wildebeests will smell me coming far away, but they won't see you until they get to the trees. Take my spear, too. I won't get close enough for a shot; you can use it."

Ash nodded. "I'll take the packs and leave them in the trees. They'll just weigh us down."

Without her bundle, Snap nearly flew as she headed southeast. She made no sound and kept as low as possible until she was directly east of the herd, when she stood up and took a good look at the animals. It was a small group, only one large male with a group of about twenty females, several with calves that looked no older than a moon. A few interrupted their grazing, nostrils flared, and began to stamp their front feet. The male snorted, and soon the entire group was milling around and staring shortsight-edly upwind. When Snap whooped, waved, and jumped, the bull kicked his rear legs and started toward her, but the cows nosed their calves in the opposite direction. Snap began to run back and forth, moving closer to the herd on each pass, and the bull soon joined the herd heading west. The animals' retreat was slowed by the cows' hanging back with the younger calves, and Snap had no trouble staying close enough to direct the herd toward the stand of figs in which Ash was concealed.

The herd did not want to run into the trees. The first few cows veered right as they approached the figs, and Snap ran around the right side of the herd to force them as close as possible to the trees. The leading animals slowed down even more, until Snap was near enough to see their eyes rolling nervously at her. A few kicked again, and Snap backed off, still whooping and jumping. As one of the first calves passed a thicket near the edge of the figs, a spear flew from the tangle of branches and hit the calf just behind the front legs. It fell and was accidentally kicked by several of the following animals. The cow stopped and sniffed at its still offspring, and then at a whoop from Snap, she charged after her comrades. At the back of the herd ran the smallest calf, apparently not able to keep up with its panicked mother. Another spear hit this calf in the hindquarters. It stumbled and limped on. Ash burst from the thicket and gave chase, the last spear at the ready. The calf bawled and one of the cows slowed, but Snap cut in between the herd and the wounded calf, bellowing with renewed enthusiasm. The cow's courage failed her, and she reluctantly rejoined the rest of the animals. By the time Ash had dispatched the wounded calf with another spear, the herd had disappeared over a low hill, encouraged by Snap at their heels.

When Snap returned, Ash was pulling the second calf toward the one killed first. "Do you want to guard the meat while I go get our bundles, or do you want to run a bit more?" he asked, jubilant and panting.

"There might be lions watching this herd; I think I'll go for the packs. Better get the spears out." Snap had run a great distance flat out but was so exhilarated by their success that she didn't feel the least bit tired. Ash directed her to where he had stored the bundles, and by the time she returned, he had retrieved the spears and found that two were usable without repair. Snap opened the packs, took out an obsidian knife, and quickly gutted the animals. Vultures were beginning to circle above, and she knew other scavengers would be on the scene soon.

Meanwhile, Ash cut two poles from the thicket and stripped them of leaves and side branches. He then tied them together at one end and fastened a hide between the poles to make a dragger. Using two more poles and the other hide, he made another for Snap. By pulling the free ends of the poles and dragging the joined ends, they could each get one of the calves back to Kura. Snap and Ash quickly tied their belongings to the draggers with the carcasses and started to retrace their steps northward as fast as they could over the rough ground.

The vultures were distracted by the abandoned entrails and didn't follow them. A lone hyena pursued them for a long while but finally gave up when Snap threw a jagged rock and hit it on the jaw. The way home seemed many times farther than the trip out, but satisfaction at the successful hunt gave Snap stamina to match Ash's tremendous pace. By the time they reached the place where they had speared the fish, twilight was deepening and Snap's feet were bleeding in several places. Her high spirits were flagging, and only her fear of twilight-hunting lions kept her running. The full moon rising to their left cheered them considerably, and when they finally arrived, it lit Chirp's uwanda so brightly that Snap could have groomed Ash's hair by its light.

As they dropped their draggers, Snap saw the door flap was arranged with one corner open, but she couldn't see the watcher within. She hooted, and Whistle came out of the door like a diving eagle, followed by Chirp in her own time. Whistle squeezed her daughter in her arms and pressed her face into the side of Snap's neck for a long time. When she finally let go, Snap signed, "I'm sorry we are so late. I hope you weren't worrying."

Whistle rumbled in wry disbelief. "No, of course not. We will definitely need to keep watch with fire in our hands tonight."

Bapoto and the children didn't stir while the others squeezed the two wildebeest calves and the bloody draggers into the deepest part of the storage alcove. Whistle volunteered to watch first, since Snap and Ash had run so far, and Chirp insisted on joining her. As Snap rolled herself into her sleeping hides, she could see the other women watching from each side of the door, Chirp holding a burning branch and Whistle a spear. Snap fell immediately into a deep sleep, and when Ash shook her near midnight, she remembered no dreams at all.

"We've had a visit from a lioness," he signed. "Whistle saw one in the shadows up on the ridge a little while ago. She appears to be gone now, but we had better not fall asleep on our watch." Whistle and Chirp looked tired, and they were asleep before Ash and Snap had finished settling themselves at the door.

The night was cold and filled with soft rustles and squeaks. The full moon was now directly overhead, and Snap saw a bat fly across its face, changing direction sharply as it did so. Clouds coming from the west slowly obscured the stars and approached the moon. Snap sat at the side of the door nearest the fire, and a branch lay at hand with one end in the fire, ready to be scooped up and used as a weapon if necessary. The best of Ash's remaining spears lay next to his hand as he scanned the uwanda. Snap's legs ached from the long journey and her arms were sore from pulling the heavy dragger. Her ragged feet had stopped bleeding, but she could think of nothing except soaking them in the cool stream until all feeling left them. The stars moved even more slowly than usual.

As the clouds began to drift across the yellow face of the moon, Snap heard a faint sound to the left of the door, downhill and away from the other shelters. A twig, bending under the weight of a stealthy foot? She caught Ash's eye and pointed. He nodded and signed, "I heard it." Snap put her hand on the branch next to her and made sure the other end was ablaze. Ash picked up the wooden spear. The small noises of leaves stirring in corners, mice conversing, the whoosh of an owl's wings continued.

An enormous lioness rounded the corner of the shelter. Firebrand in hand, Snap yowled an alarm and bounded to her feet. Ash bellowed a challenge, and both braced themselves in the door, filling it with their threatening presence. The lioness crossed and recrossed the uwanda in silence, intent on the two at the door, clearly nervous about the flames in their hands but maddened by the smell of the meat inside. Chirp and Whistle crowded into the door between them with firebrands. Over their heads, Bapoto held up the door flap to make room for a spear throw. Snap could hear Rustle herd his sisters into the back of the sleeping alcove, apparently trying to hide them among the bedding.

The lion crawled toward the door, her abdomen on the compacted earth of the uwanda, ears flat to her head, a low growl in her throat. With an astonishingly loud yowl, Chirp took a step forward and poked her flaming branch into the animal's face. The lioness roared, batted the branch to one side, and grabbed Chirp's wrist with her jaws. Snap and Whistle desperately thrust their branches at the lioness in efforts to distract her, set her fur on fire, make her drop Chirp. Ash tried to drive his spear into the lion's shoulder, but Chirp's position compromised the angle of his attack, and the blow glanced off. Bapoto heaved his spear over the others' heads but missed completely. The lion whirled around and dragged the tiny old woman downhill, into the darkness.

Snap's throat closed around a scream as she groped desperately for one of Ash's spears. *Not Chirp, not Chirp* pounded in her brain as she followed Ash downhill into the darkness, firebrand held high in one hand, spear ready in the other. She heard someone scrabbling down the slope behind her, and a brief yelp told her it was Whistle. The terrain seemed to flicker in the torchlight, and Snap stumbled and nearly fell. Too soon, Chirp's screams stopped, but they continued in the direction they last heard her. Just before they reached the stream, two long spear throws from the shelter, Snap, Whistle, and Ash found the lioness and her prey in a clearing among stunted willow trees. They were much too late to do anything for Chirp.

Snap's breath was trapped in her lungs. Whistle's wail filled her ears, but her own wail stayed in her chest, hot and expanding, unable to escape. The lioness growled and flattened her ears. A tuft of white hair fluttered from the cat's mouth.

"Too late," signed Ash. "Back away slowly, and I'll follow you." Snap followed his instructions, but Whistle, unable to see his words, stood frozen. Her unearthly scream continued to tear from her throat even as Ash took her elbow and tried to back out of the clearing with her.

As Snap backed away, the trees muffled Whistle's voice. Now she could hear a thin wail from uphill, and she instantly recognized Baby's voice. She stumbled up the hill, every breath a desperate groan, her legs and chest twisted with cramping muscles. With the moon now covered by clouds, her guttering torch made dark trees and boulders into terrifying silhouettes. Directionless without the stars, she followed Baby's cry. Finding the shelter took much longer than losing it had. As she approached the uwanda, she heard Rustle bellow and Swish scream, and then Baby's wail stopped.

The door flap was pulled half to one side and the window flap hung askew from one corner of the window gap, its fastenings dangling. The uwanda was faintly lit by flickering firelight from inside. As Snap stepped into the firelight, another lioness leapt out of the window gap. Baby hung from the cat's jaws, eyes open and staring, her neck crushed and twisted to an impossible angle. With wide night-black eyes, the lion gauged Snap's threat, apparently lumped her with mice and voles, and disappeared into the darkness. From inside the shelter, Snap could hear Swish's gasping sobs and Rustle trying to comfort her.

Bapoto stumbled into the uwanda from the west, an unlit torch in one hand, a spear with the point splintered in the other. He tucked the spear under his arm to sign. "My torch went out. Did you find—"

"Another lion took Baby!" Snap waved toward the top of the ridge. He stood frozen for a moment, his mouth open, and then stumbled after the second lioness.

An urge to run away—to follow Bapoto—to go anywhere but into the shelter seized Snap, but she charged in nevertheless. Jammed into the farthest corner of the sleeping alcove, Rustle and Swish curled into a shivering, nut brown ball. Snap dropped her spear and threw the remnant of her torch into the dying fire. With a crooning sound, she squatted next to them. The ball unrolled itself and re-formed around Snap. She tried to look for injuries, but neither would release the other. At last she freed one hand enough to sign.

"Are you all right?"

Swish nodded, but Rustle just gave her an empty stare.

"Rustle?"

His fingers shook as they slowly, painfully shaped words. "It pulled Baby right out of my hands."

Snap nuzzled both of them. "It's not your fault. We all did our best."

Rustle's face disappeared into the back of Swish's neck.

Snap pried herself from their grasp. "Stay there in the corner. I need to go watch until everyone gets back."

As Snap came out of the shelter, rearmed, Ash appeared at the edge of the uwanda, with a blank-looking Whistle by the hand. Whistle shifted her spear to free a hand and gestured, "What's happened?"

Snap gathered them into her arms, nuzzled them both, and then pulled away enough to sign. "Another lioness. She tore down the window flap and pulled Baby right out of Rustle's arms. I just got a glimpse of the lioness as she ran off. Bapoto went after her, but Baby was . . ." Snap broke off and shook her head as if dispersing a nightmare. "I'm so sorry, Whistle."

Whistle gasped and sobbed as she stumbled into the shelter.

"Rustle and Swish are all right?" Ash asked.

She nodded. A scrabbling sound on the ridge above made her raise her spear, but she lowered it again as Bapoto scrambled down the slope into the half-light, using his spear for balance. His eyes and lips were pale, and he was making a shocked-sounding rumble.

"I lost her in the dark. The lions must have followed your trail. I should have asked the spirit of the wildebeest to come to you, so the Great One would bless your hunt. It is my fault."

Snap bared her teeth and spat at Bapoto's feet. "The Great One?" Her hands shook so much her words were nearly incomprehensible. "What about you? This shelter has kept us safe for the lives of fifteen Mothers! Now you and your Great One let a lion come in the window and walk out with our Baby." She spat again and stalked past Bapoto into the shelter, Ash on her heels.

Whistle had gathered Rustle and Swish into her lap and was rocking back and forth, keening. The children were both sobbing now, but quietly. Whistle looked up as Bapoto came in. Her hands scarcely moved as she spoke, like leaves stirring in a barely perceptible breeze. "I thought you were going to stay here."

"I . . . I didn't see. . . . Did you sign to me?"

Whistle looked away, staring into the fire as if the answer to his question were there. Snap swallowed a hard lump in her throat, added a log to the fire and took a new torch, and then turned to Ash. "I'll watch at the window. You can have the door."

He nodded, took a new torch himself, and stationed himself at the door. Bapoto turned to Snap. "I'll watch. You sleep." Her jaw tightened.

Behind Bapoto, Ash gave her a small nod and signed, "Go on. We'll watch for a while."

Snap turned away from the window and crouched at the opening of the sleeping alcove. Whistle stared blankly at the ceiling, Rustle on one side and Swish on the other. Snap curled up next to Swish. Their shuddering remnants of sobs stopped as the children fell asleep, but Snap lay listening to the others breathe, to the wind rising, to the fire burying itself in its own embers.

CHAPTER 7

he night dragged on, punctuated by an occasional exhausted hiccup from Whistle and Bapoto's soft, strange whistling. Snap felt Chirp's absence like a cavity inside her, as if missing some essential part made the aches in her legs and arms engulf her entire body. The scramble after the lioness in the dark had torn open her feet, and they were bleeding again. Finally, she gave up trying to sleep and ducked out of the shelter. Ash was prodding the uwanda fire, throwing sparks into the moonless night. Around a corner, Bapoto crouched by the shreds of the window flap.

When she waved him into the shelter, Ash shook his head. "I can't sleep either. We can watch together." They squatted on opposite sides of the blaze so he could see up the slope while she scanned the downhill shadows. Every flicker of the light threatened; every shift of the gloom presaged another confrontation. For a moment, the blackness between two limestone outcrops was a crouching lioness; the fire wavered in a breeze, and the shadow became a kneeling man; she turned her head, and it was Chirp, her arms curled around her knees, her face as smooth and filled with promise as a young woman at her first Bonding. Snap shook her head to clear it.

Chirp is dead, she told herself. I saw it with my own eyes. She has been fading since fall, not really herself. She was lucky to avoid the slow, painful deaths her sisters suffered. I'm just feeling sorry for myself. I ought to be relieved her suffering was so brief. I ought to be sorry for poor Baby.

But as much as Snap had cared about Baby, losing babies—to illness, to predators, or sometimes for no obvious reason—was so common as to seem almost expected, however sad. It was Chirp whom Snap needed, whom Snap would miss most. Finally, a faint greenish glow outlined the clouds on the eastern horizon. The only incursion had been a shrew that shot across the uwanda and was scooped up by an owl before reaching cover. Snap became convinced there had been only two lionesses, and they had finished hunting. A low, scraggly sky made sunrise difficult to pinpoint, but eventually the somber light managed to wake the children. Whistle arose with them, stiff and slow, her green eyes dull and almost gray. Bapoto patted her on the arm and signed, "You sleep if you like. We can do the butchering."

Whistle looked at him without expression. "No, I can't sleep. I need to be busy." Since the kill belonged to Ash, Snap took charge of the butchering. Soon, Whistle was scraping the first hide, Ash was quartering the first carcass, and Rustle was showing Swish the best way to peel the wildebeest gallbladder from the liver without spilling bile everywhere. When Snap didn't assign him a job, Bapoto took a spear and disappeared. He had only just gone when Peep, Chirp's second daughter, came down the path and squealed greetings.

"All well? We heard a yowl in the night, but we couldn't leave the children when it was so dark."

A baby of crawling age squirmed on Peep's left hip, and she hitched the child up with an arm that was smaller than her right and bent in the wrong place, broken in childhood and healed badly. Peep was avoiding Whistle's eyes, and Snap wondered if her aunt thought the disturbance might have been a domestic disagreement. Whistle, who was squatting near the door, reached up for Peep's hand and pulled her sister down next to her.

"Lions. They took Chirp and Baby."

Peep keened and began rocking back and forth. Peep had lost four of her seven children before they were named, three with illnesses and one to a hyena, and it seemed to Snap that mourning came as naturally to Peep as eating. Whistle put down the hide she was scraping and gathered her sister and niece into her arms. They keened together until their voices drowned in quiet sobs. Finally, Peep's Baby squawked for her mother's attention, and Whistle let them go.

Peep wiped her eyes on the back of her free arm. "We're orphans." Peep used the sign for an infant whose mother died soon after giving birth. Whistle didn't laugh, but she jerked her chin up appreciatively, and Snap thought she looked a bit less gloomy.

"Ash and I went hunting yesterday, and we brought back two wildebeest calves last night," Snap signed. "The lions were probably after the meat. I hope you can use some of it." Ash had finished quartering the first calf, and Snap chose one of the forequarters to give Peep.

"Thank you. We will all appreciate this. Most of our food is gone, and what's left doesn't smell good. Your cousin has just begun to feel her baby move, and she is starving all the time."

"You're welcome. How is Bubble feeling?" Peep's daughter Bubble had become a woman the previous fall, and had always been Snap's favorite childhood companion.

"She's fine, already sticking out in the front." Peep turned back to Whistle. "Chirp did everything she should have done. The ukoo has been as peaceful as it could have been, and no hungrier than necessary. She kept all her daughters alive to womanhood. She was a fine Mother, and I'm grateful she didn't suffer long. I am sorry about your Baby. You better tie up your breasts, they're going to be pretty sore." Whistle nodded, folded up the hide she had been working on, and went into the shelter. Peep thanked Snap for the meat again and went off to share the news with Warble, her only other sister.

Shortly, Whistle came out of the shelter with a ragged strip of rabbit hide, patches of moth-eaten fur clinging to it, tied around her chest. Snap didn't laugh, but she did jerk her head upward in amusement. Whistle realized she looked silly and returned the gesture. As Whistle settled back down to working on the hides, Bapoto returned, spear over his shoulder.

"No sign of Baby anywhere. And nothing left of Chirp except blood on the ground. The lionesses must have cubs at home." Snap saw Whistle's jaw clench. Bapoto squatted by Whistle and addressed her. "I know my beliefs are not the Kura's, but I feel in my heart that Chirp and Baby are still with us somehow. I know their bodies are gone, but I am sure their spirits endure. I want to ask the Great One to take care of them, so when we die as well and our spirits go to the Great One, we will see them again."

Whistle sat staring at the hide she had been working on, which was still partly flesh covered. "Again." She repeated his last word as if she were a child learning a new sign. "See them again?"

Bapoto nodded, although Whistle wasn't looking at him, and Snap snorted. "Don't be ridiculous. They are dead, and we miss them terribly, but only people who have lost their senses talk to the dead."

They waited. Finally, Whistle looked up at Bapoto, resignation in her eyes. "All right."

Preparing for a festival while feeling so dismal felt strange, even wrong. When Bapoto asked Snap to donate the rest of the wildebeest calves for a feast, she pointed out that Rustle and Swish were both thinner than they should be and refused. Bapoto widened his eyes and snorted, but she folded her arms firmly to show she had nothing more to say. At that, he marched off to visit each family in Kura, in careful rank order.

On a trip to the spring for water, Snap happened to see Bapoto's speech at Warble's shelter. He explained his belief that the spirits of Chirp and Whistle's Baby were still present among them and his desire to help them safely go to the Great One, where all who believe in her go after their deaths. He was quite clear about the fact that Whistle had approved this idea and would be present to help send off her mother and daughter. Warble seemed bemused, but she had loved Chirp and was easy to convince. Jackal required little persuasion. He had participated in Bapoto's prehunt parties and seemed to expect this new kind of party would be nearly as much fun.

Around midday, Bapoto and Whistle walked from her shelter to the central uwanda, hooting loudly. As Whistle had directed, Snap and Ash followed at a little distance, with Rustle and Swish close behind. When they heard the hooting, the other families began drifting toward the uwanda as well. A large fire was already burning in one corner. Snap glanced around the uwanda, not sure where to sit. Finally, she and Ash drifted to the edge of the crowd and squatted near an old buffalo thorn tree. Bapoto and Whistle both climbed on the large rock where Chirp had addressed her people, and everyone's attention turned to them.

"My people." Whistle used large, slow, two-armed signs. "Last night, Chirp, our Fifteenth Mother, was taken by a lion, along with her youngest granddaughter. We miss both of them. Bapoto's people believe everything has within it a spirit, which is separate from the body. When the body dies, the spirit of a person goes to the Great One, and sees again those who have died before. All of you have seen Bapoto explain these ideas, and each of you can decide for yourself if you feel their truth. I feel Chirp and Baby inside me, and I can't imagine how they can no longer exist. It comforts me to think that somehow they are still somewhere, waiting for me. I mourn their passing, and ask the Great One to speed their spirits to her care."

Bapoto keened loudly and many voices joined his, until the sound echoed from the limestone walls above them like the sound of a great circling bird about to settle on its gigantic nest. When the reverberations had died away, Whistle climbed down from the rock and settled on the ground next to Snap, Ash, and the children. Keening softly, Bapoto used large signs to tell of Chirp's life, her children, her good judgment, her knowledge of the world, and her leadership. During his morning visits, he had learned stories about Chirp from practically everyone in Kura, including some from people nearly as old as Chirp, and he repeated the best of these.

After a touching story about how Chirp had cheered up the Naming festival in a year when there was almost nothing to eat, Snap frowned. I never knew this, she thought, and Whistle looks surprised, too. Snap could see people nodding and signing discreetly, "That's right. She was just like that," but she couldn't bear to see stories about Chirp coming from Bapoto's hands. She signed privately to Ash, "He is a stranger. How can he pretend our Mother was his own?"

Ash shook his head in agreement and squeezed her hand. After Bapoto had eulogized Chirp thoroughly, he expanded on the Great One, the existence of spirits, the need to commune with the Great One, and her ability to influence human affairs. The men began to let their attention wander, since they were familiar with this speech from Bapoto's prehunt events, but the women continued to pay attention. Finally, Bapoto encouraged everyone to join him in the quavering whistle, which many people did, including Whistle. Snap and Ash did not.

"Please share this food in honor of Chirp and Baby." Bapoto displayed two rabbits from his snares. Several responded with small contributions—a handful of dried imbe fruits, a bowl of fresh grubs—and soon the uwanda filled with cooking smells, which encouraged more people to produce a bit of their hoarded food.

Ash motioned toward Whistle's shelter, but Snap pressed her lips together uncertainly. "I certainly don't feel like celebrating. Do you think it would be rude for us to leave?"

Bapoto was signing to a group some distance from Snap and Ash, but at that moment, he moved squarely into her line of sight, although he continued to direct his remarks to the group. "Of course, there are two fresh-killed wildebeests at our shelter, but some prefer not to share on this sad occasion."

Snap leapt to her feet, growling a challenge. "How dare you accuse me of selfishness!" Her hands flapped like the bat wings. "My good fortune is already shared—a whole carcass has gone to my relatives and those with short stores."

Those nearest Bapoto and Snap backed away, faces averted but eyes on the confrontation. Whistle was nowhere to be seen. Bapoto looked down at Snap with a flicker of amusement, turned back to his watchers, and rolled his eyes.

Snap pounded the earth with her foot. "*I* would never use a death to promote foolish ideas about magical spirits." She used a word that described the sleight-of-hand tricks some traders used to attract a crowd. Amusement vanished from Bapoto's face as he turned back to her, arms folded.

Whistle appeared from the direction of the latrine pits, brow furrowed. "What is going on?"

Snap hissed, turned sharply, and strode out of the uwanda. Ash spread his hands, shrugged, and followed her. She scrambled to the top of the ridge, scraping a hand on the jagged limestone. At the western end of the ridge, she threw herself to her knees and pressed her sore hands into the fronts of her thighs. In a moment, Ash squatted next to her. He did not sign but crooned softly. Eventually, her arms relaxed, her breathing slowed, and her shoulder slumped into his.

"It is not our way, to have a celebration for the dead," Snap signed.

"No, my mother's people celebrated only the living as well. But people seemed to enjoy having a chance to talk about Chirp and Baby. And they seemed happy to share the little food they have remaining."

"It's still cold. It will be at least a moon before there is anything to harvest. Chirp would say we shouldn't finish our stored food until we see spring flowers."

The first few stars faded into view above them. Snap saw Ash draw his brows together and purse his lips. "They want to believe Bapoto's story about seeing the dead again when we die."

Snap snorted. "Well, if my feet and my legs hurt this much after I'm dead, I don't know if I will be too pleased to be around forever. Let me do my best for my family and my ukoo, and then let me die without suffering. I can't imagine a worse fate than having to continue to struggle forever."

Ash gave a sharp upward jerk of his chin and nodded.

Snap twisted Ash's beard into neat spirals. "How do you suppose Bapoto's people came to believe in living dead people and invisible spirits?"

"Suppose a Mother was afraid to die, and invented the story to comfort herself. Maybe she was particularly powerful and trusted by her ukoo. She might have used the Great One story to predict a successful hunt, or an unexpected recovery. People could be convinced."

Snap frowned at his beard and tucked in an errant hair.

"Magicians like that come in the summer, sometimes. They pretend to cure boils or rheumatism, in return for food and other things. We always chase them away; only an idiot would believe them. But Bapoto doesn't ask for anything; he truly believes this foolishness and believes he is helping us."

"Do you think Bapoto wants to be the Mother?" asked Ash, feeling her handiwork.

"Bapoto is a man!" Snap laughed, and Ash's mouth twisted in a half smile. As they stood up, the last streaks of gold and pink left the sky, and it seemed to her they were leaving for the last time, gone forever.

CHAPTER 8

After Chirp's death, Snap watched her mother. Whistle settled disputes, collected food for those whose stores had run out, planned the spring Naming, and Snap compared her mother's acts to what Chirp would have done. When Whistle joined Bapoto's warbling or ignored his frequent men-only gatherings, Snap frowned to herself and hoped her mother's changes would disappear with the men when they left for summer journeys.

As the ukoo preoccupied its new Mother, Snap's family responsibilities multiplied. She set the watch, planned meals, kept track of her brother and sister. The prospect of becoming Mother of Kura seemed to drift in from the far distant future to lurk somewhere close by, and she wanted to set a good example for the children. She took to gathering several girls together for impromptu lessons on reed gathering or snare setting, and was pleased to find that the boys accepted her solemn judgment of their wrestling contests. Every decision Whistle made gave Snap a chance to hone her own judgment in private.

Spring was late. Cold rains hung on longer than usual, and the early crop of tiny gwaru beans was poor. The women had to search far and wide to find any spring greens, and those they found were afflicted by a brown, scaly blight. Snap wished for better weather so people could start to fatten up again, but spring would bring the Naming, about which she had decidedly mixed feelings. After the Naming, the men would leave on their summer journeys and the women would follow the harvests. She was anxious to be rid of Bapoto, but expected saying good-bye to Ash would be a new experience she would rather not have.

She had grown accustomed to having Ash around, someone taller and stronger, someone who didn't require an explanation when she rolled her eyes or jerked her chin upward, someone ready to mate at a moment's notice. The older women always seemed more than happy for the summer respite from the men's presence, and she certainly would be glad to be free of Bapoto's influence, but she would put up even with Bapoto to keep Ash around longer.

Finally, the last drizzles stopped, the low areas near the stream dried out, the Kura women began returning to their shelters with baskets of baby kinanas and early berries, and Whistle proclaimed the Naming would be held in three days. That night,

Bapoto and Whistle sat up late at the uwanda fire and discussed the Naming while Snap, inside the shelter, tried to position her sleeping hides so she could see their words.

"But this is exactly the time of year when it is obvious to people how much we owe to the Great One," Bapoto was signing. "When we are celebrating growing children and the return of warmer days, it is easy to convince people of the power of the Great One. We can't let this opportunity go by."

Whistle's brow creased. "People are upset by change. They enjoy seeing the same words at every Naming. Honoring our children gives them hope for the future. Eating the first foods of spring reassures them spring will always come. If we tell them that spring is a gift from the Great One, that they should feel gratitude, they will not be pleased to add obligations to a pure celebration."

Snap snapped her fingers in support of Whistle's words. Bapoto turned away from Whistle, shot Snap an unpleasant look, and pulled the door flap closed so Snap saw no more of the conversation.

The next morning, Snap, along with the rest of the village, went into a frenzy of activity. Although food was still scarce, the Naming feast would be as sumptuous as possible. Most of the men, led by Bapoto, set off to hunt for antelope and zebra a day's journey to the southwest, with plans to return for the Naming. Ash, Rustle, Wart, and three other men headed north to a lake of which Ash knew, with seines that had taken a full moon to make. The women combed all the nearby places where they might find early fruits or vegetables, set snares everywhere, and made sure their best containers were in good repair.

To prepare for the Naming, Whistle had identified six families with a Baby to be named. Snap accompanied her mother as she visited each of these families in order to verify that each child was seeing a fourth spring, and to ascertain that each of the mothers planned to choose a proper Kura name not being used by a living person. The highest-ranking mother with a child to be named was Warble, who would have first choice of the available names. Snap was exceptionally pleased when Warble chose Chirp for her daughter's name, and she noticed Whistle had to blink some imaginary dust out of her eyes when she learned Warble's choice.

By the afternoon before the Naming, Snap was exhausted. She and Swish had dug on hands and knees for marama roots for most of the previous day, and had retrieved a basketful. That morning, she had ground the last of the stored bambaras from last fall and made the flatbread for which she was becoming known. Her hands were raw, her knees ached, and shortly after midday, Snap went down to the stream to soak her hands and feet in the icy water. As she sat at the water's edge, she saw a strange procession approaching from the north. Six people trotted in pairs, each carrying the ends of two long poles on his shoulders, his partner with the other ends of the same poles. A flapping, silvery black curtain hung from each pole.

Snap stood up, stepped from the water, and cocked her head to listen. A faint Kura hoot drifted across the uneven ground from the distant parade. She hooted in response and began to run toward them. As she neared the procession, she recognized Ash and Rustle carrying the first pair of poles, Rustle's end much lower than Ash's. On closer inspection, she could see that the curtain comprised many fish of various sizes. They dangled from the poles in a long line, and brought an unfamiliar smell of the distant lake.

Exhaustion banished, Snap whirred in hunger as she approached them. "Wonderful! Let me take your poles, Rustle." With barely a pause, she took the ends of Rustle's poles and easily matched Ash's long strides. Rustle dashed ahead, hooting, and by the time Snap and Ash reached Whistle's uwanda, Rustle had located his mother and they had already begun assembling the smokehouse. The other fishermen, unable to sign with both hands holding poles, made respectful sounds of leave-taking and carried their fish toward their mates' shelters.

Snap and Ash propped the ends of the poles on sticks. Hands now free, Ash turned to Whistle. "Rustle is an amazing fisherman. Even though he held the smallest seine, he caught more fish than any of the rest of us, and he cleaned all the fish on that pole. We will be sorry when he grows whiskers and leaves his mother's shelter." Rustle pretended he hadn't noticed Ash's words, but he shook out the hides for the smokehouse in a businesslike way. Whistle snapped her fingers in approval, and Snap thought her mother's eyes seemed less empty than they had for the last moon.

Whistle and Snap mixed most of the remaining salt from the round mungomu box with water in the largest wooden bowl. They reserved some of the fish to eat immediately, and began brining the rest, while Ash and Rustle made a small, square, peaked-roof smokehouse from hides stretched on poles. By dusk, most of the fish were hanging over a smoldering fire in the smokehouse, the reserved fish had been cooked and eaten, and

Bapoto's hunters had still not returned. Rustle fell asleep next to the shelter fire with his last bite still in his mouth, and Whistle had to prod him until he staggered to the sleeping hides she had rolled out for him.

Snap offered to take the first watch. She did not expect much interest in the smokehouse from the local predators, since most of them had had some experience with fires and were deterred by the smell of smoke. Ash dropped into his sleeping hides gratefully and fell asleep immediately. After he was asleep, Snap noticed he had left his feet uncovered, even though the nights were still quite cool, and they looked rather the worse for wear, although neither was bleeding. Snap's watch was uneventful, and when she woke Whistle near midnight, she signed, "Ash is exhausted and his feet look like a rat has been gnawing them. Let him sleep. I can take the third watch."

Whistle agreed. She woke Snap when the stars had just begun to fade above the horizon. "I just need to sleep until it's light," she signed. "Everything is quiet."

Snap was excited about the Naming, and had no trouble shaking herself awake. Too keyed up to just sit and watch, she checked the smokehouse fire and began to sweep the uwanda. By the time the sun hit the summit of the ridge, Snap was preparing a special food for the Naming festival, bambara flatbread rolled around fuu berries. Whistle and Swish awakened, and Swish began to help Snap without being asked. Swish remembered her own naming the previous spring quite well and was thrilled that her cousin, Warble's Baby, would be named that day. Whistle went to the central uwanda to start the large fire and supervise the roasting of two rabbits, three hyraxes, a hedgehog, and a porcupine, the only game available for the festival. There was still no sign of

Bapoto or the other hunters. When Ash and Rustle came out of the shelter, yawning and rubbing their eyes, Snap was working on the flatbread rolls in bright sunshine.

"Rustle!" signed Snap. "Run over to Peep's and Warble's shelters and see if anyone knows anything about the hunters." He dashed off, pleased not to have been given a boring food preparation task, and came back with Whistle as she was returning from the uwanda.

"No news. I visited Peep, Warble, and three of my friends; none of the hunters are back."

Snap looked at Whistle. "What about the Naming? Should it be postponed until the hunters return?"

Whistle considered. "Spring has been late, and people really need a festival now. The children are all stirred up, and the meat is already roasting."

"Some people will think us rude if we don't wait for the rest of the men."

"The Naming is mainly for the children, anyway, not for the men. We will not wait."

At that moment, Snap thought Whistle truly looked like the Mother, decisive and assured, and she wondered if Whistle was relieved to have an excuse to avoid changing the Naming to suit Bapoto's ideas about the Great One.

At midmorning, Whistle's family started for the central uwanda, carrying food for the festival and hooting their loudest. Rustle proudly carried some of the partly smoked fish to contribute to the feast, Snap brought her special fuu-berry rolls, and Whistle had a large basket of greens, made more interesting with some stale dika nuts and a liquid made from last year's imbe fruit that had accidentally fermented. Snap thought the morsels of meat roasting on the large fire in the central uwanda gave the impression of a poor feast, but at least they smelled good. Whistle chopped them into as many pieces as possible, so everyone would get a portion.

Mats were spread on the ground around the large central rock, and the food was arranged as attractively as possible. Everyone lined themselves up in rank order, as usual, each person with his or her own plate, and served themselves. Snap thought the food would be barely enough for breakfast, but since most of the men were in the absent hunting party, everyone was able to fill their dish at least once, and the six children who were to be named each got seconds as well. Snap especially liked the partly smoked fish, as it had acquired the tangy flavor of the wood but was not yet dried to the leathery consistency necessary for preservation.

After the remains of the feast were cleared away, Whistle climbed onto the rock to address her people. She was impressively tall compared to Chirp, and her long arms made striking signs. Snap thought she looked dignified, almost grand, definitely a Mother of whom the ukoo should be proud. "People of Kura! My people. Spring has come, and we again have food for our stomachs. We have endured another winter." Whistle gurgled relief, and the sound that rose from the assembly was like a huge waterfall.

"Today, we will name those children who are greeting their fourth spring. They have already survived the most dangerous journey they will take: infancy. They deserve reward, and we reward them today with this feast, and with their names." People began to snap their fingers as a sign of respect, not with any sort of rhythm, but like an armload of green wood thrown on a hot fire. Whistle waved at the first of the six children, and Warble lifted her daughter onto the large rock. The little girl stood shivering solemnly in the warm morning sunshine, all her hair on end, and looked over the crowd to the distant line of the river.

"Who is your mother?" Whistle asked, with two-armed signs, and looked kindly at the child.

"Warble." The child used large signs for the first time in her life.

Whistle turned to her sister. "What shall this child be named?"

"Chirp," signed Warble.

Whistle stood behind the child, turned to the crowd, and raised both arms, fingers spread wide. "This child shall be named Chirp." Everyone snapped their fingers again, and many purred to show respect for the child. Whistle's face was impassive, but Snap thought her eyes seemed brighter than usual. "Chirp, go back to your mother."

"Thank you," signed the terrified Chirp with both arms. Her mother lifted her down, and Whistle waved at the next child, a boy who belonged to one of her cousins.

And so each of the grave, anxious children were named without incident, except for the last one, who had to be reminded to thank Whistle for her name. Whistle declared the Naming complete, and a storm of finger snapping filled the uwanda. As the sound died away, Whistle signed again.

"And now we take leave of our winter mates. The men must begin their journeys to faraway places. They must hunt the animals we need, and trade for useful and wonderful things from far away. We women must pack up our summer tents and follow the harvests, so our storerooms will be full next winter. In the fall, we will all be pleased to see one another again."

The finger snapping that greeted these words was scattered and uncertain. Some of the women whose winter mates were not present looked at one another with questions in their eyes, and the few men looked over the crowd as if wondering which female might like a visit from one of the remaining men, now that they were free.

"Safe return," Whistle signed, and the crowd responded with the same sign. The women stood up and collected their children, mats, and dishes. Soon the uwanda was empty again. As Snap walked back to the shelter with Whistle, Warble caught up with them and tapped her sister on the arm.

"What about the hunt?" she asked. "Jackal may return with meat intended for the Naming."

Whistle gave her sister a wry look. "I don't think the men will be especially upset about missing the Naming, except maybe Bapoto. If they have been successful, I'm sure Jackal will give you a share, even if he isn't exactly your mate any longer. And if he doesn't, you won't starve. Look around you! The long rains are bearing fruit already."

Warble raised one eyebrow as if skeptical of Jackal's generosity, and turned toward her own shelter with a grumble.

CHAPTER 9

Snap was restless. After the Naming was over, she settled in a corner of the uwanda and tried to turn a rabbit hide into a leather pouch, but the cured hide stubbornly resisted her attempt to shape it into something useful. Swish pointed out to her sister how the dust motes sparkling in the gauzy spring sunshine formed flowers and animals, but Snap only growled and complained that the dust made her rabbit hide even more difficult to handle. Ash, who was planning to leave the next morning, tried to avoid attracting her attention as he collected his gear and packed his bundle, but every time he passed in her peripheral vision, she found the leather even more uncooperative.

Near midafternoon, when she was about to abandon the hide and start over, she heard a distant hoot, barely identifiable as Kura. A figure, just in hooting range, was approaching at a slow lope, hardly more than a walking pace. She asked Rustle to watch the smokehouse and trotted off in the direction of the figure, whom she soon recognized as Pike, Peep's winter mate. One arm was bound to his body with a strip of hide, and another strip was tied around one thigh. His hair was matted with mud and possibly blood, and he ceased hooting as soon as he saw someone approaching.

"Pike!" Snap signed as she approached. "What happened to you? Where are the others?"

Pike stopped and leaned forward with his free hand on his thigh; each breath looked painful. "We had a disagreement with some strangers over a herd of zebra. Cascade and Gorge are dead. Most of us are injured. I came ahead to get draggers for the two or three who are worst off."

"Mother's blood! Can we get them back before dark?"

"They are probably not too far behind me. I don't think I'm moving much faster than the others."

Pike described the route he had taken, and Snap sprinted back to the village. At her news, Rustle, Ash, and Whistle dispersed to get help, and Snap began assembling a dragger large enough for a man. Almost immediately, she saw Peep and Whistle dash toward Pike, and before she had finished the dragger, Ash returned with a group of rescuers, including Warble and Hum. They were carrying two draggers, a pile of soft, old hides, and an ownerless crutch. While she finished assembling her dragger, the others filled water bags, and then they departed together, leaving Rustle in charge of Swish and the smokehouse. In a few minutes, they passed Whistle, Peep, and Pike, and he made a gesture of thanks. They hooted in response.

In fact, Pike had been making much better time than the remainder of the hunting party. The rescuers followed Pike's directions at a strong, constant lope, until their legs ached and the sun was not much above the high ridge to the west. Snap was beginning to worry they had somehow missed the injured men when they came to the top of a low rise where Ash stopped, pointed, and sent a loud, deep hoot echoing from the ragged limestone slope in the distance. Far away in the direction of Ash's pointing finger was a straggle of twenty or so people, some of whom appeared to be waving. She heard a faint answering hoot, and a rush of relief flooded through her.

When they reached the men, she was shocked. She had seen people injured by animals and accidents, but these injuries had been inflicted by spears and stone axes, skillfully and purposefully wielded. Many of the men were pale around their noses and lips, and their breathing was fast and shallow. Those with more severe injuries leaned on those who were stronger, and the band shuffled along at a crawl. With neither energy nor free hands with which to sign, the hunting party greeted them with weak squeals. Jackal appeared to be nearly unconscious, and Bapoto was carrying him on his back. Warble hurried to Bapoto and helped him lower Jackal to the ground. When Jackal opened his eyes and recognized his mate, he buzzed a confused mating sound. Warble gurgled with relief and then laughed.

Starting with those who looked worst, the rescuers distributed water, tied up the wounds with strips of old hides, and helped the three most badly injured get settled in the draggers. Bapoto was in better shape than most of the others. He had been slashed from the corner of his mouth across his cheek, and also had a gash on his left upper arm, similar to Snap's leopard injury, but he wasn't pale, nor as weak as the others.

"What happened?" Snap asked Bapoto, using a little of the water to clean the wound on his arm.

Bapoto squatted to rest his legs and looked at the ground in front of his feet. "It's a long story. We were driven away from a herd of zebra by a hunting party from another ukoo. Cascade and Gorge fell, and they. . . ." His hands faltered and he turned his face away from her. "They took their bodies. We have been walking since midday yesterday, but so slowly, I was afraid we would have to spend another night in the open. The hyenas are not far behind us."

Snap glanced in the direction from which they had come, and indeed, a large female hyena stood boldly in the open, barely outside the range of a spear, and looked straight at her.

"Well, I think we can get back before dark. It's not so far to Kura."

Soon they started off again, by way of a smoother route than the one they had taken from Kura. Two people pulled each dragger and exchanged positions frequently, so they were able to move much faster than the injured hunters had and thus arrived at Whistle's shelter just as the last rays of the setting sun left the top of the limestone ridge above them. The injured men were delivered to the shelters of their mates without discussion about when they must leave. Snap was grateful to find Whistle had prepared some of the partly smoked fish, roasted several yams, and filled all the suitable containers with water, clearly ready for every sort of need on their arrival.

A subdued Bapoto accepted the food and water gratefully and allowed Whistle to clean his injuries and wrap his arm with a soft old rabbit hide. When she questioned him gently about the attack, he shook his head. "It's all my fault. We should have left the zebra to those savages." Immediately after eating, he unrolled his sleeping hides next to Rustle and Swish, and fell asleep instantly. The others built up the uwanda fire and sat gnawing bones left over from the earlier feast as disquieting darkness collected beyond the reach of the flames. Although the stones of the shelter and the packed earth of the uwanda still radiated some of the day's heat, a nebulous unease chilled their conversation, and Snap sat closer to Whistle than she normally would have done.

It was almost completely dark when a man passed by the uwanda and signed a greeting. Snap recognized Thunder, a bearlike man whose fearsome appearance was at odds with his genial nature, and who was one of the least injured members of the hunting party. Whistle waved an invitation for him to join them at the fire. He did so, accepting a porcupine bone with respectful thanks.

Thunder fidgeted with the small thighbone. "I've been up to the ridgetop to have a look around," he signed. "No sign of any visitors. I wonder if some of us men who aren't hurt badly should scout around once or twice during the night." Thunder's status had never been high enough to organize any men's projects; his proposal was almost apologetic.

Ash jumped up. "You're absolutely right, and I'm sorry. I'll go around and see who can do a patrol or two tonight."

Thunder saluted him with the bone. "Just let me know when it's my turn."

Ash signed a good-bye and disappeared into the dusk.

"Tell us what happened," asked Whistle. "Bapoto said you fought with a hunting party from another ukoo over a herd of zebra. He told us they killed Cascade and Gorge and took their bodies, but I couldn't understand why."

Thunder wiped his mouth on his arm. "We were planning to drive the zebra into a blind canyon when the other group of hunters arrived. They seemed friendly at first. They greeted us, and introduced themselves as Fukizo."

Whistle's eyebrows crowded together. "Where is Fukizo?"

Thunder shrugged. "No idea. Anyway, the herd was more than large enough for all of us, so we invited them to cooperate in the hunt, and they agreed. When Bapoto started to explain our plan, some of them looked angry, and they made signs to one another that we didn't understand. Bapoto pulled us away from them and tried to convince us to abandon the zebras, but we were there first, and we were hungry. While we were debating among ourselves, the strangers attacked."

Whistle shook her head. "I don't understand. Bapoto has such nice manners; everyone likes him. Why were they so unreasonable?"

Thunder shook his head. Snap frowned. "Maybe he's not all that charming," she signed.

Whistle shifted nervously. "I suppose the men will have to stay a bit longer. We certainly will get a late start on the harvesting this summer, won't we?" Snap wondered if Whistle was worried about something other than the harvest.

That night, Snap took the last watch, as usual. She squatted by the uwanda fire, which was welcome but not really necessary, and watched the sky lighten from black to thin grayish blue. The conflict with the Fukizo had unsettled her. She wasn't alarmed by death, sad but commonplace, an ordinary woe; nor was killing prey or predator particularly disturbing, but a battle with another ukoo was almost unimaginable. How could any woman hate an ukoo to which her brothers and uncles, her past and future mates, might belong? How could any man attack an ukoo to which he might have belonged in the past, or to which he might belong in the future? Two ukoos might have a disagreement over a harvest, easily resolved by the two Mothers, but she could not imagine a conflict that would need to be settled with spears. Nothing like this had ever happened before. By the time she heard Whistle stirring in the shelter, she was still confounded by the Fukizo's aggression but hadn't come up with an explanation that would allow her to blame Bapoto.

"I think the fish is nearly ready," she signed to Whistle as she emerged from the shelter. "Do you think the Fukizo will come after us, like the strangers in the story about the Seventh Mother?"

Whistle yawned and stretched. "They must live at a great distance. Why would they come here? We have done nothing to make them angry. There is plenty of game for everyone. I don't think they will bother us." Snap scrunched her mouth to one side doubtfully as she watched Whistle open the smokehouse and bite into one of the fish. "Let's wait for Rustle to get up before we store the fish. He is very proud of them." Whistle waggled her eyebrows in amusement and gnawed at a tough bit of fish skin.

Bapoto seemed much more like himself when he awoke and invited everyone to join his morning warbling. With an indistinct remark about gathering reminiscences about Cascade and Gorge, he trotted off downhill. Whistle sent Snap to visit Warble and check on Jackal's injury. She could hear him roaring with pain before she reached Warble's small uwanda, and when she arrived, he was lying on a mat with his head in his mate's lap. Warble was cleaning a wound that extended from his right temple above his ear to the back of his head, destroying the effect of his well-tended Kura hairstyle. She was trying to remove the matted blood from his hair without making it bleed more, but he didn't seem to appreciate her efforts.

"How are you today, Jackal?" Snap asked.

He bellowed as Warble pulled a clump of loose hair from the edge of the wound. "Miserable!"

"He's much better, thank you," signed Warble, and added to Jackal, "you know the wound won't close if all that hair is hanging into it. Now hold still."

"What do you think about these Fukizo, Jackal?" Snap asked, trying to distract him from Warble's ministrations. "Did they stay to hunt after the fight, or do you think they followed you here?"

He roared again. "How would I know? I remember the fight starting and getting hit in the head with a hammer. The next thing I saw was Warble."

Warble shook her head perplexedly. "I don't see why they would attack you to begin with. A larger group would have made it much easier to contain the zebras. You would all have had more meat."

Jackal snorted. "They got their meat without chasing any zebras."

As Snap climbed back to Whistle's shelter, she flung pebbles downhill with her toes and watched them skitter to new, but probably permanent, resting places. Jackal would be himself soon, but what about the Fukizo? Kura's familiar environs had become foreign, capable of hiding an army of strangers. A spear's throw below Whistle's uwanda, she heard hissing and low growls, so she crept cautiously up the slope and peered around a bush. Whistle and Bapoto faced each other, both signing energetically and making the sounds she had heard as she approached.

"It's too late!" Whistle's words were almost too vigorous to interpret. "We will miss the early peas if we don't leave right away, and we have to beat the Panda Ya Mto to the kunazi fruit. Anyway, the Naming is over, winter has passed, and Cascade and Gorge are no longer Kura."

"Not Kura!" Bapoto's hands were equally vehement. "They may be men, but they are still people. Their spirits will go to the Great One, just like Chirp's and Baby's, if we just ask her to accept them."

With a final hiss, Whistle threw her hands up and sighed. "Fine. Have a funeral. But as soon as the men are rested and able to travel, we will all be on our way."

With help from the last mates of Cascade and Gorge, Bapoto planned a funeral for the following afternoon. Shortly after midday, people gathered in the central uwanda. Bapoto gave an eloquent description of the lives of Cascade and Gorge, although he avoided the circumstances of their deaths. Before long, he segued smoothly into an explanation of his beliefs about the spirits of the dead living on in the company of the Great One. It seemed to Snap that his ideas about the afterlife had expanded since his remarks at Chirp's funeral. She got the impression he expected Cascade and Gorge to be rewarded by the Great One after their deaths because they had, according to Bapoto, believed in the power of the Great One and joined Bapoto's rituals enthusiastically. His remarks appeared to comfort some of his audience, especially the women who had been their mates.

Snap examined her own hands as her thoughts drifted away from Bapoto's solemnly flapping appendages. How could this Great One be so powerful, if she allowed Cascade and Gorge, her strong supporters, to be killed by strangers? Where does one keep one's spirit, and what does it look like? It was all so ridiculous, and so clearly the result of wishing somehow to avoid death, to control the inevitable. She caught Ash's eye and thought about trying to sign privately to him, but realized her words might offend an unintended audience. When everyone began to keen, she realized Bapoto had stopped talking, and added her voice to the wail that rose from the assembly. Bapoto jumped down from the large central rock, and Whistle solemnly replaced him.

"People of Kura! Our hunters have returned. They have missed the Naming feast, and many of them are hurt. Let us share what food we have left with the men who returned last night." As food was prepared for the injured hunters, Snap and Ash slipped through the crowd and started toward Whistle's shelter.

As they came around the corner of a limestone outcropping, Snap saw Peep's daughter Bubble, her favorite cousin, talking with

Hum. Bubble stood with one hand on her hip, as if presenting her round belly to the world, and signed, "I guess Bapoto forgot to ask his Great One to protect the hunters, huh?"

Hum jerked her chin upward and looked amused. "Maybe he asked her for something else. I've never been to any of his magic shows; I'll never know."

Just then, Bubble noticed the pair approaching them and turned to greet her cousin enthusiastically. Hum made a polite gesture and headed toward her own shelter.

Over the next several days, various traders visited Kura. They brought news and fabulous tales, which were sometimes difficult to tell apart, as well as small collections of food, tools, and interesting objects, which they offered in trade. It was clear that the men had left the other ukoos in the region. Snap noticed that Ash spent time in conversation with each of the traders, and with each one, he had discussions that involved much pointing into the distance and scratching marks in the dirt with sticks. His bundle still lay half-packed in a corner of Whistle's shelter.

By the eighth day after the attack, the injured men were recovering. Jackal's head wound had closed, but left a wide livid slash through his hair that he seemed to think made him look valorous and manly. Warble told Snap he was now unaccountably tractable, his notorious temper as tranquil as a summer sky. Pike had been struck on the front of his left shoulder by a stone hammer, and he still had excruciating pain and a grinding noise when he tried to move his arm. Snap had accompanied Whistle when she went to look at it. Whistle told him the bone was moving in a way it shouldn't, and to keep his left arm bound to his body. On the way back to the shelter, she told Snap she wouldn't be surprised if his arm healed as badly as Peep's had. Snap knew a weak arm would make it impossible for a man to find a mate under normal circumstances, but she suspected Peep would be willing to overlook it, especially since he was right-handed.

Ash began to hint about leaving. Snap agreed miserably and helped him organize his supplies and food and finish packing his bundle. Late one afternoon, they climbed to the top of the Kura ridge, and Ash considered the view in several different directions, as if he were reviewing in his head what lay beyond each of the horizons. He was looking westward when Snap addressed him. "Which way do you mean to go?"

"I will start toward the sunset and away from the Great Desert, the same direction Tor and I took last summer. I once met a far-walker, a man who had come much farther than any other traders, and who had a strange-looking face, short legs, and light eyes. He told me if one carries on the same direction, one will always learn something worth knowing, sooner or later. Anyway, the traders have suggested I will find something interesting in that direction."

Snap pressed her lips together. "Very well. I wish you safe return."

Ash looked intently into Snap's eyes. "I will come back. I mean to find out why the Fukizo have become our enemies. I don't know where I will go or what I will see there, but I will see you again." She nodded, and Ash cut off her words by putting his arms around her. As she pressed her face against his chest, vistas opened in her mind, filled with high, cold mountains, caves full of dangerous beasts, waterless plains populated by lightning-fast, unfamiliar predators. Coming back is harder to do than to say, she thought.

In the morning, everyone was awake even before the sky began to lighten and soberly hurried to finish last-minute preparations without conversing. At Whistle's shelter, the summer tents, a variety of empty containers, and tools needed for the harvests were packed into a dragger. Whistle gave the men some dried fish, early kinana, and a few moldy nuts, which they packed into their bundles. Everything not needed for summer was packed into the storage alcove, which was sealed with a temporary rock wall and caulked with mud. The roof, door, and window flaps of the shelter were tightly closed. Snap prepared the stone fire-carrier with a few lumps of glowing coals, and tucked her now-empty salt box into a secure spot in the dragger. By the time it was light enough to walk safely, everything was ready.

Ash left first, with formal farewells to the women, a perfunctory wave to Bapoto, and hugs for Rustle and Swish. With a lope that would never tire him, he started out southwest, toward the ridge where Snap's leopard had been struck by lightning. She watched him out of sight, and then made proper farewell signs to Bapoto. He signaled farewell to them, lifted his bundle to his shoulders, and started north, much slower than Ash. As usual, neither of the men carried a fire; Snap knew spears and axes would serve them for defense, and like most men with sound teeth, they were satisfied with uncooked meat.

Snap thought Rustle looked like he was repressing great glee. Sure enough, when Bapoto was out of sight, Rustle broke into an energetic dance, accompanied by hoots and laughter. Swish joined him, and they danced until both fell over exhausted. Whistle and Snap had to laugh as well, but soon Whistle was hooting loudly to warn the other women of their imminent departure. As they passed through the village from west to east, groups of women and children followed them. Some pulled draggers, others carried infants, and most had bundles tied on their shoulders. The most responsible woman of each family held a fire-carrier in her hand or fastened one carefully to the handles of a dragger.

With the blindingly bright sun just clearing the horizon in front of them, the caravan started east at a pace suitable for the smallest walkers. Snap and Whistle pulled the first dragger, with Rustle and Swish close behind. Peep came next, with her Baby in a basket on her back. Peep and her two daughters, Bubble and Murmur, took turns pulling a dragger. Warble's family followed, and so on, in order of their status. Hum, with a small dragger and a pack, brought up the rear. Snap wondered if Whistle was nervous about leading the summer harvest for the first time, and sneaked a sidelong glance at her. She thought her mother looked more cheerful than she had since the lion attack, with purpose in her measured stride and hope in the gaze that swept the horizon.

"Where first, then?" Snap asked with the hand not pulling the dragger pole.

"You know. Where are we going?" Whistle asked, amused.

"Spring beans on the banks of the Kijito, half a day downstream. Camp right above the river where the white rock turns to gray." Snap had followed Chirp every summer of her life, and not with her eyes shut. Twelve summers was not long enough to know every alternate site; she didn't know where to go when a crop didn't grow when or where they expected it to, but she knew the usual routine. Snap felt pleased, and at that moment, she felt something strange in her middle, a fleeting sensation, like a tongue pushing out against a cheek. She nudged it to the back of her mind and started to think about setting up camp, how they would have a single large campfire tonight, and maybe danc-ing that evening. Watching would be much easier with so many women sharing the duties, although sleeping would be harder, with all these children in such close quarters.

Whistle looked at her daughter with an expression that might have been pride or fear. "What?" signed Snap. "Isn't that right?"

"Quite right. That's what we will do, unless we have to do something else. The Kura must eat in the winter, and so some-times plans have to change." She raised her eyebrows at Snap pointedly. "Isn't that so?"

"Right." As they walked on, she wondered to what, exactly, had she just agreed?

CHAPTER 10

*B*y *midday,* Snap's neck and shoulders felt as if they had been roasted, and she was only too happy to drop the dragger and collapse in the shade. At the first harvest camp, a grove of morojwa trees covered in yellow flowers shaded a space large enough for six big summer shelters and a central uwanda. Whistle went to make sure the spring beans were indeed ready to pick. Snap propped herself up on her elbows to watch out for children playing too near the river while she contemplated a dinner of fresh beans followed by a long, sociable summer evening. At Whistle's sign, some of the women began to set up shelters, some went to pick beans, and others collected downed wood for the common fire. Snap helped erect the largest shelter, which would hold Whistle, Peep, Warble, and their families. Long flexible poles supported woven mats, covered by two joined hides in case of a rare summer rain.

Dusk found most of the children already rolled up and asleep, stuffed with spring beans and exhausted after their long walk. Snap was tired, but the cool summer-night breeze carried novel smells and whispered of the kinds of stories only told by women around the fire during harvest time. She squeezed into the circle next to her cousin Bubble, who merited a stump to lean against because of her unwieldy pregnant belly. Bubble made room for her with a chirp of welcome and offered her hair to be tidied, which Snap undertook with pleasure. Someone started a story about a child's funny misunderstanding. Summer stories weren't faithful reproductions of ancient tales like the stories told at the Bonding, but reprised and interpreted bits of life, told by anyone with a talent for stories or with something to say. Next followed a gentle rehash of a long-standing disagreement between two cousins, and then a humorous performance of a mate's peculiar sleeping habits.

After the stories had wound down, Whistle and two other women took the first watch. Snap tucked herself into her space next to Swish and fell asleep instantly. Near midnight, she woke to Whistle's soft tap on her shoulder and silently exchanged places with her. Warble's back was framed in the shelter door as she emerged for the next watch, and outside, Hum was stirring up the fire and causing bits of ash to shower the crisped, flattened grass around the fire. The three women greeted one another with silent signs. Snap turned away from the fire and searched the darkness beyond the circle of shelters. The half moon outlined the morojwa trees and made boulders, bushes, and stumps into immobile beasts, stalking the women's camp. Snap shivered and retrieved her short spear from near the shelter door. The sound of the fire and the distant splash of the Kijito were interrupted by a *chht* from Warble.

"Shall we walk?" she asked. Spears in hand, they followed Warble away from the fire between two shelters and waited for their eyes to adjust to the moonlight. The night breeze was cool on Snap's face, and she tightened her grip on the spear as she heard rustling and the whoosh of unseen wings. Through the whispering gloom, the women walked three abreast around the circle of shelters. On the second trip around the perimeter, the uneven shapes were familiar, less threatening. The shadows became possible sources of a midnight snack by the third round, and Snap poked her spear into bushes and likely-looking animal holes, but didn't flush anything either threatening or edible. They returned to the fire and squatted around it, evenly spaced so as to keep watch in every direction.

"So, will you choose Jackal again in the fall, Warble?" Hum asked. Although Hum squatted even with Warble and looked directly at her, Warble didn't appear offended.

Warble looked at the moon. "He's strong and fast, and we ate more meat this winter than we have for a long time."

Hum whirred hungrily.

"But it's not easy to be cooped up with him. He hisses when Chirp cries, and he roars at the kids when they run around and squeal. I'd say no, except that he did seem like a different man after he got smacked in the head." Hum laughed softly. Warble glanced at Snap and continued, "Bapoto is the best hunter. Maybe he will be available next fall."

Snap rolled her eyes. Did her aunt know something about Whistle's likelihood of choosing Bapoto again, or was she just speculating? "As far as I'm concerned, you're welcome to him. I wouldn't put up with him for any amount of meat."

Hum raised her eyebrows. "He does believe that he's helping us by sharing his ideas. The Mother seems to believe him."

"Indeed. My own senses have served me pretty well so far, and the old ways have served our people for a long time."

Warble contemplated her niece, and her tiny mouth tautened. "One day, you will be Mother, Snap. You may see things differently when you must think of others before yourself."

Snap's nostrils flared. She was usually pleased to learn how the older women managed their domestic affairs, but Warble wasn't the Mother, and Snap was not inclined to take her advice on this subject. Should she thank her aunt for the advice? Sincerely, or with a hint of sarcasm? Should she kneel up, reminding her aunt who was daughter of the Mother? In the end, she folded her arms and pretended to listen for an imaginary beast. Warble observed Snap's disregard for a moment, and then turned to examine the shadows as well. Hum got up to prod the fire, an amused look in her eyes.

❦

Spring beans were easy to harvest and store, and the days sped by in a miscellany of full stomachs, companionship, and warm sun. When the riverbanks had been cleared of anything worth eating upstream and down, the shelters were dismantled, the draggers were packed, and the caravan reassembled itself. Whistle led them northeast to the next camp, home to medlar and imbe fruit trees and small wild potatoes, where they spent almost a moon.

By the time they reached the third camp, which was shaded by a grove of mpingo trees, the days were hot and the longest of the year. The cool, pale grass of spring had become brittle, and a great variety of fruits and vegetables were ripe. The least worthwhile, Snap thought, were the amaranth leaves that would be shredded and buried in tightly covered containers made from gourds. In the depths of winter, when other food ran low, the fermented leaves could be eaten, if one were hungry enough.

One day, near midsummer, the women planned to return to Kura before setting out on a second trip for the late summer crops. Bubble and Snap were working together to pack a large dragger. Eating their fill every day had made everyone rounder, but Bubble's middle was now impressively large, and she struggled to get a bundle of dried fruit into the dragger.

"Let me do that," signed Snap. She lifted the bundle from the top of her cousin's belly and helped her lower it into the dragger.

"Thanks." Bubble sighed and squatted for a moment to rest. "I suppose this baby will be just as heavy after it's born, but it'll be nice to put it down once in a while." Snap snorted, and Bubble winked at her. "You're looking pretty womanly yourself. I never thought my little cousin would grow breasts like those. And look at your belly!"

"Nothing like yours, though." Snap threw back her shoulders a bit.

The caravan was led by Whistle and Snap as usual. Because of the blisteringly hot midsummer day and the heavily loaded draggers, they didn't reach the planned camping place until dusk. After a makeshift dinner, the women arranged their sleeping hides in a circle around the draggers and the children. Three watch fires defined the camp's boundary. Snap, Bubble, and Hum had the third watch, each of them stationed at one of the fires.

Snap felt livelier in the cool night air than she had all day, and as she squatted by her fire, an idea presented itself. Working quietly, she collected all the twigs and dried grass she could find in the light of her fire and twisted them into the mat on which she had been sitting. Covered with the bristling mat, she crept away from her fire in a wide circle around the camp, so she could approach Bubble's fire from outside the perimeter. She slunk from bush to bush, approaching as close as she could get without rousing Bubble. Bubble squatted at her fire with her hands folded over her immense belly, her chin drooping and her eyes nearly closed. With a hiss loud enough to startle Bubble without awakening the entire camp, Snap leapt from her bush and danced wildly toward her cousin, encased in her prickly disguise.

Bubble tried to jump up, but one foot slipped and she fell onto her back, both feet in the air, like a flipped turtle. Snap stifled her laughter with one hand as she threw off her camouflage and offered the other to Bubble to help her to her feet. At first Bubble looked put out, but after a brief pout, she began to giggle as well. They exchanged a few rapid signs and then quickly fashioned another disguised mat for Bubble. The younger women slipped silently around the encampment in opposite directions in order to approach Hum's watch fire from opposite sides. From the shelter of a dense shrub, Snap saw Hum squatting close to her fire, rocking slightly and making indistinct, low-pitched sounds, as if she were crooning to a baby. Soon, she heard Bubble's signal, the hoot of a wood owl, and responded with the same sound. Together, the two cousins jumped from their hiding places into the light of Hum's fire and repeated Snap's performance, hissing and dancing madly. Hum raised her chin and surveyed them.

"Very good," she signed. "If I hadn't heard Snap laughing a while ago, I would have been scared to death."

The younger women giggled and joined Hum in a drink from her water bag. The moon had set, and the muttering of leaves and scrabbling of nocturnal beasts repeatedly tested Snap's vigilance. Hum inclined her head to her left as she listened to something, and then turned to Snap. "Prick up your ears, Snap. Pay attention to the small things."

Snap lifted her eyebrows. "What do you hear?"

"Wood owls aren't always what they seem. Nor are people. I think you will be a good Mother one day, but not everyone agrees with me."

The fire flared up as a log fell. Sparks flew toward stars that seemed to have shifted into unfamiliar shapes. "Who?"

Hum suddenly turned her head and held up a finger. For a moment Snap heard nothing, and then she heard a soft footstep in the dry grass beyond the circle of firelight. Hum picked up her spear, and the other two pulled torches from the fire. Snap squinted into the silky darkness, but the moon had already set, and not even her racing imagination could distinguish the shapes of bushes from anything more mobile. The sound of steps faded away, and the watchers felt no desire to follow them. For the rest of the night, the three women circled the camp from fire to fire. Snap heard no more worrisome sounds, but her own thoughts churned like the pool under a waterfall. When gray streaks of dawn began to stretch over them, the anticipation of seeing Kura again crushed her worries.

Well past midday, the high white ridge of Kura was finally drawing near, and the caravan sped up. Draggers seemed lighter

and tired arms and sore feet barely noticeable as the white limestone of Kura, and then the individual shelters, came into view.
Snap loved the summer harvest for its food and socializing, but returning to the shelter that had protected her family from so many
winters evoked a feeling of security never possible at a camp. At
the eastern edge of the village, the caravan began to disperse as
each family headed toward its own shelter. Snap's family did not
walk through the village, but pulled their heavily loaded dragger
up the slope and above the uppermost shelters to Whistle's, which
was nearer to the top of the ridge than any of the others. As they
entered the uwanda, all four of their mouths fell open.

The door and window flaps, which had been tightly closed,
had been pulled down from their fastenings and lay in heaps
on the ground. The uwanda was strewn with household goods
that had been taken from the carefully closed storage alcove, and
many were damaged.

Snap and Whistle lowered the dragger to the ground and
Snap stared at the shambles angrily. "Mother's blood! What kind
of animal did this?"

"I don't know. I've never seen anything like it," signed Whistle. Eyes wide and lips pale, they made a path to the shelter door,
sorting the chaos into piles as they went. Rustle and Swish both
dropped their bundles and threw themselves on the ground in
exhaustion.

The inside of the shelter was revolting. Rotting animal entrails were spread across the floor. Excrement was smeared on the
walls and piled in the fire ring. The storage alcove had been completely emptied, and part of the side wall had been pulled down,
leaving a jumble of irregular limestone. Shocked, Snap knelt just
inside the door and picked up a ragged rabbit hide that was stiff

with something brown and fetid. As a small child, she had been inseparable from the soft hide, sleeping with it and dragging it around until her brother was old enough to tease her about it, after which Whistle had put it away carefully so that Snap would always know it was safe. Rising tears made her blink, and she complained that the dreadful reek was irritating her eyes.

As they started to sort usable things from those irreparable, Snap heard a scream from the direction of the central uwanda. "Now what?" she signed as they hurried out.

"Watch the dragger, Rustle." Whistle flashed the words at him as the women pulled small spears from the side of the dragger and started downhill toward the main uwanda, following the continuing screams. They passed two other shelters that were in as much disarray as their own and reached the edge of the main uwanda behind a crowd of other women. Snap couldn't see over them, but Whistle, teeth clenched, edged her way through and Snap followed in her wake. As she emerged from the crowd near the large central stone, Snap saw it was Warble who was screaming. She lay curled on the ground in front of the stone, her arms over her head, and screamed as if she were being beaten. The other women seemed to have been carved from boulders.

Snap felt nauseated. On the large central stone, someone had constructed a pyramid of several large slabs of limestone, daubed with disgusting filth like the inside of the shelter. On top, the empty eye sockets of a blackened, fleshless human skull stared at the horrified women. From the open, silently screaming mouth protruded the butt of a short spear. Remnants of hair and beard that clung to the skull were clearly in the Kura style. A slash interrupted the hair, from the right temple, over the right ear, to the back of the head.

Warble, after she ceased to scream, seemed paralyzed. She did not respond to anyone who addressed her, but climbed to the top of the ridge above the shelters and sat staring into the west. She, as Jackal's last mate, should have taken his remains to the cave of death, a small limestone grotto to the northeast of Kura, but she refused to move. Her oldest daughter, ten-year-old Trill, bravely wrapped Jackal's head in a fragment of ragged hide, put it in a small dragger, and pulled the dragger to her mother at the top of the ridge, but neither sound nor movement disturbed Warble's expressionless vigil.

When the sun set, the shelters were not yet habitable. Snap and several of the younger women started a large fire in the central uwanda, Whistle organized a watch schedule, and by dark, the uwanda was filled with sleeping hides rolled around nervous women and children. Trill spread her sleeping hide between Snap and her own younger brother and sister. In the morning, Warble was still sitting on the ridgetop, and it was clear she was not going to fulfill her responsibility. Trembling, Trill announced she would go to the cave of death for her mother.

Snap patted her cousin on the shoulder. "You are brave, and you know your responsibilities, but whoever did this to Jackal could still be around. I will go with you."

In the end, the group consisted of Trill, her seven-year-old brother Rattle, Snap, and Rustle. Rustle, as the oldest male, carried a hand axe and a spear that was much too long for him, and Snap made sure there were two more spears tucked into the dragger. She was glad of her brother's company, but even though

Rustle was big for nine, she didn't really expect he could protect her from anything fiercer than a recently fed cane rat. As they prepared to go, Snap saw Whistle give her a look that might have been pride, but she only signed a perfunctory farewell.

The cave wasn't far and the way relatively smooth, so Snap started out running faster than the lope she would have used for a long journey. Trill and Rattle pulled the dragger and kept up without difficulty. Rustle followed at a short distance and paused often to watch in all directions. They made good time and met no one. Just as Rattle was beginning to tire, they began climbing a gentle slope to the small dark aperture of the cave of the dead.

Before they reached the opening, Rustle stopped. "I'll climb to the top of the rise and set a watch." Snap agreed and watched him climb to the nearest lookout, cross his arms, and try to look fierce. She suppressed a snort of amusement and continued up the slope with Trill and Rattle. The day was hot, and Snap was sweating profusely, but she shivered slightly as she reached the mouth of the cave, her hair bristling.

The cave mouth was so low Snap had to stoop to enter. She peered into the dim, cool interior, determined it was empty, and stepped inside. The cave was about a man's height in width and in depth, and the ceiling just high enough for her to stand. Snap smelled musty old death, but no hint of any recent occupants. When she had come here with her mother and Peep, after the death of one of Peep's children, Whistle had explained afterward that hyenas denned nearby, and took care of whatever they left in the cave. "Illness comes from dead things, Snap," Whistle had said. "Never eat an animal if you don't know when it was killed, and when people die, bring them here as soon as possible."

Snap turned and waved Trill and Rattle into the cave. They

followed with the dragger, but stopped immediately inside the door, unable to see much in the sudden darkness. Snap took Jackal's head from the dragger and placed it on the floor near the rear wall where Peep had left her baby.

As she was standing up and turning around, Rustle burst in through the entrance and flattened himself against the wall. "I saw somebody. Far away. Three people, I think, but too far away to tell if they were men or women or what ukoo." He was sweaty and making himself look as large as possible.

Snap edged up to the opening and peered out with one eye. "I see them. Three men, I think. Can't see their hair very well. They're not coming this way. I don't think we should hoot."

Trill and Rattle moved away from the door without being told and stood quietly behind Snap. Snap watched from the shadow of the cave entrance for what seemed like an eternity. Finally, she signed, "They've on their way to Kura, I think. Let's go. We'll follow them and stay hidden, and if they attack the village, we can come up from behind and surprise them."

Rustle narrowed his eyes. "You're crazy. They might be the ones that got Jackal, and he was huge."

Snap gave her brother a sharp look. "And what do you think they'll do to Swish?"

"And Chirp," added Trill.

Rustle kicked the wall with his heel and kept his eyes on the floor. "Fine. Let's go."

With a spear in one hand and both dragger poles in the other, Snap left the dim cave and started after the men. The others followed closely. They approached the top of each rise carefully and occasionally got a glimpse of the three men in the distance, but couldn't get near enough to identify them. As they approached the village, they heard hoots and at last realized the three were Kura men. The men appeared to be heading for Whistle's shelter. Snap sent Trill and Rattle to Warble's shelter and then signed to Rustle to follow the three men with her.

Snap and Rustle found Pike, Owl, and Hawk in Whistle's uwanda, where Whistle and Peep were cleaning up. The three ill-at-ease men greeted Whistle as if they were returning in the fall. Hawk, Jiti-born and Bubble's last winter mate, was sturdy and determined-looking, with coal black hair and an open expression that turned easily from a frown to a laugh. His cousin Owl, who had also bonded with a Kura woman for several winters, was very like Hawk in both appearance and temperament. Pike, who had been Peep's mate, seemed able to use his injured left arm nearly normally, and although he correctly addressed Whistle first, he kept looking at Peep. None of the three appeared to be sporting any new injuries, although all looked thinner than they had after the Fukizo attack. Swish danced around them, trying to hug the men's legs without getting stepped on or kicked. At the door to the shelter, Whistle made a show of confidence, but Snap saw her wipe her eyes on the back of her hand.

"Welcome," Whistle signed with both arms. "Please share my fire." The fire was, in fact, banked, but Snap dropped the dragger and spear she was holding and rushed over to stir up the uwanda fire. The men squatted at one side of the fire, and Whistle squatted at the other. Snap, eyes lowered, rummaged in the partially unpacked harvest and produced a basket of recently collected carissas, which she offered to the three newcomers. They tore into the fruit as if it might try to escape.

"How do you return so early?" Whistle asked.

Pike answered one-handed, eating with the other hand.

"We met a trader seven days ago, far to the west. He told us he had come to trade at Kura and found it had been ransacked and mostly destroyed. We have run here as quickly as we could." Pike waved his carissa to indicate the entire village. "We are happy to learn he is a liar."

Whistle rocked back and forth. "Not a liar. When we returned yesterday, every shelter had been ransacked, some walls were pulled down, and disgusting filth was everywhere." She looked down and waved her hands as if the words burned them. "And Jackal is dead. They left his head in the big uwanda, with a spear in his mouth."

Pike keened sharply, and the others joined in. "Who did it?" asked Owl.

Whistle shook her head. "You know the people of Jiti, of Panda Ya Mto, of Gange. Our mates are sons of these ukoos, and our sons are their mates. I don't think any of them could have done this. Only the Fukizo have ever harmed us."

Peep snapped her fingers in agreement. Hawk bared his teeth and rubbed a scar that zigzagged across his thigh. "Those Fukizo are all sons of hyenas."

"We are nowhere near finished harvesting," Whistle continued. "Once we have finished cleaning up and storing our food, we have to go out again, or we will starve this winter."

"We will not travel far," signed Pike, and he looked at the other men for confirmation. "We will hunt near your camps." Owl and Hawk nodded. Whistle formally welcomed the men to sleep in the men's shelter, and they went to see how it had fared.

Well after midday, Warble appeared at Whistle's uwanda, apparently having regained control of herself. Whistle and Snap had already cleared up the worst of the wreckage and had a good start on repairing the shelter's damaged wall. Whistle greeted her sister kindly and put an arm around her, which only made Warble begin to sob again.

Finally she managed to sign, "I want to have a funeral for Jackal."

Whistle patted her shoulder and keened sympathetically, but her expression led Snap to suppose her mother was thinking of the cleaning and harvesting yet to do. Eventually, Whistle decided a funeral would help Warble control her emotions and agreed. Whistle and Peep set snares in preparation for a feast in the morning, and the men contributed three large catfish.

The next morning, Snap went to the central uwanda at first light, started a large fire, and began roasting the fish and two snared rabbits. When the sun had risen enough to strike the large central stone, people began to assemble. Whistle arrived at the uwanda to find Pike, Owl, and Hawk standing together near the central stone, shuffling their feet, and looking around at the crowd. Whistle raised her eyebrows and approached the men, and Snap left the fire to join her mother. She felt the women and children who had been spreading out their mats watching.

"Thank you for bringing the fish," signed Whistle.

Pike stepped forward slightly. "We are happy to provide food for Jackal's funeral. And we would like to address the ukoo as well. Jackal was enthusiastic about Bapoto's beliefs, and I was, too. We'd like the funeral today to be as much as possible like Bapoto's funerals."

"Of course, you may if you like. Which of you will it be? I will call you to come up with me."

The men looked at Pike expectantly. "We would like to lead the funeral. Bapoto thinks the old rituals should be led by the Mother, but the new rituals, like the hunting ritual and the funerals, should be led by men."

Whistle pressed her lips together. She looked at her own hands, at the ridgetop above the men's heads, at the fish and rabbits sizzling over the glowing embers of the fire. Snap had never seen Bapoto assert that rituals should be led by men, but her mother didn't seem surprised by the men's request. At last, she nodded assent. As the men clambered onto the stone, the Mother and her family spread out their mats and sat down. It seemed to Snap that many people were signing to one another in such a way she couldn't see their hands.

The funeral was similar to the one for Gorge and Cascade. Jackal had been born in Jiti, as had Owl and Hawk, and the two held forth movingly about Jackal's life. Next, Pike related stories of several of Jackal's many successful hunts, and then went on to assure them that Jackal was safely with the Great One and awaited the arrival of his family and friends. It seemed to Snap that Pike had paid attention to Bapoto's sermons, and reproduced his ideas closely. He even expanded on them as he described the meeting between Jackal, Gorge, and Cascade, all now in the company of the Great One, and finally left Bapoto's idea behind altogether as he finished with a graphic description of what would happen to the Fukizo if he ever saw them again.

Warble, whose family was sitting near Whistle's, cried silently, except when she keened along with everyone else, and seemed to pay close attention to Pike's words. After Pike had yielded the stone, Whistle climbed up and invited all those present to share the food. By midday, the event was over. The three men packed their bundles and departed. The women finished cleaning up, repaired enough containers for the remainder of the harvest, and resealed their household goods into their storage alcoves. By bedtime, the women's draggers were lined up in their uwandas, ready to leave in the morning.

CHAPTER **11**

As *Snap* watched that night, sitting by the uwanda fire under a nearly full moon, a west wind came up. It was dry and warm, with no hint of rain, but smelled sharp and tangy, like lightning. She left the fire and climbed partway up the side of the ridge in the moonlight. The western stars were obscured, and it seemed to her that a cloud hovered just at the horizon, neither approaching nor retreating. She squatted on the ridge where she could see both the western sky and Whistle's uwanda, and watched for a long time.

The night was empty, sound muffled. No owls hooted,

no hyena whooped. Even the usual sounds of the Kura were absent—no baby cried, no watcher hissed at a pair of eyes in the darkness. Apprehension twisted in her chest, visions grew in her mind of her family, butchered like Jackal, lying silently, in pieces. Her breath came faster as she hunted for any movement below, any misplaced shadow. She moved to a better vantage point and crouched in a deep shadow. As she did so, she felt a strange sensation in her belly, like a gentle poke with a round stick just under her navel. In the last few weeks, something similar had happened now and again, but never so strongly. She pushed on the spot with her hand, and it happened once more. Three times she prodded her middle; it prodded back. Sure she understood now, she climbed down the ridge and tapped Whistle awake.

Whistle murmured sleepily, and then threw off her hides in one motion and leapt to her feet. "What is it?"

"Something is moving." Snap touched her belly just below her navel. "In here."

Whistle nodded. "Finally." She put her arms around her daughter. Snap buried her nose in her mother's sleep-warm hair and smelled hope, absent since Chirp's death. Whistle might be inexplicably tolerant of Bapoto's strange ideas, she thought, but she was still her mother.

A peripatetic breeze disturbed the dawn. Snap tried to hurry through her morning chores, but her attention was distracted again and again. A rock in the newly repaired shelter wall was uneven and a bit loose, and she worried at it until it seemed secure; the central uwanda seemed untidy until the flat stones that had formed the pedestal for Jackal's head were scattered far from the village. Every small reminder of the Fukizo rampage needed her attention, needed to be erased before she could leave Kura again.

Everyone seemed to move in slow motion—coals for the fire-carriers, a final check of the packs, a misplaced child—by the time the exodus began, the sun was high and Snap was pleased to be leaving. Whistle, a fire-carrier in her hand, set a pace that seemed much too slow to Snap, on her heels with the nearly empty dragger. Their unshaded route headed southwest, through dried mavue and the occasional lone acacia tree. Aromatic shrubs and gray dust prickled Snap's nostrils. Near midmorning, they rounded the end of an east–west ridge, where she recognized a partly burned snag. No sign remained of the leopard carcass.

One by one, the toddlers were picked up and carried or tucked into draggers, and their speed slowed even more. The afternoon was old and already slightly cooler when they arrived at the usual camp. A steep north-facing slope shaded a spacious clean-swept clearing not far from the Kijito, which was wide and slow here.

Whistle examined the clearing and turned a sour face to Snap. "The Jiti have been here." All the nearby kunazi had been collected, leaving only a few late-ripening fruit. Even the baobabs were tiny and nearly inedible, but the Kura could walk no farther. The shelters had to be erected on empty stomachs.

At dusk, the women were planning the watch when they heard Kura hoots. Pike trotted into the women's camp, asked to light a branch at the fire, and departed without exchanging formal greetings. Snap frowned, unsure if the lack of greetings was rude, or if the situation was too foreign for ordinary manners to apply. He climbed the ridge just within hooting distance and joined two other figures. They built a fire and seemed to settle down for the night. Snap went into the shelter and told Whistle the three men were camping nearby.

"Good." Whistle nodded as she arranged sleeping hides. "I don't suppose those three can protect us from the Fukizo, but I'm glad they're there."

Snap had the first watch. After the camp had quieted and the watchers had made their first rounds, she found her eyes drawn to the twinkle of the men's fire. Somewhere, Ash was sleeping, or watching. Did he have a fire? Was he hungry, cold, injured, alone? Had he met any Fukizo? What would he think about all that had happened at midsummer, and what stories would he have to tell? Would he return in the fall at all? She pushed that thought firmly away and concentrated on trying to feel her baby's flutters. Would the baby come during the winter, in Kura? Would Ash be there? Resignedly, she hoped he was safe, or at least as safe as a far-walker could be.

Pike, Owl, and Hawk often camped within hooting distance. No traditions governed interactions with the women in the summer, and so they simply stayed at arm's length. Sometimes they quietly borrowed a fire, but they didn't pay their respects to Whistle as they would on returning to the village, and they didn't bring game or gifts. During the day, walking, digging, eating, and packing away the harvest distracted Snap from their presence, but whenever she watched, she remembered they were nearby, and why.

The evening storytelling had been Snap's favorite part of the harvest, but now the women had almost nothing to say around the fire in the evening. Very soon after the children were asleep, the women rolled up next to them and listened to the sounds of the night. The watch was set as always, but the watchers were never the only ones listening for a footstep in the dark or an imitation animal call.

The long winter rains made the harvests a bit later than usual, but larger than usual as well. The draggers became enormous, each pulled by two women who exchanged positions often. Returning to Kura at the end of the harvest with the huge draggers was slow and tedious, and even the smaller children were weighed down with bundles as large as they could carry. When finally the white ridge above Kura began to loom nearer and nearer, Snap's footsteps slowed. Hand shading her eyes, she searched the ridges and mesas that interrupted the savanna around the village, and then turned to Whistle. "Do you think we should wait for the men to catch up before we go into the village?"

Whistle's mouth twisted uncertainly. "We haven't seen any sign of the Fukizo since we set out on this trip. Nor have the men. Two days ago I walked out to let them know when we planned to return, and they haven't seen even a footprint." After examining the vista in all directions, she set her jaw. "We will go into the village. I expect the men are not far behind anyway."

Snap nodded and turned toward Kura again. With the goal in sight, the speed of the entire caravan increased. Even the smaller children, most of whom had been asking all day how much farther to Kura, were energized, and they soon reached the environs of Kura. Whistle's shelter looked just as they had left it; the door and window flaps were securely closed, and there was nothing unexpected in the uwanda.

"I'll check the big uwanda." Snap dropped her pole and proceeded to do so. The square appeared undisturbed, but she made a circuit of the large space nevertheless. As she passed the center rock, she noticed a small object lying in the center, so she approached the rock and picked up something small and white. At first she thought it was a pig's tooth, possibly left in the vicinity after last fall's feast, but as she looked at it, she began to think the tooth was a bit too small, and too white to have belonged to a pig. She felt her nape hair stand up and flung the tooth away as hard as she could. The sound of the tooth skittering downhill went on and on. As she returned to her mother's shelter, she inspected every corner and shadow but found nothing untoward.

Whistle and the children had opened the door and window flaps. Snap poked her head in and saw they were unsealing the storage alcove. "Everything is fine," she announced, and started to unpack the dragger. After the necessary unpacking was finished, however, she visited several relatives and reassured herself that they had found things just as they had left them as well.

The next morning, Pike, Owl, and Hawk entered the village and came straight to Whistle's shelter, just as they usually did in the fall. The formal greetings were made, the requests to stay in the men's shelter were granted, and all three bounced off to greet the other women who were of particular interest to them. Everything seemed unnaturally normal to Snap and she couldn't relax, even though no one had seen the Fukizo. Finally, thoughts about Ash's return began to accompany her fears of threatening strangers.

One day, Bubble asked the question Snap had barred from her thoughts. "Do you think Ash will return?" The mat Bubble was repairing refused to balance on top of her enormous belly, and Snap propped it up for her cousin before she answered.

Snap was finishing a new basket—tightly woven and finished

with beeswax on the inside so spoiled food wouldn't spoil the basket as well. "This wax cools too fast. I can't get it into the weave before it clumps up. Of course he will."

"Will you choose him again?"

"Mother's blood, now it's too hot. Of course."

Bubble studied her cousin's face. "It's hard to get used to a new mate, isn't it? Hawk's not exactly a lion killer, but at least he's not too disagreeable when he's hungry. I expect I'll keep him. Ash is even smaller than Hawk, though, isn't he?"

Snap wiped off the wax and started again. "Ash is big enough. I'm sure he would do as well as any of the others if the Fukizo come back. He just . . . he feels right."

Bubble snorted. "I hope he gets back for the Bonding so you can feel him some more."

Snap frowned at the basket and decided it didn't need to be waxed after all.

The men arriving at Kura greeted Whistle with small gifts and obvious erections, and Snap found their smells and their stories extremely interesting. Only a few had anything for Snap, and she wondered if her pregnancy made her less appealing. Would Ash find her equally uninteresting?

One morning when she had been the last to watch, she sat by the uwanda fire and watched the sun struggle to light up an overcast sky with gray-green streaks. The women had been in the village for a half-moon, the harvests were stored, and she had received only two small gifts from returning men. Her middle was now quite round, and the tiny movements had become un-questionable kicks and punches. She often took naps, which was unusual for her, but also was often awake at night, and sometimes watched when it wasn't her turn, since she was irresistibly up anyway.

It was impossible to tell when the sun actually rose, but the sky became brighter and gradually metamorphosed from gray-green to gray-purple to just gray. The vague light didn't wake the others, and she saw no reason to disturb their sleep, so she sat on, scraping a dried hide. Footsteps made her reach for a small spear and scramble to her feet, surprised anyone would approach without hooting. Bapoto trudged slowly up the slope to the uwanda, pulling a dragger so heavy it gouged a deep furrow into the earth behind him. His arm had healed with a scar similar to her own, and another scar extended from the corner of his mouth to his ear, as if it were part of the thin white line of his set lips. Unlike most returning men, he looked thinner than he had at the beginning of the summer, but he had found time to keep the hair on his head trimmed short, as usual.

"Bapoto! Have you been walking in the dark?" Snap leapt up to help him with the dragger.

He dropped the dragger poles at the edge of the uwanda and staggered toward the fire like an elderly toddler. His hands formed barely comprehensible words. "Just the same." Bapoto dropped to his knees at the fire, apparently too tired even to squat. "Was it here? Just the same."

Snap stirred up the fire and scooped up a gourd full of water from the bucket near the door. "Drink." He swallowed the water.

"Where's Whistle?" he signed with a fraught look at the shelter. "Is she all right? She's not . . ."

"Still sleeping."

A long breath, almost a moan, escaped him. "I tried to get here last night, but there was no moon or stars and it was too dark. I camped near the Kijito and started again as soon as it was light."

Whistle came to the door of the shelter. She opened her arms in welcome, but when she saw that Bapoto seemed about to collapse, her eyes narrowed and her hands flew up. "Bapoto! What happened?" He began to make the formal signs of greeting, but Whistle didn't assume her usual pose. She fussed around seeing that he was comfortable and began to inspect him. "Are you injured? What do you need?"

Snap brought another dipper of water and Bapoto drank it before he answered. "I'm not hurt, just tired and hungry. I'll be fine after I have a rest. There were rumors about the Fukizo being here in Kura, and I've been trying to get back as fast as I could."

Whistle told him what the women had found at midsummer. She described how Pike, Owl, and Hawk had led the funeral, and he nodded approvingly. "We were pleased to have them nearby, just in case the Fukizo should return."

"They camped with the women?" he asked, nostrils flaring.

"No, not at all. We just knew they were not far away." She stroked his arm soothingly. "Just in case."

Bapoto didn't look completely placated but seemed too tired to pursue the issue. Instead, he waved at the dragger. "Most of a wildebeest in the dragger, for you. Killed yesterday."

Whistle signed formal thanks but didn't go immediately to the dragger. "What would you like to eat? It wouldn't take long to cook some of that wildebeest, and our storeroom is full."

Bapoto accepted a handful of tiny sour annona fruit and, without asking permission, took his sleeping hides into the sleeping alcove, which the children had already vacated. Whistle shot a look after him that would have made any of her children think again about what they were doing, but she didn't call him back. Whistle and Snap had to ask Rustle and Swish to help them get the wildebeest carcass out of the dragger, as it weighed as much as all four of them together. Peep, Bubble, Pike, and Hawk came to help with the butchering and were rewarded with portions of the meat. Peep's Baby toddled around the uwanda, getting in the way, and Swish was enlisted to entertain her. At midday, they rested and admired their work while slices of liver broiled on a spit over the fire. The smell of the cooking meat brought Bapoto out of the shelter, and Whistle invited him to join the feast. Peep raised her eyebrows pointedly when she saw him emerge from the shelter, and Whistle hurriedly explained how Bapoto had arrived that morning, exhausted, and had only been napping.

Several times during the morning, Snap thought Bubble looked distracted. Her meat slices were uneven, she nearly cut herself out of inattention, and Snap saw her stop and stare into the distance often. When the liver was ready to eat, Bubble looked nauseated and declined. Peep gave her daughter a shrewd look. "You had better eat something. There's a basket of marulas at home."

Bubble nodded, struggled to her feet, and waddled downhill toward her mother's shelter. Hawk started to get to his feet, but Peep shook her head and waved him back. "I'll look after her. Stay out of her way for now."

Whistle leaned toward her sister and signed, "Just send Murmur up to get us when you need us."

"Thanks." Peep sent an apprehensive look after her daughter. "The first baby is so hard."

Bapoto seemed back to normal. He ate heartily, laughed at Pike's jokes, and after lunch, helped finish the butchering. As they were cleaning up, Pike turned to Bapoto. "Can I use your dragger to help Peep take home her part of this meat?"

Bapoto folded his arms and leaned against the limestone wall into which the shelter was built. "There's something I think you should all know first. Something has happened." The others looked at him, and Snap narrowed her eyes. "In the spring, about a half-moon's travel south of Kura, I came upon a single gazelle grazing in the early morning. There was no herd in sight, but she seemed unconcerned. As I was planning how I might be able to get near enough to throw a spear, I saw a lion cub following her. At first I thought a lioness was teaching her cub to hunt, and was somewhere nearby, so I kept myself hidden. After a while, though, the cub walked up to the gazelle and nuzzled her, and she allowed the lion cub to nurse. After I saw this, I couldn't bring myself to try to take the gazelle. No gazelle would ever suckle a lion, and so I realized this must have been a vision from the Great One."

Snap was about to rumble in disbelief when she realized the others were nodding solemnly. Bapoto went on, "I sat for some time, considering what this vision from the Great One might mean for us. Eventually, it became clear to me the vision was telling us there is something about the way we live which is wrong, and we need to change. The lion, the hunter, undoubtedly is meant to stand for men, and the nursing mother gazelle undoubtedly represents women. The change in the relations between the lion and the gazelle must mean we are to change something about the relations between men and women. In some way, we are to make the weak stronger, and the strong weaker."

Snap expected Whistle to say something agreeable, but make no promises. She was surprised when her mother wrinkled her brow uncertainly and left her hands in her lap while Bapoto went on.

"Finally, I realized the true meaning of the gazelle suckling a lion was this: men and women are meant to live together. We men should stay nearby to fight against the invaders. We shouldn't leave to trade or to look for better hunting; we should be making sure our mates and their children are safe."

"What a peculiar story!" signed Snap. "That would be funny to tell at the Bonding. Don't you think so, Whistle?"

Whistle glanced around at the assembled faces and then at the fire, biting her lower lip. Snap went on, "We know Whistle will make sure we have peace and enough to eat."

Peep's eyes flickered around the uwanda uncomfortably, as if she wanted to avoid looking at Snap's words, but couldn't help herself. Pike suddenly became interested in cleaning his fingernails, and Hawk started backing slowly toward the downhill side of the uwanda. Even Rustle and Swish seemed to be uneasy with their sister's lack of deference.

"I need time to think about this. Go to the men's shelter for now. In a day or two, I will know what to do." Strangely, Whistle used a jumble of ordinary signs and large two-armed signs. Bapoto dropped his gaze and impassively began to help Pike pack meat into the dragger.

When the others had departed, Snap gave Rustle and Swish a few handfuls of berries and herbs to pound into paste, and she began slicing the wildebeest meat to prepare it for drying. Whistle squatted by the fire and watched ash cloak the glowing coals. After a while, when the children had begun pounding their finished paste into the slices of meat, Whistle rose and joined her daughter at the large stump on which she was cutting the meat.

The stump was stained dark red, and flies were buzzing over the slices that were piled between Rustle and Swish.

"They will kill one another, if we don't kill them first." Snap divided the hindquarter and gave part of it to her mother.

"The flies?" Whistle picked up a hand chopper and began to cut slices.

"The men. They are so agreeable in the fall, but you know what happens by spring; they argue about everything, some hit their mates, some sneak off with other people's mates, they're impossible."

Whistle handed a slice to Rustle. "Spring is hard for everyone. None of us are agreeable when we're hungry."

"No, we're not. And that's why we need that time in the summer; to remember why we need one another, to make us appreciate one another again. This is how we are, and it works, vision or no vision."

Silence and the smell of the wildebeest's blood filled the space between them. Snap began to worry she had offended her mother, but Whistle didn't look angry.

"I am afraid of the Fukizo," the older woman signed, but the younger one thought it was misery that lined her forehead, not fear. Whistle closed her eyes, and her features smoothed into a blank mask. "We need to protect our children, and we need the men to do it. These Fukizo are probably like the strangers in the story of the Seventh Mother, the ones who kidnapped our women during the summer harvest. They have returned to torment us again, and we must drive them away, as was done in the time of the Seventh Mother. If we are working with our men against the Fukizo, we can avoid the disagreements that come from too much time too close together."

Snap drew her mouth into a thin line and cut the next slice with so much force it became imbedded in the stump and she had to loosen it with her fingernails before she could give it to Swish to be pounded. Whistle shook her head. "Chirp was always sure she knew better than anyone else, and today I can see Chirp looking out of your eyes. It is enough to make me believe in Bapoto's spirits."

Snap raised one eyebrow at her mother, and Whistle went on. "Our traditions are good, but we must do what is best for the ukoo. And that will be that." Whistle made her last slice with a flourish and handed it to Rustle.

By the time Snap hung the last slice of wildebeest meat on the drying rack, the sun was setting. A shower of pebbles made her look around, and she saw Peep's daughter Murmur scrambling up the slope. Her short, seven-year-old legs were poorly matched to the steep path, and she was waving her arms incoherently. Snap caught the girl in one arm as she threw herself into the uwanda. "Slower. I can't understand a word."

Murmur squeaked in alarm at her own bad manners. She pulled herself upright and gave a short purr of respect. "Peep thinks the baby might come soon."

Snap gave a click of interest. Whistle looked up from rinsing blood from the stump on which they had been working. "Tell Peep we'll come right over. Rustle and Swish can go to Warble's for the night."

Murmur nodded and started back down the slope to her mother's shelter. Whistle collected some things into a sling and started for Peep's shelter, while Snap took Rustle, Swish, sleeping hides for the children, and the drying rack filled with meat to Warble's shelter. Warble was pleased to know Bubble's baby was coming and cheerfully agreed to watch the children and the meat. Her children, Trill, Rattle, and Chirp, were not interested in Bubble's baby, but were pleased about their cousins' visit. Snap thanked Warble and headed up the slope to Peep's.

At Peep's shelter, Snap gave a soft hoot and ducked under the door flap. The twilight was deepening, and a fire filled the shelter with flickering shadows. As her eyes adjusted to the firelight, Snap recognized three kneeling shapes in the middle of the room. A trench had been dug into the floor, a large hide spread over it, and the depression filled with dry moss. Bubble knelt between the other two women, one knee on each side of the trench, eyes closed, hands resting palm up on her thighs. She looked tired, but intensely focused, not sleepy. Whistle and Peep watched Bubble silently. Murmur crouched in the sleeping alcove, her arms around a rolled sleeping hide, and stared at her sister.

Snap had been present at the births of her three younger siblings, as well as at the other births Whistle had attended in the last several years, and she wasn't frightened by the looks of concentration on the faces of the three women or by the peculiar smell she associated with births. Whistle looked up at her daughter as she entered and signed a greeting. The new arrival went to the sleeping alcove, squatted next to Murmur, and patted her cousin's shoulder gently. The girl gave Snap a brief, searching look, and then turned back to her sister.

In a moment, Bubble took a deep breath and shifted her weight from her knees to her feet. As she squatted, she curled her body around her huge abdomen, supported on each side by the two older women. After several slow, deep breaths, a deep rumbling sound escaped her, then several more slow breaths, and then a sigh as she returned to kneeling. No one made a sound or a sign. Just as at the other births she had attended, Snap felt the deep concentration of the mother engulf each of those present in the vortex of her labor, as if the laboring woman was using the strength of the other women present. Bubble kept her eyes closed, and it seemed to Snap her cousin was in a sort of waking dream, between consciousness and unconsciousness.

Snap sat next to Murmur through several more contractions, and then got up to stoke the fire. As she moved, a torrent of tiny kicks erupted in her own middle, as if provoked by Bubble's labor, and she absently patted her belly as she returned to the sleeping alcove.

"Why is it taking so long?" Murmur asked. "When Baby was born, I ran to get Whistle as fast as I could, and he was born almost as soon as we got back."

"Oh, this isn't long for a first baby. The first one always takes much longer." Snap signed with the authority of a witness to a dozen previous births.

Murmur shook her head. "I don't think I will have any babies, then."

"How are you going to arrange that?" Snap asked, jerking her chin upward.

The girl shook her head again. "I'll think of something."

By the next time Snap got up to stoke the fire, Bubble's rumbles had evolved into grunts, and with each contraction, she pressed her hand against her bottom, as if to hold the baby in. Whistle bent down to look during one of the louder grunts, and after that contraction, she made a *chht* sound so Bubble would open her eyes. "I can see the head," Whistle signed. "Almost there."

Bubble looked exhausted now. "It burns."

Three more contractions, and the next grunt turned into a squeal. Peep caught the slippery, brown-haired infant before she could fall into the moss-filled trench, and handed the tiny girl into her daughter's arms. Bubble looked astonished as the baby sneezed into her face and then began to scream. Snap realized she had been holding her breath for some time, and let it out. She had thought little about her own labor, but suddenly it loomed over her, and she hoped desperately it would be short.

Eventually, the squalling stopped. Peep and Whistle helped Bubble, still kneeling over the trench, get the baby into a position to nurse, which stretched the umbilical cord to full length. The baby had scarcely latched on to the breast when Bubble's face returned to its former state of intense concentration, and she began to push again.

Murmur directed a worried look at her cousin. "What is it?" she asked.

"The afterbirth will come next," signed Snap, knowledgeably. "A thing like an antelope liver. Whistle says they are delicious. Bubble will get to eat it herself. She doesn't have to share, because she's the mother."

Murmur looked disappointed and returned to watching the baby nurse. Bubble's expression became more and more intense, and she grunted louder than she had before. Whistle drew her brows together and leaned down again to look.

"Take the baby, please, Peep," she signed as the contraction ended. "I don't think it's the afterbirth." Both Bubble and Peep stared at Whistle. With a finger in a corner of the baby's mouth,

Peep broke the suction between the baby and the breast and took her from her daughter as another contraction started. Another wet, brown head emerged, and Whistle held out her hands for the baby, a boy. Bubble knelt with her mouth wide open and gaped at the screaming infant in Whistle's hands.

CHAPTER 12

Everyone had something to say about the twins. When Warble visited Whistle the day after the twins' birth, she observed that Peep was lucky to get two grandchildren at once, after losing so many of her own children, and Whistle agreed. Snap told Hum that Bubble had her sympathy, and she hoped to escape the same fate. The men seemed to be discussing the twins almost as much as the women. Bapoto, on his daily visits to Whistle, propounded the idea that the birth of twins was undoubtedly another message from the Great One. Whistle attended patiently while he explained that the birth of a boy and a girl at the same time obviously meant his interpretation of his vision had been correct; men and women should live together. Snap rolled her eyes and watched for a chance to meet her mother alone.

Several days later, Whistle proposed a trip to collect shea nuts. Rustle seemed to think nut collecting was unmanly, so he marched slightly ahead of his family with his small spear held at the ready, as if he were only there to protect them. Walking short distances was as much as Snap could manage, and running almost impossible. As she waddled at Whistle's side, Snap attracted her mother's attention with a *chht* and signed, "What are you thinking about Bapoto's vision? He seems eager for you to make a decision."

"Is that right?" Whistle's sarcasm was atypical but unmistakable. "He's tried to bring his sleeping hides up to the shelter four times. He's been to every single shelter in the village to explain his ideas in every possible way. He's had three of his men-only prehunt parties, even though all they ever do is talk and snare rabbits. Everyone expects me to announce that the Bonding this fall will be permanent, and no more summer journeys for the men. They are going to stick to us like tree sap."

Maybe she's coming around, Snap thought. Surely Whistle could see Bapoto's plan would be disastrous. "Terrible idea, don't you think?"

Whistle flattened her lips over her teeth. "Having the men around all the time will be troublesome, but being attacked by the Fukizo would be worse. Our ways have worked well for us for a long time, but it's possible that doing things differently might be safer, just for a year or two, until we are sure the Fukizo will leave us alone."

Swish was leaning around her mother in order to see what

she was signing to Snap, and stumbled on a loose rock. Whistle pulled her younger daughter upright, and her older daughter stopped to take a few deep breaths. As they started again after an impatient Rustle, Snap looked at her mother. "I don't think this would be good for the ukoo. There would be less hunting, less meat, more of the children would be hungry. Men would fight more, and mates would argue more. And what's more, if our boys are raised like this, women in other ukoos will think they're peculiar, and they won't be able to find mates."

Whistle didn't respond immediately. Her lips were still drawn tightly, and she walked as if she were choosing footholds on the side of a steep cliff. Finally she signed, "Bapoto tells me he met men from Panda Ya Mto during the summer, and they are changing as well. Thump has taught some of them the hunting ritual and the healing ritual, and told them about the Great One. Soon the Great One will be known in every ukoo."

Snap wasn't sure if she believed this. Thump? Her sensible brother? He might have been intrigued by Bapoto's odd ideas, but he couldn't possibly believe them. He wouldn't want to destroy the traditional ways. Would he? She looked again at Whistle, who was still picking her way slowly and determinedly.

"You are my mother, and you are the Mother of Kura. Whatever you decide, I will support you, but I will continue to believe my senses, no matter what anyone else thinks. I will never try to send messages to invisible people, even one with the unlikely name of Great One, and nothing will convince me dead people are not really dead."

"You are my daughter, and you will be the Mother in your time. What goes on in one's head is one's own business, isn't it? The Kura have met all sorts of threats before; we can handle a little thing like men in the summer." Whistle's words were reassuring, but her hands shook uneasily.

Snap attempted a hum of approval, but the result sounded more like a whimper. Rustle had reached the edge of the grove. He turned and announced with large two-armed signs that he would reconnoiter the area to make sure they were safe. "Fine," responded Whistle.

"He won't be back soon," signed Snap. "He hates collecting shea nuts." Whistle nodded and began to show Swish which nuts were worth putting into her sling.

❧

The next morning, Snap corralled Swish and Rustle to help her to shell the shea nuts. Whistle went off to confer privately with each Kura woman and with each man staying at the men's shelter. By the time she returned, it was past midday, there was a nearly roasted cane rat the size of a crawling baby over the fire, and the nuts were all shelled and ready to be ground. As Whistle squatted by the fire and sniffed, Snap saw the lines on her mother's face smooth.

She squatted next to Whistle. "Thunder brought the rat. It's for you. He agreed I should cook it for you. It's nearly ready to eat. Have you talked to everyone?"

"Yes. The women are worried about the Fukizo. The men have been away from the women all summer, and any plan that involves staying with us longer sounds good to them. We will have the Bonding in three days, and I will make it clear I expect the men to stay with us through next summer, until the Bonding next fall."

Snap was disappointed, but not surprised. Whistle wanted

consensus. Chirp had been the Mother forever and made decisions without consulting anyone, but Whistle was different.

"Three days! It is still warm, and not a hint of rain. What's the rush?" Snap turned the rat and prodded the meat with a nut-stained finger. She signed casually and didn't look at her mother, but Whistle registered her unexpressed objection.

"There are already more men here than returned last fall for the Bonding. Ash is a far-walker; who knows where he might be?"

She couldn't object to her mother's reasoning, but neither could she pretend to be pleased. All of the returning men had formally greeted Whistle, and a few presented gifts to Snap as well. Their drying rack was constantly occupied with meat and fish, prepared with new obsidian knives. Thunder even brought her a tiny packet of dirty salt, but she knew at least six other women had received the same. The prospect of living with a squalling infant had probably deterred most suitors, but apparently a few were more interested in her status.

The next three days were filled with the usual madness of preparing for the Bonding. Whenever she could spare some time from the feast preparations, Snap climbed the ridge above the shelter and searched the distant landscape for a moving dot that might be approaching Kura, but saw nothing of interest. Bapoto almost seemed to be standing guard at Whistle's shelter; he greeted the steady stream of male visitors with an expression remarkably like a wolf's snarl, even those who claimed to be visiting Snap. After a day of this, an annoyed Whistle suggested he organize a hunt to provide meat for the Bonding feast. He held a particularly elaborate prehunt ritual that night and managed to convince nearly all of the men to join him the next morning in a boar hunt. Two desperate bachelors wanted to have as much time as possible to impress the women of Kura, and so remained behind, along with the two old men who no longer hunted anything that couldn't be snared.

On the night before the Bonding, the hunting party returned with two large boars. The feast seemed likely to be the best in Snap's memory, but she wished it was not quite so imminent. She took the first watch that night, kept the fire burning high, and listened for the sound of a distant hoot that never came. When the sky began to lighten, Whistle came out of the shelter and stretched, and Snap reluctantly went to sleep until sunrise.

The feast was, indeed, unmatched in her memory. The delicacies offered during the morning procession were diverse and plentiful. The boars roasting in the pit in the great uwanda with Whistle's special selection of fruit, nuts, and vegetables made their mouths water while Whistle told traditional tales nearly as well as Chirp had done. Snap watched and ate and hooted at the appropriate moments, but her attention was elsewhere; one ear listened for a faraway hoot, and at each pause, her gaze swept the horizon for a speck that might have moved since her last check.

By the time the two oldest men started the drumming, her hope had faded away, and she helped organize the nursery where the older children would supervise the younger ones with an expression as blank and hard as the limestone that towered over them. Then it was time to dance, and she stood woodenly between Whistle and Peep until forced to join in by sharp elbows in the ribs from both sides. She joined the women's trill automatically, pounded the baked gray earth with her feet unthinkingly. The previous fall flooded her memory; she had diligently examined each face passing her in the outer circle as she convinced herself she was making the right choice. This time, the faces of the men seemed to her to be as expressionless as the faces of lizards, indistinguishable and emotionless. The drums and the singing filled her mind and occupied her body, but no vision of spending the next year with any one of these men engaged her passion.

At last, Whistle stepped forward, seized Bapoto's hand, and left the circle. Snap noticed they did not leave immediately, but stood just out of the firelight to watch the others dance. It was time to step forward, time to choose, and she forced herself out of the women's circle and stood facing the men. As Thunder passed her, he slowed his steps, waved his hands at his waist, and warbled with what appeared to be sincere ardor, but she remained impassive as Thunder was pushed on his way. Several other men also tried to remain in front of her as long as possible. Finally, the men completed a revolution of the uwanda, and Thunder passed again. She stepped forward. Thunder raised his arms in triumph, but she didn't take his hand. She walked through the men's circle and left the uwanda, just as Chirp had done the previous fall.

She could hear a number of men and some of the women hiss behind her, but she continued into the darkness. Her vision gradually adjusted to the moonlight as she climbed the Kura ridge to a level area at the top. Facing west, she squatted with her back against a large rock and methodically examined the regions she could see, just as she had been doing since Whistle had announced the Bonding. A bat flickered across the stars, and below the village, a hyena splashed across the stream, but she saw nothing that looked even vaguely human. A breeze blew away the last warmth of the day, and she smelled a breath of moisture; finally, fall was coming. Would Ash come, too? Somewhere, she was sure, he would smell the same first breath of fall air, and it would remind him he had somewhere else to be.

She sat on. A cloud made its way across the stars, shredded into wisps, and gathered again, and then another joined it. She heard the singing fade as couples left the central uwanda, and finally even the sound of the drums died away. Only a few night noises reached her; a baby cried, and one of the old men returning to the men's shelter had a coughing fit that echoed across the village. When it seemed to her everyone except the watchers must be asleep, she heard another sound. Somewhere on the north side of the ridge, away from the village, a dislodged rock rolled downhill. Slowly and silently, she peered around the rock against which she had been squatting. The darkness on the north side of the ridge was almost impenetrable, but she managed to make out a number of figures, darker black against the limestone, warily climbing the back of the ridge.

Yowling an alarm at the top of her considerable voice, Snap blasted down the path toward Whistle's shelter, which was the highest and most westward. People spilled from every shelter, and as she scrambled down, Snap waved, "Strangers on the ridge!" with both arms. Before she reached Whistle's shelter, she met Bapoto and Rustle running uphill, spears in both hands. Still yowling, she gesticulated wildly, "Strangers! Climbing the back of the ridge! I saw them!"

Bapoto gave her a brief nod and joined the stream of men and bigger boys who tore up the ridge to the level area at the top. Some added to Snap's yowls, but most were hooting, even those who had learned to make the Kura hoot only that day. She flung the door flap aside and burst into the shelter. Whistle, with the biggest obsidian chopper in one hand, appeared to be trying to hide Swish under every last sleeping hide in the shelter. As her older daughter rushed in, Whistle waved at several spears leaning against the wall. "Enough yowling. Everyone has heard you. Now take a spear and be silent."

Snap selected the strongest of Bapoto's remaining spears and arranged the door flap so she could see the uwanda without being seen herself. When Whistle had hidden Swish to her satisfaction, she picked up a burning branch in her other hand and moved to the opposite side of the door, careful not to disturb the flap as she took her position. Snap could still hear Kura hoots from the top of the ridge, occasional alarm yowls, and finally, a scream. The two women stood silently and watched faint shadows cast by moonlight creep across the uwanda. The hoots and alarm calls faded, but no normal night noises replaced them; silence rang in Snap's ears. Her cramping fingers slipped on the sweaty spear shaft. Whistle's firebrand burned down, and she dropped it into the fire with scorched fingertips.

Neither of the women moved. Whistle prodded the flames with another branch, and took the new torch back to the door. Swish peeked from under the hides, and Snap waved her back. A cloud began to move across the moon, and the uwanda darkened. Something small rustled in a bush near the shelter, and a bird wakened in the night and gave a sleepy twitter. At last, Rustle stumped into the uwanda and announced his presence with a soft hoot as he approached the door. Whistle pulled back the flap, and he ducked into the shelter. "Well?" she signed.

He squatted next to the fire, eyes wide with exhilaration, but the knuckles clutching his short spear were pale. Swish crawled from under her pile of hides, sat next to her brother, and touched his knee, as if to confirm his presence. "There were at least ten strangers on the top of the ridge when we got up there," he signed. "They roared and ran at us, but when they saw how many of us were coming, they backed down the north side of the ridge. Hawk got one of them in the arm with his spear, I think, but he ran away with the others. The men are going to patrol around the village tonight, and they sent us boys back to guard the shelters."

"Very wise." Whistle kissed Rustle on the top of his head. "You and I can take the first watch, if you like."

He nodded, straightened up, and took his sister's position at the door. Snap made a gesture of thanks and relinquished her place with a grateful pat on his shoulder. It was late, she had had little sleep the previous night, and now that they seemed to be safe, exhaustion rolled over her like a late-afternoon thunderstorm. She crawled into her hide next to Swish and fell asleep.

When Whistle woke her, she saw that Rustle had fallen asleep at his post and his mother had covered him with his sleeping hide. A dream twitched his sleeping face. With a yawn, Whistle took her daughter's place in the sleeping alcove, and Snap squatted next to the door. The moon was low. Whispery night noises and an occasional muffled hoot were the only sounds she heard. Finally, the eastern sky became smudged and colorless, and a soft Kura hoot announced someone's approach. Rustle's head jerked up and he pretended to have been awake as Bapoto entered.

"Have you seen anything?" Snap asked. Bapoto turned slowly to her with his eyes narrowed and his lips clamped between his teeth, but did not answer.

"Was it the Fukizo?" she pressed on.

He still did not answer, but bared his teeth in a peculiar way, rolled himself in his hides, and fell asleep.

By the time the sun had risen fully, Peep and Pike had come by to share some scorched marrow bones left over from the previous day's feast. Whistle and Bapoto were still asleep, and Snap saw no reason to wake them. Pike complained that between Bubble's babies, Peep's baby, and midnight invaders, he might never sleep again, but he sat close to Peep and nuzzled the back of her neck. After they had departed, Snap carried a stack of leftover flatbread to Warble and Thunder, who looked as tired as Pike and Peep, and equally pleased with their new family circumstances.

When Snap returned to Whistle's shelter, Rustle and Swish were lazing in the sun, and Bapoto was absent. Whistle was squatting on the shady side of the shelter, frowning at an antelope hide as if it worried her, and she didn't respond to her daughter's greeting. Snap settled down next to her with a partly finished basket. "Are you all right?"

Whistle nodded.

"What is that going to be?" asked Snap.

"A new covering for a baby board, I think. You are welcome to use my old baby board, if you want it, but I've had that one since Rustle was born, and I think it's better to have a new one for your first baby." Snap nodded gratefully and worked on in silence.

At Whistle's *chht*, she looked up from the nearly finished basket. "Bapoto is angry." Her hands folded on the antelope hide like a nesting bird, Whistle focused on something far down the valley.

"About what?" She had a good idea what Bapoto was angry about, but produced a bemused expression for her mother's benefit.

"The vision he saw over the summer has affected him powerfully. He feels it is essential for men and women to join together right now, for our safety and because the Great One wishes it. You haven't chosen a mate, and he thinks this has offended the Great One and brought us misfortune in the form of an attack by the Fukizo. This morning, he suggested a mate should be chosen for you, in order to fulfill the wishes of the Great One and prevent a disaster."

Snap dropped her basket with an angry yelp. "What! How can you say this? *You* didn't take a mate once. Didn't you defend me?"

Snap felt as if the sun had suddenly shifted in the sky, and the appearance of everything in the valley, everything in Kura, was subtly different. "Think about this, Whistle. There is no invisible person telling Bapoto I must take a mate. Bapoto is forceful and persuasive, but he is wrong. The Fukizo will not be turned away by my accepting a mate I don't want."

"You don't know that. Bapoto may be right. The Great One may be punishing us, and you could save us, just by taking a mate. How hard would that be? Next year, when the Fukizo are gone, Bapoto will forget all about the idea of permanent mates, and you can have Ash again, if he comes back."

Snap stood up and walked away from the uwanda, uphill toward the ridgetop. Whistle picked up the hide and began punching holes along one side with a stone awl.

Snap felt as if she had become invisible to all the adults in Kura. The children still ran up to her and asked to feel her baby moving, invited her to join their games, and helped her with chores her growing belly made difficult. However, neither Whistle nor Bapoto addressed her, looked at her, or shared the watch with her. Whistle prepared food for herself, Bapoto, and the children, and left the remainder where Snap would find it later. The other adults ignored her when they met her and silently stepped around her if they found her in their paths. Only Bubble gave any sign she recognized her existence when she burst into tears as her cousin walked by Peep's uwanda.

At first, Snap was a bit annoyed, but mostly amused. She got ready for the baby, talked to Rustle and Swish, and waddled alone to ridgetops where she could watch for distant specks that might be Ash. On her walks, she occasionally met men, who ignored her, but never any women; the women and children kept close to the shelters now and went to the latrines and to the stream for water in groups. After seven days of this treatment, Snap began to find it less funny, but also less annoying. She almost appreciated the fact she didn't have to discuss Bapoto's ideas with anyone, and she expected it would all blow over when the baby came. Returning from the latrines one midday, she was startled when Whistle addressed her from the uwanda fireside.

"Snap, come join me."

She squatted next to her mother and noticed that Whistle had nearly completed the new baby board. "That hide turned out very well."

"Yes. I want you to know that everything has been worked out. We've found you an acceptable mate. Bapoto and the Great One will be happy, I'm sure you'll be satisfied with him, and anyway, you only have to be sociable until spring."

"What do you mean?"

"He is waiting in the shelter. Go in and meet him."

Whistle put her work into a basket, stood up, and steered Snap toward the shelter with a nod. Snap ducked under the door flap and was surprised to find two men inside: Bapoto and Burrow, the large, dull-eyed man whom she had seen performing the hunt ritual with Bapoto and Jackal. Just like the previous year, he had arrived in Kura for the Bonding and departed the day after, not chosen. Bapoto moved to stand between her and the door, while Burrow eyed her as if she were a rabbit.

"Snap, this is Burrow," signed Bapoto. "He has kindly agreed to return to Kura to be your mate. This will protect us from the attacks of the Fukizo. You will accept him." Burrow gave her an unpleasant expression that revealed his two missing incisors and a raggedly broken canine and moved toward her.

Snap bared her teeth and growled. She backed away from Burrow and found her path to the door blocked on one side of the fire by Bapoto and on the other by Burrow. As the two men started toward her, she jumped as high as her cumbersome belly allowed, between the men and directly over the fire. The fire had smoldered down to embers, and Snap wasn't burned, but they caught her easily by her arms in midair, stepped away from the fire, and threw her onto the hard earthen floor on her hands and knees. Bapoto put his foot on her neck and pushed her face into the floor. She fought to turn her head so that she could breathe and felt the baby kick violently.

Bapoto held his hand at floor level so she could see his words. "Calm yourself. Accept the will of the Great One."

She growled again, but didn't move. Searing anger blinded her, numbed all feeling, filled her throat with a bellow of fury. Neither the leopard nor the lion had provoked such a fierce reaction in her, but Bapoto's foot crushing her neck precluded any struggle.

"It is not your place! What are you thinking?" Snap couldn't see Burrow's face, but she tried to direct her one-handed words at him as best she could. Bapoto made a sound like the quavering whistle with which he addressed the Great One. Burrow buzzed a mating sound and seized her hips. As he clumsily bounced on the balls of his feet behind her, she roared, not in pain, but in anger and humiliation. Her words were barely intelligible. "I am the daughter of the Mother, and you are a hyena. Get out! No wonder no one ever chooses you for their mate!" Almost before her seething brain could think of any more insults, she realized Burrow had finished grunting, removed his offending organ, and rocked back on his heels. Bapoto released her neck, turned, and left her alone with Burrow. She backed up into the sleeping alcove to get as far away from him as possible.

Burrow showed her his broken teeth again. "Mated for life, Bapoto says. We saved the ukoo, he says. Everybody will treat me better now."

Snap hissed, and Burrow's leer faded into a vacuous stare. Finally apprehending her frame of mind, he stood up and lumbered out of the shelter. Snap took a few deep breaths and tried to collect her thoughts. Outrage still roared in her ears like a cloud of locusts, and her fists lay clenched on the floor beside her. The crumbling limestone ground into her back as she considered, and discarded, one plan after another. What could she do? No one in Kura would defy the Mother; no one would even acknowledge her presence. Silence from outside gave her the courage to check the uwanda. It was empty. Apparently, Bapoto and Burrow had gone to give the rest of the ukoo the good news, and Whistle probably didn't want to face her daughter until she had calmed down.

An empty water bag and a pouch of dika nuts lay near the

shelter door; Snap snatched them up as she hurried across the uwanda and down the slope as fast as her ungainly shape allowed. Scrubby trees west of Kura provided cover on her way to the stream, but when she reached it, she found Hum filling gourds at the water's edge. The older woman raised her eyebrows but made no sign. Snap filled her water bag, slung the carrying strap over her shoulder, and started downstream, away from Kura. She heard Hum snap her fingers several times and turned to see the woman watching her leave with overbright eyes and an anxious frown.

The sun was just past its zenith as Snap swayed south. Her anger boiled down to a simmer; some order returned to her thoughts. She was first daughter of the Mother. She would not accept a mate chosen by anyone else, especially not by Bapoto, and especially not a repulsive buffalo like Burrow. Isolation hung around her neck like a load of firewood. Head down, she dug her toes into the light gray dust with each step. Where would she be safe? Not at Kura, not any longer. What Whistle thinks best for the ukoo was no longer best for Snap. She knew the land well in all directions, she knew what could be eaten, what might be used, and what ought to be feared. She also knew she wouldn't get through the winter without any stored food, or through the birth of her baby without any help.

One thing at a time, she thought. First decide where to go.

Maybe Thump returned to Panda Ya Mto this fall. Maybe his mate could spare a little food for an unrelated woman.

Snap frowned skeptically at her toes and turned southwest.

CHAPTER 13

B*y the* time Ash thought to stop for a last look back at
Kura, it was gone, lost behind the last outcrop of serrated
karst. His long twists sprayed over his shoulders as he turned
and ran on. No slower runners held him back, no need to return to camp before dark limited him; the pleasure of stretching
his underused muscles spurred his pace far beyond his usual
long-distance lope. His conversations with traders informed his
plan; follow the Kijito upstream, southwest, until it dwindled
to a trickle, and then cross the stream and turn south. His
back was soon matted with sweat, so that he shivered when he

stopped for a drink in the shade of an enormous baobab. He ran with a short spear in his hand in case he surprised any small game, for which he was rewarded shortly after midday, when a squirrel hiding under a low bush lost its nerve and darted into his path. Cooking was a winter luxury, and he was soon on his way again, a fresh squirrel hide flapping on his pack. By nightfall, he was in an unfamiliar region, far to the southwest of Kura. Savanna intersected by limestone ridges had given way to towering, open forests interrupted by broken granite and scrub. It was cooler than it had been at the lower elevations near Kura, and by the time the diurnal birds had fallen silent and bats were beginning to appear, Ash was pleased to find a dense thicket under which to roll up in his sleeping hides.

The next day was very similar, and the next, and the next. The Kijito, still on his left, shrank at each tributary. He spent an afternoon hunting, a morning fishing, and an entire day climbing a local summit for a better view. He met a few hunters and traders, with whom he exchanged greetings and information, and came upon several ukoos, where he traded his small supply of goods and his larger supply of stories. Days became a moon, and he began to meet people whose signs were slightly different from those he had seen before.

When he had traveled from Kilima the previous summer, the long days of walking were filled with storytelling. He and Tor had embellished the old tales, expanded their repertoire, and honed their skills as raconteurs. Stories he told on this journey, however, always seemed to include Snap, or had a similar character, or recounted an adventure like one he had with her. Fall was never far from his thoughts.

He had long since crossed the Kijito and was heading south

when he met a trader who had had dealings with the Fukizo, and who directed him through a pass in a mountain range visible at the horizon. High on a shoulder of these mountains, he passed through a grove of trees, no more than knee high, contorted by cruel winds and winter storms into fantastic shapes that inspired especially fearsome monsters in the next tale Ash concocted. An intriguing piece of this wood lay broken in his path, and he added it to his bundle. During his brief rests and before sleep each night, he considered the convolutions and intricacies of its form from every angle. Finally the contour of the wood suggested a shape, and he began to add a groove here, smooth an edge there.

Two days after crossing the mountain pass, he emerged from a stand of stunted, twisted trees to find a large lake, its calm water reflecting piercingly blue sky and cold, bright, midday sun. The trees continued around one side of the lake, while the other was an open meadow that swarmed with flying and hopping insects and burst with tiny pink flowers. The meadow was occupied also by four large and dripping-wet men, who were working at extracting a mass of uncooperative fish from a tangled net.

He hooted respectfully and proceeded around the rocky shore toward the men. The largest of the four returned the hoot and started toward him, while the others continued their efforts to turn the fish out onto the grass. He halted and assessed the intentions of the approaching stranger. He was about Ash's height, but broader. Like the other three, his hair was carefully twisted into a series of concentric rings around his head, and he was wearing an expression Ash interpreted to be welcoming, although he was showing more teeth than Ash thought strictly necessary for friendliness. When he was near enough for easy conversation, Ash tucked his spear under one arm and greeted him with two-armed signs he had found were generally understood, even among ukoos with many idiosyncratic signs.

"Greetings! I am Ash, of the Kilima."

"Welcome, Ash. I am Dika, of the Fukizo." Fortunately, Dika seemed to be using ordinary signs, and he had no weapon. As Dika continued to approach, Ash made sure of his footing, shifted the spear slightly, and tried to imitate Dika's toothy smile. He shot a glance at the other men, who were watching the encounter while they straightened and folded the net and retrieved straggling fish that tried to flop toward the water.

"Good fishing today." Ash waved a hand at the wriggling heap.

"Very good. It will take us the rest of the day to get them ready to smoke. Why don't you eat with us? We would like a story, if you have one." Dika used clear, familiar signs, but at such a deliberate pace that Ash had to pay close attention to avoid losing the meaning of his words. Dika's smile had relaxed into an expression more like curiosity.

"Thank you. I would be pleased to help you with the fish, and to tell a story or two, in exchange for a meal." Ash put down his pack and his spear, and held up his hands in a gesture of trust. Dika beckoned Ash to follow as he turned and walked back toward the other men.

Ash made an open-palm gesture of greeting as they approached the other three men, and each of them returned the same sign. Ash introduced himself, and Dika introduced the others. Agama was short, wiry, and had the most elaborately styled hair of the four, and to Ash, seemed a bit suspicious. Granite had a wide, friendly face and was as tall, as thin, and as young as Ash. Falcon was strikingly handsome and greeted Ash with a sad, introspective gaze. Almost before Ash could keep them straight, Dika had organized the five of them into a sort of assembly line, and they began to clean and string up the fish onto long poles. The work was repetitive and required neither strength nor much thought, but prevented conversation. Soon the fish hung gleaming in silvery rows from the poles.

They invited Ash to accompany them to their shelter and share a meal, and he accepted gratefully, since he had not hunted for two days. Carrying the poles on their shoulders, they soon arrived at a large, clean-swept uwanda, which curved around a sizable shelter. A neat fire ring in the center of the uwanda contained a banked fire. The shelter had apparently begun as a shallow cave about ten feet deep, surmounted by a natural arch in a crumbling granite wall. The cave had been extended by a framework of bent poles, tucked securely into notches in the granite, and roofed with joined hides. There were no other shelters visible, nor any other people. Ash complimented the design and construction of the shelter, and thought this was undoubtedly the best kept bachelors' shelter he had ever seen, and the only one he had ever seen with summer occupants. Falcon looked pleased.

Falcon chose a basketful of fish, stirred up the uwanda fire, and began to prepare a meal. A smokehouse stood ready to receive the rest of the fish, and the remaining four pairs of hands made short work of hanging the fish in the smokehouse, building its fire, and arranging its flaps to allow the correct draft. By the time the smokehouse was closed, twilight was gathering, and the smell of food cooking made Ash's mouth water.

The men each found a dish; Ash rummaged in his bundle for a wooden bowl. Falcon passed out the fish, each stuffed with tiny onions, spring beans, and unfamiliar herbs, and cooked over the fire in slings made from the same fibers of which the seines had been constructed. The other men appeared to be as hungry as Ash; although each of them received three sizable stuffed fish from Falcon, there were no leftovers to be seen when Ash looked up from his empty bowl, except for a feathery pile of fish bones next to each of them. Granite was chewing on one of the cooking slings, and Ash found that the sling in which his fish had been cooked was quite tasty as well, although too tough to swallow.

By the time they had finished eating, the night was cool and quite dark, but Agama coaxed the fire into a blaze that allowed Ash to see that the others were clearly not ready to sleep. Dika climbed to his feet and located a short spear leaning against the shelter.

"I will watch first." Dika bared his teeth in the same strangely friendly way he had earlier. He climbed onto a large flat rock near the edge of the uwanda and squatted facing the fire. "Please tell us of your travels."

Ash launched into the story of how he had grown up in Kilima, left his mother's ukoo, and then was not accepted by any of the women of nearby villages. They seemed to find this entertaining, so he continued with the story of his trip with Tor the previous summer, Tor's death, and his arrival in Kura. Ash watched the four men for signs of recognition when he mentioned Kura, but they attended to his story with no perceptible change in their expressions.

Ash pulled a sleeping hide around his shoulders and leaned back against a stump. "I need a chance to think of another story. Does someone else have one?"

The other men settled themselves around the fire and looked expectantly at Falcon, who began a story similar to one told in every ukoo, in which a mountain smokes, coughs up ashes, and vomits a hot liquid that burns everything it touches and then turns into black, shiny rocks that make excellent tools. Next, Granite told about catching a lizard by the tail. The tail had came off in his hands and allowed the lizard to escape. Ash noticed Agama roll his eyes at Dika, but Falcon nodded his approval of the story, and Ash remarked that he had seen stories of such lizards before. Then Ash described how he came to be accepted in Kura. He gave a humorous imitation of tiny Chirp, bossing around the much larger members of her ukoo, and brought Agama and Granite nearly to tears with the story of Chirp's death. When he described how Bapoto had invented a funeral for Chirp, Dika shot Granite a glance Ash couldn't interpret, and Ash noticed Agama was grinding his teeth.

"Tell us about this Bapoto," signed Agama.

Ash told them how Bapoto had arrived at Kura the previous fall with a belief in a spirit called the Great One, how he performed a healing ritual for Snap's infected wound, and how many people were thus convinced of the truth of his ideas. Ash described Bapoto's beliefs as he understood them: the Great One brings good luck and bad; the Great One heals some wounds and causes others to suppurate and spread; the Great One makes some animals come peaceably to be slaughtered while others become invisible to the hunters; and finally, how dead people don't really die, but go, in some changed form, to live with the Great One. "By spring," Ash finished, "most people were convinced. Or at least, the new rituals seemed popular."

Dika grunted, and the others looked at him as he squatted above them on the rock at the edge of the firelight. "I believe we know Bapoto," he signed, his words large and slow, so they could see them in the dim light. "I was born in Fukizo, thirty springs ago. My mother was named Aster, and her sister was Hibiscus, the Mother of Fukizo. I was well fed and grew large. When I had about eight springs, Bapoto came to Fukizo for the Bonding. He was a grown man, with perhaps twenty springs, tall and strong, and even a child like me could tell all the women wanted him for the Bonding. He was chosen by the Mother, my aunt Hibiscus, although she was much older than he was.

"Soon after, things began to change. Even though they were bonded, the men began to gather in the men's shelter in the evenings to play drums, dance, and make strange sounds. My mother explained to me that Bapoto was teaching the men something that would make the hunts more successful, and it did seem, at first, there was more meat than usual. Next, Bapoto showed us a ritual for people who were injured or ill, which was supposed to make them well. It seemed to work most of the time. People started to regard Bapoto as a sort of secondary Mother and asked his advice on all kinds of things. Many things that had been done only by the Mother, like telling the traditional stories at feasts and judging disputes between people, were now done by Bapoto, with Hibiscus's full support, of course. Eventually, I came to understand that the new rituals for hunting, healing, and death were all part of Bapoto's belief in the Great One.

"By the time I became a man, Bapoto controlled our lives completely. He told each woman whom the Great One wanted her to choose at the Bonding. He informed every mother what name the Great One had chosen for her child. He was revered and loved by nearly everybody. People were only too happy to fulfill the wishes of the Great One, to improve their own chance of good luck now, and life with the Great One after death.

"In that spring when I became a man, and was to leave my mother's shelter, my aunt Hibiscus died. She had had many sons, but only a single daughter had survived to be named, and that daughter had only six springs, too young to become the new Mother. My own mother, Aster, should have become the new Mother of Fukizo by our tradition, but something happened. On the night of my aunt's death, Bapoto didn't join the family to sit with her body, but left the shelter and the village. When he returned in the morning, he told a remarkable story of having met a full-grown male lion, who, instead of attacking him, lay down on its belly and slunk away, tail between its legs. Bapoto interpreted this strange occurrence as a vision sent from the Great One, and declared the Great One wanted him to be the new leader of the Fukizo."

Dika did not use the word *Mother*, since it implied a woman with children, but another word meaning *first in line*. Ash stretched and added a log to the fire. "That does sound suspiciously like the Bapoto I know. And did he become the Mother, I mean, the leader, then?"

"Sort of. Most people liked and respected Bapoto, and had been comfortable with the way he had gradually assumed Hibiscus's duties, as long as he was acting in her name, but quite a few would not accept a male leader. It was spring, and time for the men to leave the village. When we men left, a group of women, including my mother, left Fukizo as well. They walked to a place that had been one of our summer harvest camps, built winter shelters there, and called it New Fukizo. My mother became Mother of the New Fukizo, while Bapoto was leader of the Fukizo who remained. This seemed to be a good solution, and at first, both villages seemed happy with it.

"I spent the summer hunting and trading, and wintered at a men's shelter not far away. I occasionally visited my mother, and talked with people from both villages. Those who stayed at Fukizo continued to revere Bapoto as an intermediary to the Great One. Those who had moved to the New Fukizo continued to believe in the Great One, and continued using Bapoto's rituals, but they rejected the idea that the Great One was sending messages by way of Bapoto. Time passed, and conflicts between the Fukizo and the New Fukizo began to ferment. There were squabbles over who would harvest what, arguments between groups of hunters, and both ukoos were absolutely sure the Great One was on their side.

"Eight springs ago, my mother died, and my sister Nerina became the Mother of the New Fukizo. She led well, and the New Fukizo prospered, but conflicts with the old ukoo increased. Three summers ago, after the women had returned from the harvests, Bapoto and a group of women from the old ukoo came to New Fukizo and told them the Great One had declared the two Fukizos must be reunited. My sister thought he was condescending and reproachful, and the women of New Fukizo evicted him from the village with willow switches.

"As the men of both villages returned from their summer journeys, they learned of the altercation. Both sides felt the integrity of their own women had been insulted, and since the Bonding was in the offing, both sides felt it was an excellent time to display their bravery defending the honor of the women with whom they wanted to mate. Parties of men set out from both villages, heavily armed. They met in a narrow pass between two steep hills. I witnessed the fight from the top of one of the hills."

Eyes closed, face twisted, Dika's hands shook as he signed. "The roaring and bellowing and screaming were earsplitting. It was nothing like any hunt I have ever known, nothing like an attack by animals. Both sides were fighting for their beliefs and for the honor and reputation of their women, and neither side was willing to back down.

"Most of the men from old Fukizo died, either that day or later. About half of the men from New Fukizo died. Bapoto's body was never found, but we assumed it had been dragged away by a leopard or hyena before it was identified. We didn't know he had survived until you told us your story. That winter, both villages suffered from hunger and cold; many more died. The following spring, the women of the two villages met again, with a great many tears on both sides. Whether or not Bapoto could communicate with the Great One was no longer an issue. Grief and hardship had humbled everyone, and the women reconciled."

"You must have had family and friends who died in the battle. I'm sorry for your losses." Ash directed his remark to all four of the men, and he keened briefly. Dika nodded in thanks, and the others keened as well. Ash remembered the Fukizo attack on the Kura hunting party, and could easily imagine the battle and the injuries Dika described. The reason for the Fukizo attack on the Kura men was clear to him now: when the Fukizo recognized their enemy Bapoto, the Kura men happened to be in the way. When Ash realized the four men around the campfire didn't resent him personally for his contact with Bapoto, he decided it was safe to tell them about the attack on the Kura men.

"A group of Fukizo men met Bapoto hunting with the Kura this spring."

Agama growled, and Ash noticed his hands were balled into fists next to him.

"What happened?" asked Dika.

Ash recounted Thunder's story of the Fukizo encounter with the Kura hunting party. Agama watched with his jaw clenched, Granite's eyes were narrowed, Falcon seemed about to cry, and Dika chewed his lower lip. When Ash finished describing the Kura's injuries, he asked, "I wonder how the Fukizo came to be so far from home?"

"Many of the Fukizo men are far-walkers, and hunting was poor last winter," signed Dika. "Some of them may have gone much farther west than usual after game. The Fukizo are not, as a rule, belligerent, especially away from their usual lands, but finding Bapoto leading a new group of men, well. . . ."

Ash nodded wryly. "Of course."

CHAPTER 14

P *anda Ya* Mto was farther away than it used to be, Snap thought. Although women didn't visit other ukoos except under extraordinary circumstances, she was quite sure she knew the way; the village was easily visible from a grove of morojwa trees where she had picked fruit. Adrenaline had carried her for most of the afternoon, but now the sun was setting, her feet were as heavy as an elephant's, and she was sure it would be dark before she could reach the village. Her stomach growled, but she was afraid to deplete her small supply of dika nuts and only ate one. On a rise above the stream she had been following, she spotted a low-growing copse that might provide some shelter, so she filled her water bag and struggled up the slope. As she searched for a place to hide, the sun dropped below the horizon and she shivered. The thicket she finally chose was prickly and made it impossible for her to watch properly, but she judged its brambles to be her best refuge.

Curled on her side, she felt exhaustion burn in every muscle and hunger pinch her stomach. A small arm or leg thumped a tender spot in her back, and she squirmed into another briary position. The last remnant of her courage disappeared with the light. Surely that sound was a footstep—something large. A twig snapped—undoubtedly a lion. That hiss—was it Burrow? Her heart beat faster and faster, her muscles tensed, and her own pulse pounded in her ears. An unmeasurable amount of time later, she heard a distant howl, and sometime later, the shriek of a rabbit. More darkness, a sharp rock in her side, a gust of wind that disguised all other sounds. More interminable darkness.

Snap's eyes flew open. Dull light trickled through the brambles. Silence. Her entire right side was asleep, and she moved her leg clumsily to shake life into it. The movement rattled the entire thicket, and she froze, listening for a response to the announcement of her presence, but she heard nothing. As the feeling screamed back into her limbs, she crawled out of the thicket, nostrils filled with the smells of dried leaves, broken twigs, grass gone to seed. She stood and breathed deeply—no hint of woodsmoke, no people, no midden, not a whiff of stored food— she had left all the smells of her ukoo behind. A flat gray sky gave no hint of the sun's location, and she surveyed the landscape uncertainly until she was sure she recognized the withering stream she had followed the day before.

Too stiff for another attempt at rest, Snap nibbled a nut, filled her water bag, and plodded on. The sun did not appear. Her feet were even heavier than the previous day, and she wondered if the landmarks she thought she recalled were taking her not to Panda Ya Mto but to some other, vaguely remembered spot. It might have been midday when she spotted shelters in the distance. Was that it? It didn't seem to match her memory of the village with the morojwa trees overlooking it, but there was nothing to be done now; she must ask for help. When she announced herself with a Kura hoot, several people appeared and stared curiously at the singular sight of an approaching woman. She saw their hair was styled in the Panda Ya Mto fashion and sighed with relief. The nearest uwanda held three women, two men, and several children. Snap addressed the woman who looked oldest with informal, one-handed signs.

"Greetings. I am Snap of the Kura. I am looking for my brother Thump; is he wintering with the Panda Ya Mto?"

The two younger women crossed their arms, rolled their eyes at each other, and looked toward the older one. The men hid their expressions with their hands. The oldest woman narrowed her eyes and signed with rigid fingers.

"The Mother of Panda Ya Mto is Spring. Her shelter is that one." She turned and pointed at a large, sturdy-looking shelter nearby.

I'm an idiot, she thought. Failing to greet the Mother—I should be switched. Mortified by her own bad manners, Snap thanked the woman profusely and made her way to the uwanda outside the indicated shelter, where a tall woman stood, arms folded, eyes wide. Using the formal gestures of greeting used by men returning in the fall, Snap introduced herself.

"Welcome, Snap." The tall woman used an odd combination of the informal signs used between women and the formal signs she would have used to greet a returning man. "I am Spring, Mother of Panda Ya Mto. How do you come here?"

"I am looking for my brother Thump. He has bonded with Dew in the past; is he here now?"

"Thump is with Dew again. My son Lightning will take you to the shelter of Rain, Dew's mother." She waved at a boy who looked to have about seven springs, and he scurried off with a backward glance to make sure Snap followed him.

Snap made a purr of respect and bowed her head slightly, and then followed the boy between two shelters and around a rock outcrop. He made no gestures or sounds as he led her to a small shelter on the far side of the village and abandoned her in the uwanda. Snap hooted softly, and a tiny, fine-featured woman just a few springs older than Snap came out of the shelter. She was holding a toddler's hand and was followed by Thump, who looked even burlier than he had the last time Snap had seen him.

Snap grinned broadly at Thump, but addressed the woman first. "I am Snap, of the Kura. I am Thump's sister."

The tiny woman examined Snap with wide eyes, and then checked Thump's face before she answered. "I am Dew, of the Panda Ya Mto. Welcome to my mother's shelter. She is away at the moment." The toddler was straining to wiggle out of Dew's grasp, and she picked him up against his will. Thump winked at Snap, but seemed uncertain about whether he ought to greet her.

"He is a handsome boy." Snap waved at the child in Dew's arms. "Is he yours?"

She wrapped her arms around him, crooning, and considered Snap over his head. "Yes."

Snap gave Thump a desperate look. His mate showed no sign of inviting her into the shelter, but he finally bobbed an apologetic nod at Dew and addressed his sister anyway. "What's brought you to Panda Ya Mto, Snap?"

"I've left Kura. You wouldn't recognize it. Did you know Whistle's Baby and Chirp were taken by lions last winter, and Whistle has become the Mother?" He shot another glance at Dew and nodded, and Snap went on. "You remember Bapoto, don't you? Whistle chose him at last fall's Bonding, and he has used her rank to convert nearly all the Kura to his ideas. There are rituals for everything, and bonding is supposed to be permanent now. Bapoto claims he gets messages directly from the Great One, and tries to use that authority to control practically everything in Kura."

Thump's eyebrows drew together, and he clicked with concern as Snap went on. "I gather things are changing here as well." She raised her eyebrows inquiringly, and Thump shrugged.

"Some of the men are interested in the hunting ritual. We tried to do it a few times, and once we tried to do Bapoto's healing ritual, but it doesn't seem to work for us. Nothing like Kura, I think. But you didn't answer my question. What's happened?"

"The mate I preferred didn't return in time for the Bonding this fall, and I refused to choose anyone else, so the Great One sent a message to Bapoto that I must accept Burrow. Bapoto actually forced me to mate with that warthog!"

Dew made a noise of disgust.

"Exactly," signed Snap. "I ran away with only this water bag and these dikas."

Thump didn't seem to want to meet Snap's eyes, and Dew

looked at Snap's large belly sympathetically. At last she seemed to realize this lone woman was not after her mate and needed urgent help.

"Please stay with us." Dew's hands moved with every sign of real enthusiasm. "We have plenty of food, loads of extra sleeping hides. Don't even consider going on tonight." She bustled Snap into the shelter, built up the fire, and began to pull food from the storage alcove, which was brimming with smoked fish, dried meat, and every kind of fruit and vegetable. Snap felt as if she had been pulled from the jaws of a hyena just before her neck was snapped, and she gurgled relief.

"Thank you." Snap squatted at the fire. The warmth washed over her, and she shivered, although she hadn't been very cold. Thump offered his sister a dipper of water and settled himself next to her.

Just then, Dew's mother, Rain, appeared. Introductions were repeated, Dew retold Snap's story, and Rain repeated Dew's invitation to stay in her shelter. Rain was even smaller than Dew, and might have once been equally beautiful, although she was now wrinkled and missing a number of teeth. Snap helped Dew and Rain wrap dried meat and fruit tightly in a fresh hide with some herbs and several sorts of root vegetables, and bury the whole thing in glowing embers. Snap paid close attention to the procedure in hopes she might have a chance to duplicate it one day. Dew's sister Mist, her two children, and her mate, Rabbit, were invited to share the feast, and they joined the group at Rain's fire just as the shelter was beginning to smell heavenly.

The conversation was congenial, and Snap was asked for news from Kura. She related the events that had led to her leaving Kura and told them about Bubble's twins.

"Do you know about Jackal?" Snap asked hesitantly. Dew shuddered and Thump nodded grimly. "The first Fukizo attack was just, well, men fighting over zebras." Snap glanced at her brother. "But the destruction in Kura, and what happened to Jackal—no animal would do something so horrible."

Rabbit shook his head. "I think I might have been one of the last to see Jackal. Last spring, I left Panda Ya Mto and headed northwest, in the direction of Kura, but I fell and injured my ankle. I was resting in a thicket when two men passed. My injury put me at a disadvantage, so I didn't attract their attention, but I could see their words. They had left Kura several days previously, but had had no luck hunting. One of the men was trying to convince the other to return to Kura, because the first man had forgotten a spear he needed. Eventually the second man agreed, and they turned back in the direction of Kura."

"Did you know the two men?" Snap asked.

"The second man was Jackal," signed Rabbit. "I didn't know the first, and I couldn't recognize his ukoo."

Eventually, the embers died down and the packet was opened. In high spirits, Thump proclaimed that Dew had made his favorite food in the world and promised to bring her a wildebeest the following day. She snorted and nuzzled him behind the ear. The group ate, licked clean their dishes and fingers, and Dew's relatives departed. Dew located an extra sleeping hide and unrolled it near the fire for the guest. Snap knelt at Dew's knees, overwhelmed with gratitude, and took her hand.

"I can't thank all of you as I should," Snap signed.

With a dismissive sound, Dew waved away Snap's thanks, but she was clearly beginning to think more highly of Snap's manners.

The next morning, Rain's family and Snap had already rolled up their sleeping hides and breakfasted on the remains of the previous night's feast when Spring arrived in Rain's uwanda, accompanied by Lightning, who was pulling a small dragger, and two other women. By the women's superior bearing, Snap guessed they were close relatives of the Mother of Panda Ya Mto. Eyes downcast and knees bent, Rain greeted the arrivals and invited them to share her fire.

"Thank you, Rain, but we have come to sort out the Kura woman." Snap, squatting near the door of Rain's shelter, saw no hint of displeasure in Spring's smooth, cool gestures, but none of congeniality either. She stood up and approached Spring with a purr of respect, eyes down and hands open meekly.

"You have quarreled with the Mother of Kura." Spring addressed the statement to Snap.

"Yes." Rabbit and Mist must have passed on her story, she thought. Snap's heart raced, but her show of humility was just as it should be; she had always received respect from every woman in Kura except her mother and grandmother, and she reproduced exactly the proper expression and posture.

"You are not of Panda Ya Mto. Thump is bonded here, and is part of us until the Naming. His guest is welcome as long as Rain wishes to share her shelter, but you are not of Panda Ya Mto, and never will be. You must find your own way." A hint of solicitude crept into Spring's expression as she continued. "You may need some things. Please accept this dragger with our hope for your good fortune." Spring gestured at Lightning. He pulled the dragger to Snap and lowered it carefully.

A hurricane of emotions swirled through Snap, though she kept her face impassive. Charity! Distributing charity she understood—she had learned from the Mothers before her the tricky job of judging who needed a handout to get through the winter, who was hiding the extent of their stores, who was the softest touch when it came to helping the hungrier members of the ukoo. But receiving charity was as humiliating as having the brute Burrow forced on her. The baby kicked hard into Snap's ribs and forced Snap to think of the approaching arrival.

"Thank you. You are a wise Mother and gracious host." Snap forced herself into a deep bow, blinking furiously. Spring and her retinue politely took leave of Rain and departed.

By the time Snap could bring herself to look around, Rain and Dew had busied themselves with repairing baskets and Thump was engrossed in sharpening a spear. Snap attracted their attention.

"It is still early in the day, and the weather is good. Thank you for your hospitality." She bowed to Rain and Dew, and threw her arms around Thump. He cleared his throat uncomfortably and patted her on the back. Snap pulled away from her brother, trying to swallow a lump in her throat, and found Dew surreptitiously tucking an antelope hide and some dried meat into the dragger while Rain prepared a stone fire-carrier. Snap signed polite farewells, picked up the dragger and the fire-carrier, and left Panda Ya Mto, as directionless as a twig in the Great Water.

CHAPTER 15

Without a specific purpose, Snap's feet took her generally west. She ate a handful of dika nuts and refilled her water bag each time she passed near a stream, but didn't unpack the charity dragger. Her thoughts stretched no farther than the next few steps, the next water, the next hilltop. I am nothing, she thought. A woman without an ukoo, what is that? No more than mist that burns away in the sun.

Just past midday, she passed within a spear throw downwind of a small herd of antelope. Clenching her fist around the spear she wished she had, she stared after them when they finally scented her and stampeded away. After that, she carried a fist-size rock ready for an unlucky lizard or bird, but none presented itself. Two days of travel with a little worried sleep between them took their toll, and she labored on at a glacial pace, emptied of emotion and nearly drained of strength, oblivious to her haphazard route. Near dusk, she stopped for a momentary rest and recognized the ridge where the leopard had attacked her the previous fall, far from both Panda Ya Mto and Kura.

A shallow cleft in the base of the towering limestone ridge suggested a refuge, and she approached it cautiously. There was no sign of a recent occupant, and she pulled the dragger into the cleft while she searched for downed wood and tinder. There would be no second chance at starting a fire if the first failed. In front of the recess, Snap built a minute tent of pine needles and dry leaves and scooped Rain's coals into the center. Only the tiniest glow shone when she blew over them, but eventually the tinder exploded in orange flames that pushed back the unsettling darkness. She finally opened the dragger and took out a few bites of dried fruit and smoked fish, as well as Dew's antelope hide. Curled up in the hide at the back of the cleft, she could see only the fire—it illuminated nothing of what lay beyond. The walls of the limestone cleft, the dragger, the fire—they might have been all that remained on earth.

As tired as she was, Snap still couldn't sleep. Over and over, she dozed off, but worry about the fire, or the distant bark of a hyena, or a sudden gust of wind awakened her. When the day dawned pink and gold, it found Snap huddled in her hide, glassy-eyed and unmoving until the sun was high enough to shine into the recess and prod her into life. She rubbed the crusts from her eyes and crawled to the fire. The downed wood had lasted through the night, but just barely. She must prepare the fire-carrier if she was to go on, or collect more wood to keep this fire burning.

But she sat on. The fire burned lower, the sun inched upward, and Snap stared at the dying flames. Finally, a tiny brown-and-white hyrax peered around a rock near the dragger. It didn't seem to see the unmoving Snap, and it began to worry at the dragger fastening with its teeth and front feet with stubby toes like hooves. After a time, two even tinier hyraxes appeared, nosed at the dragger, and joined the first in a concerted attempt to bite through the ties. Snap's attention was at last pulled from the fire, and as she watched, her spirits began to rise as if the animals' earnest efforts were for her benefit. Finally, she found she had energy enough to shoo the hyraxes away and get to her feet.

All the nearby, dry, downed wood was gone, so Snap clambered over a large area of the ridge in order to collect enough fuel to prod the fire into life before it burned down entirely. In so doing, she found that the ridge containing her little refuge was similar to Kura's, although not as high. It stretched away into the mist-obscured west and then gradually dwindled into a jumble of karst.

Once the fire was tended, she ate a few bites and drank the last of her water. No streams had crossed her path during the search for firewood, so Snap left the covered dragger in the alcove, climbed laboriously to the top of the ridge, and followed it west in search of water. Sections of the gray-white, crumbling rock were broken into jagged spires, which slowed her considerably. The sun was high when she finally saw it: a tiny stream that sprang from the rock and gurgled downhill a short distance into a small, clear pool with no aboveground outlet. Not far above the spring was a relatively level step about halfway up the southern side of the ridge.

Desperately thirsty but exhausted by climbing along the rugged ridge, she sank to her knees on the ridgetop and stared down at the water sparkling in the sun. Finally, she pulled herself to her feet and scrambled down to the water. Her knees and palms were scraped and bleeding by the time she reached the small pool, and she plunged her body into the ice-cold, knee-deep water, slurped up her fill, and then lay back in the water, staring blankly at the colorless sky. When the aches in her limbs lessened and the baby began kicking furiously, she filled the water bag, struggled down to the bottom of the ridge, and returned to her dragger and her fire. Now the sun was well past the zenith, and Snap's spirits had returned to the morning's nadir. She revived the fading fire, chewed on a piece of antelope jerky, and wedged herself into the cleft with the dragger for another night alone.

A desolate half-moon crept by. Misery filled Snap's thoughts, precluded rational planning, distracted her attention even from her own actions. Automatically, gradually, a camp grew on the level area just above the spring. A sharp chunk of granite served as a hammer—a storage niche appeared in the limestone wall. The same sharp granite cut a strong, straight sapling and sharpened it into a usable spear. The dragger yielded its zebra hide and two bent poles—a makeshift shelter covered the niche. A fire ring protected the precious embers. By firelight, mavue fibers twisted into a snare—a gray-brown hyrax became the first food cooked in the fire ring. Oblivious to everything but her own isolation, Snap barely noticed how the ridge was becoming hers.

The only thing that prodded her into awareness was the baby. Every protruding foot, every thump that took away her breath, every thud that made her rush to the latrine pit brought her into the present with a surge of panic. The baby. Most babies, she knew, came into the world without help. Whistle had shown her ways to make things easier, tricks to slow down bleeding, what to do with the mess, but Snap couldn't help thinking of the new mothers who were helpless for a moon or more, and of Whistle's cousin who had bled to death three springs ago. Unconsciously, Snap twisted her arm hair into tiny tufts whenever she thought about the baby. By the time Snap had spent a half-moon alone, her arms looked like underfed porcupines.

From her makeshift uwanda, Snap had a wide view of the valley to the south of her ridge and paid close attention to its inhabitants, but none were immediately threatening or likely prey. Flocks of ducks squawked across the ridge, solitary eagles regularly patrolled the skies above the valley, and small herds of antelope, wildebeest, and impala grazed along the valley, but Snap found no occasion to use her new spear either for defense or in pursuit of dinner, until one evening when a group of gazelles passed very close to the base of the ridge just below her shelter.

Snap had just banked her fire for the night and was returning from her latrine pit when she saw them grazing obliviously upwind around a solitary blackwood tree only a few spear throws away. She scooped up the spear she kept standing at her shelter door and made her way as quietly as possible down the path to the base of the ridge. The tall grass hid her as she crept toward the gazelles on her hands and knees, belly nearly touching the ground. When she judged that she was close enough for a good spear throw at the nearest gazelle, she stood up, took aim, and threw with all her might.

The spear hit a small female just behind the front legs. The injured gazelle leapt into the air and sprinted north, along with the rest of the herd. Snap ran after them as fast as she could manage. Before she had run ten steps, she stopped short, face-to-face with a grazing white rhinoceros calf that had been hidden in a stand of tall grass. The calf squealed, and Snap heard an answering bellow behind her, followed by the unmistakable sounds of an adult rhinoceros picking up speed. Without a glance behind her, Snap considered running for her shelter—the distance wasn't great and she could probably climb faster than the mother rhinoceros, but if her pursuer made it up the ridge to the shelter, there was nowhere to hide. The blackwood tree was nearly in arm's reach and had low-growing branches she could reach.

In a flash, Snap was pulling her ungainly body up the tree. She clung to the curved branches with her toes, pulled herself up with her arms, twisted madly to balance her ridiculous belly as it tried to push her away from the trunk. As the great herbivore reached the tree, Snap barely yanked her foot up and out of the way as the horns slammed into the blackwood trunk and sent it rocking madly. The calf wandered over and began to nurse. Its mother stood motionless, nostrils flared and pointed at Snap.

An hour later, it was dark. The moon wouldn't rise for some time, but Snap could see enough to know that the enormous black mass at the base of her tree hadn't moved. She tolerated discomfort as well as most people—lots of things hurt, and there's nothing to do about most of them—but this discomfort was extraordinary. She shifted from one lumpy branch to another every few minutes, stood up, tried to sit, even took her weight on her arms for brief periods. The mother rhinoceros waited. Being pregnant, Snap was forced to relieve herself several times during the night, and did her best to hit her tormentor, but to no effect.

After a night that lasted as long as three or four ordinary nights, the sky began to lighten in the east. The calf grunted and wandered off to the south, and its mother followed. Snap waited until they were both out of sight before she lowered herself stiffly to the ground and struggled clumsily up to her shelter. Though she was exhausted, hunger kept returning the wounded gazelle to her thoughts. After a brief rest, and some food and water, she climbed back down to the valley and set off to the west in the direction the gazelles had fled. Drops of blood and recent spoor were not hard to track, and she found the carcass in practically no time, not yet discovered by vultures and with her spear still hanging on.

Hints of fall started to arrive. Thunderheads gathered in the afternoons, and occasionally she heard distant rumbles, but no rain fell. One cool, damp morning she woke to thick, gray overcast. Snap scowled at her pitiful shelter, which seemed to emanate an aura of imminent disaster. With a resigned shrug, she retied the hide roof as securely as she could, jammed her storage alcove with wood, and checked her snares. By late afternoon, no rain had appeared, but a small, bright fire crackled in the improvised shelter where she squatted.

At the sound of an indistinct hoot, barely audible over the sound of the fire, she stumbled out of the shelter and climbed onto a rock outcrop to look for the source. A figure pulling a dragger was approaching from the east along the base of the

ridge. The light was already too dim for her to recognize the figure. Snap's heart hammered. The fire had obviously announced
her presence. Was someone coming to steal her miserable little
cache of food? To attack her? To drag her back to Burrow?

Snap gathered an armful of dried gazelle meat into her sleeping hide and scrambled uphill as fast as she could. Once on the
other side of the ridge, out of view of her camp, she slowed down
and began to search for a hiding place. Several spear throws west,
on the lower part of the ridge, a jumble of rocks overgrown by
brambles hid a crevice into which she squirmed, pushing her
bundle before her. The crevice was dark, but not damp, and she
felt nothing that suggested she had disturbed a previous occupant. Snap lay on her side, waiting. Sometime later, she thought
she heard another faint hoot, and then another. Time crawled
on, her legs cramped, and her stomach rumbled. Finally, after an
interminable silence, a real owl hooted, and she decided that she
must move before she was too stiff to ever move again.

She backed out of her hole and found the last remnant of
dusk fading. The moon rising through broken clouds lit her way
back to camp. The fire had burned low, but wasn't out. Snap made
it blaze up, and in the light, she saw that a dragger had been left
in the tiny uwanda. The corners of her eyes stinging, she pulled it
close to the shelter and opened it. A small hog, already drawn and
quite fresh, lay on top of a disassembled summer shelter. When
she moved the hog to a large flat rock for butchering, she recognized the summer shelter: it was Hum's.

Tears splashed onto the meat as she worked by firelight. Hum
had no meat to spare, and certainly no extra household goods.
Why had she done this? What was happening in Kura? The
work took all night, but the life that had abandoned her when

she left her mother's shelter surged through her again. Grilled liver and kidneys at midnight and the prospect of dried meat to come made the long night pass in a blur of purpose. When the sun rose through a low-lying mist, it warmed the hog's hide already stretched on an improvised rack, began to dry the slices of meat already hanging from a makeshift frame, and revealed an exhausted Snap snoring on the summer shelter's folded mat.

The brown-and-white hyrax with her two young appeared often in Snap's uwanda. The comings and goings of the local group fascinated her; their dens were complex arrangements with entrances everywhere to allow a quick escape when the hyrax on guard screamed an eagle alarm. Snap's snares confounded them, however, and captured one almost every day. The brown-and-white hyrax that frequented the uwanda knew something the others didn't; Snap watched her teach her offspring to circumnavigate the carefully arranged loops.

The summer shelter, so humble last summer, seemed extravagant now, with its three hides over newly mended mats. Two fire rings, one inside and one out, lit the night. She had neither the time nor energy to look for Ash. Each task completed, each bit of housekeeping, reified the baby's arrival and pushed Ash further into the best-forgotten past. In her dreams, she walked with the women of Kura in the summer, ate at a feast, danced at the Bonding, and met Ash walking along the ridge, but she permitted no thoughts of the past in her waking mind. A moon passed, and Snap began to call her ridge Asili.

Days dragged on, the first rain came and went. No overlooked kinanas remained in the dry washes, not a single nut hung on the trees, even the grubs she dug from the banks of the pond were scarce. She tried a bit of the moss that grew over the stream, but it was so bitter she spat it out. Climbing over the ridge to check her snares left her panting and made her huge belly harden and ache off and on. The morning of the new moon dawned gray, dark clouds punctuating a flat colorless sky. The air was brisk, with a breeze that stirred up the fine dust into a palpable fog. After her morning chores, Snap sat down to finish a baby bunting. The tiny hyrax skins were so small and thin as to be hardly worth tanning, but she had nothing else, and they were, at least, very soft. As she sat in front of her shelter door, a large raindrop plopped onto her work. She scooped up the bunting and carried it into the shelter.

She stirred up the fire, carried in a supply of wood from her woodpile, and set to work again by the firelight. The rain gradually intensified, the wind increased, and Snap heard distant rumbles of thunder. She noticed the contractions she had had occasionally for the last moon were more frequent, and some made her stand up and walk around her fire ring. The shelter began to feel uncomfortably warm, and the drafts of cold air that came in around the door flap felt refreshing, rather than chilly.

Soon the wind had begun to howl around the rocks above her shelter, and the rain pounded on the shelter roof like the drums at the Bonding. After days of silence, the rooftop cacophony confounded her senses, a fitting accompaniment to her increasingly hectic contractions. Drops of water began to run down the inside of the hide covering and drip into a small trench she had dug around the perimeter of the floor. Between contractions, Snap slipped her bowl under the edge of the roof hide to catch some of the rainwater.

The day was so gloomy, it was not obvious when the sun set,

but it was quite dark and very cold by the time the rain slowed to a drizzle and she went outside to urinate. The contractions were stronger and closer together now. She rocked back on her heels, panted at the uniformly black sky, and hoped this baby would know how to get into the world by itself.

She had two more contractions while she filled her water bag and got back to the shelter. She couldn't concentrate properly on anything other than the contractions and on resting in between, but eventually she located a digging stick and started making a new trench in the shelter floor like the one Bubble had used when she delivered her babies. By the time she had lined the trench with her oldest, most ragged hide and filled it with dried moss, the rain had picked up again and was pounding a tattoo on the shelter roof.

Thought became impossible. Wave after wave crushed her awareness, and the universe shrank to the size of her womb, her legs, and her voice. The baby kicked, the only communication Snap could perceive in the instant of intensity. And then the tide ebbed, like a great snail pulling its head into its shell, and the world was revealed again. The shelter came back into focus, the rain outside as oblivious to the storm inside as if it were a distant part of the sea.

Time passed, but Snap was not aware of it; every moment commanded all her attention. Again and again, breakers washed over her. Pressure waxed and waned, every effort exhausted her, and she was overwhelmed, alone. A watermelon was swelling inside her, and she must evict it. Sounds like an elephant in musth issued from her and transcended even the noise of the storm. Yet another surge began, and she felt the baby's head, encircled by fire. Her roars became squeals, energy flooded through her, and an uncontrollable compulsion overtook her. The world split in two.

Silence. Snap stared down at the wet, dark hair covering the back of the baby's head, reached down, and lifted the baby as the rest of her appeared, slippery and blue. Eyes blank and open wide, like a fish, limp as a spiderweb, the baby lay in Snap's arms, cradled against her shrunken belly. Dead, thought Snap. Too drained to wail, she croaked a hoarse sob and started to clean her daughter with her tongue. The tiny knees drew up, the little arms waved, the face screwed itself up and filled the shelter with angry screams.

Snap clutched the ear-piercing infant and wept as she finished cleaning her up. In a bit, the baby stopped screaming and began to root around hungrily. After years of watching other women nurse their infants, Snap soon had her latched on to a breast and smacking noisily. The afterbirth delivered, and Snap gave no thought to cooking it or even waiting for Baby to finish nursing; she devoured it one-handed, leaving the tough umbilical cord dangling from Baby's belly.

Baby fell asleep. Still wide-awake and exhilarated, Snap detached her daughter, wrapped her in a leather diaper stuffed with dry moss, and settled her into the sleeping hide. A similar, but larger, diaper served for Snap. She gulped rainwater from her bowl, and then pushed the soaked moss from the trench down the hill as far as she could to distract predators from the shelter. The ragged hide that had lined the trench was bloody as well, so Snap spread it out on a flat rock where the rain would rinse it. Then fatigue and dizziness forced her back into the shelter.

Curled up around Baby, Snap examined the tiny face a hand's breadth from her own, and saw the future marching across the perfect eyelids. This baby will be strong and wise, she thought, brave and beautiful. A traditional ukoo, free of misguided theories, will grow here at Asili. At the feasts, my daughters will tell the story of how the first Mother came to this place. A frown creased her forehead. Unless we starve, or are killed by the Fukizo, or maybe by the Kura. Snap slipped into a dream in which Whistle's shelter collapsed into rubble while Bapoto stood on the uwanda stump, arms upraised, warbling his strange whistle.

When she woke, it was light. The rain was still thrumming on the shelter roof, and Snap's bowl had refilled with rainwater. She crawled from her sleeping hide leaving Baby asleep and pulled herself to her feet, sore and light-headed. The fire crackled and hissed as she added a new log, momentarily louder than the noise of the storm. In the midst of the fire's pops, she turned her head to listen. Was that another sound, muffled by the rain and wind and fire? She checked the baby, still sleeping soundly, and lifted the door flap. A definite hoot—an unfamiliar one—drifted through the rain. Four bent figures with foreign hairstyles and large bundles on their backs were climbing the path, less than a spear throw away. Snap bit her thumb and tried to pull her scattered thoughts together. No place to hide—the shelter and its fire were obvious. No way to run—just standing up made black spots appear at the edges of her vision. She pushed Baby wrapped in the sleeping hide into the darkest corner of her storage alcove, dumped a few slices of dried morojwa fruit into the bowl of rainwater, and stood outside the open door flap, as tall as she could make herself, arms folded. Her short, roughly made spear leaned casually against the shelter wall next to the door.

❖ 213 ❖

The men stopped on the path, still some feet below her shelter, and the first one looked up and bared a number of well-preserved teeth. She did the same, unsure if she was returning a threat or a greeting. The man was tall and burly, with a prominent brow ridge and hair twisted into perfect concentric rings around his head. He spread his arms to show that his hands were empty, but Snap was not distracted by that; she scrutinized all of their fists for signs of flint axes and all the bundles for protruding spears. The first man used slow, formal signs.

"Greetings! I am Dika, of the Fukizo. This is Agama, Granite, and Falcon." He waved at the other men in turn. "May we approach?"

Her muscles tightened imperceptibly and she instinctively checked her footing, but her expression was unchanged. She raised both arms to answer, mind racing. Did these men attack Kura? "Greetings, Dika. I am Snap, of . . . of . . . Asili. Please share my fire."

The uwanda seemed much smaller when the four soaked men reached it. She returned their greetings and gestured them into the shelter after her. Planted in front of the storage alcove, Snap waved them to the fire, which hissed as they stretched their hands over it. As they knelt and untied their bundles, she looked them over. The tall, skinny one, Granite, kept showing his teeth, which unnerved her. Agama, the small, tough-looking one, scowled at the fire and seemed to be watching Dika. Falcon had fine, perfect features and long tapering hands.

"Your shelter is well made," signed Falcon. "The way you've joined the roof hides will keep out rain nicely, and the drainage trenches are cleverly done."

She signed thanks without a hint of suspicion.

Falcon turned his attention from the shelter to its owner. "Are you alone? Do you need help?"

"No, my sisters are checking the snares, and my mate is hunting. They're not far away." She signed briskly, trying to radiate conviction, and offered the bowl of water and fruit to Dika. He thanked her, took a ceremonial sip, and passed it on to Agama.

As the others tasted the fruit and water, Dika went on. "We are looking for an ukoo called Kura. Do you know it?"

Snap's heart pounded in her throat. She shook her head.

"And a far-walker called Ash."

She shook her head again. "Sorry."

The crowded shelter warmed up fast, and the visitors were soon dry. They passed the bowl around until it was empty, and then began to tie their bundles to their shoulders again. Snap stood in front of the alcove, arms folded, and listened for any sound from behind her, but the rain and wind were too loud.

"Thank you for your fire and your food," signed Dika. "Do you know of a men's shelter nearby?"

With the help of lines she scratched in the floor with a stick, she explained how to get to the men's shelter near the junction of the Kura stream and the Kijito. Agama, who was apparently the best navigator among them, nodded his understanding and they set off.

After the visitors had gone, Snap unrolled the sleeping hide and found her new daughter shivering. She built up the fire, replaced the moss in both diapers, and wrapped up with Baby next to the flames. They slept.

Days and nights went by in a blur of aches, Baby's cries, exhaustion. The time of day lost meaning; Snap woke, slept, ate, nursed Baby, collected moss, whatever had to be done, whenever it needed to be done. Checking the snares was impossible—the ridgetop was too far, and if she felt stronger, then it was raining. Even the latrine pit seemed much too distant. Her little supply of dried meat and fruit dwindled, and the pile of firewood shrank alarmingly fast. Some of her hair fell out, and the rest, untended, began to escape its Kura twists.

The simplest tasks overwhelmed her. She was hungry, but finding something to eat was beyond her. Digging for grubs frustrated her, going to the spring exhausted her, even chewing the dried meat she had left required more effort than she could muster. She slept more and more. Baby slept too, her cries became weaker, and she rarely needed moss in her diaper. When it rained, Snap drank what water she could collect, but after several dry days in a row, she woke one morning with no water in the shelter. A trip to the spring was inevitable.

Where were the empty water bags? Where was Baby's sling? Even in the tiny shelter with its nearly empty alcove, nothing was where she expected it to be, nothing looked familiar. Tying the sling around her shoulders took forever—she had forgotten how to make the knot, the ends kept unwinding themselves. Baby opened her eyes blankly as Snap wriggled the limp infant into the sling.

Getting down the path to the spring took all the concentration she could summon. Filling the water bags was impossible—Baby was in the way, the bags too heavy, the bank too slippery. She finally got one filled, but it slipped from her hands and sank in the shallow pool. A rest, she thought, I just need a little rest. Mud oozed around her as she lay down on the bank of the pond. In front of her, a beetle struggled across the mud to a blade of grass, began to climb it. She caught the beetle and ate it.

Finally, she pulled herself up, waded into the frigid water, and dredged up the water bag. With both bags filled, she started back to her shelter. Baby was as heavy as an elephant, the bags as unwieldy as zebra carcasses. On her knees now, she pulled the bags up the path at caterpillar speed. Her back cramped, a rock tore into one knee, at last she reached the top of the path. The uwanda, usually so tiny, stretched interminably before her—it was too much trouble to stand up, too painful to crawl.

At last, the shelter, the fire, the sleeping hides. Untie the sling. Curl around Baby. Who was that, squatting on the other side of the fire? Snap pulled herself up to her knees, her back cramped again, her torn knee throbbed, and she signed to the invisible someone.

"I'll put that water away in a bit, Bapoto, after I rest. Baby is fine there." Her hands lay on her thighs for a moment like curled-up dry leaves, and then formed words again. "Yes, the wood will be gone soon, but I'm so tired. I'll have a rest, then I'll go out for wood." Her hand fluttered to her side, and she peered into the shadows and nodded. "Tell me again about the healing ritual. What do I do to bring back the milk?"

At midday, Snap staggered out of the shelter and crawled onto the flat rock she used as a work surface. Unable to get to her feet, she knelt, raised her arms, and turned her closed eyes into the warmth. A weak, quavering whistle came from her mouth, and she sank into a heap. The sun passed behind a cloud. She slid off the rock and disappeared back into the shelter.

Snap woke lying on her side in the dark. Baby was at the breast, sucking feebly. A single spark in the blackness was the last stick of firewood, burned down to an ember. As she watched, it disappeared. She sighed, closed her eyes, went back to sleep.

CHAPTER 16

inding the shelter was the hard part. The ridge was exactly where Agama had told Ash it would be, but no sign of a fire hinted at occupation, no hoots answered his. He walked along the base of the ridge, east to west, until it disappeared into crumbling scrubland, and then climbed to the summit and followed it in the other direction. His right arm ached, and he held it very still, close to his body. The sun was well past the zenith when he finally chanced upon a snare set with a twitch-up, as Snap usually did. An unfortunate hyrax wriggled in its noose. He killed it and took it along. Agama had described the north side of the ridge clearly.

He studied every irregular shadow, every suggestive shape on the slope below him. Not far from the snare, he spotted a ragged hide roof and scrambled down, whooping and hooting.

The unkempt uwanda and shelter stopped him short. Snap, destined to be headwoman, had grown up in a rock shelter fit for a dozen people, used tools made by the best craftsmen, eaten from the most plentiful pantry in Kura, but this place was barely recognizable as a human habitation. A few ragged hides topped a disintegrating summer shelter, a fire ring had been disturbed by animals and contained no recent ashes, and a reek of human waste rose from a latrine pit dug much too close. Ash picked his way across the uwanda and stood silently at the closed door flap, willing his hand to open it.

He managed a soft Kura hoot and lifted the flap. The sun shone into the west-facing door. A tattered, bunched-up hide on an unraveling mat curved around the cold, empty fire ring. An empty water bag lay near the door, and a partly full one near the mat. A few scraps of dried meat had been dragged from the barren alcove and were strewn across the floor. Ash stood frozen at the door for several heartbeats until he could force himself to move. As deliberately as a stalking leopard, he approached the ragged heap, knelt, and reached out.

A high-pitched wheeze startled him, and then the thin, weak cry of a baby escaped from the rolled sleeping hide. Ash pulled open the roll. Snap's eyes flew open, her pale, cracked lips parted, and she grunted what might have been a threat. One hand flicked, but formed nothing comprehensible. Baby's wails became muffled as she tried to nurse. Ash gurgled relief and signed clumsily with his left hand, although he usually used his right.

"Mother's blood, what happened to you? What do you

need?" Snap's puffy eyes closed and a stertorous breath escaped her. He dropped his bundle and the dead hyrax and let a few drops from his water bag fall onto Snap's lips. She licked them off. With her head propped on his leg, he dribbled water into her slack mouth and watched her swallow, until she finally opened her eyes and looked at him with a hint of recognition.

"Ash." Her hand moved stiffly, as if she had forgotten how to make words with it. "Did the Great One send you?"

Ash gaped at her. Was she ill, delirious, deranged? Could she possibly have come to believe Bapoto's nonsense? Snap's eyes closed again, her mouth fell open, and her dry, swollen tongue protruded. Delirious, he thought. With his awkward left hand, he held the water bag to her mouth again, and she sucked desperately. When she seemed to have drunk enough, he lowered her head to the mat and started to untie his bundle. A new obsidian knife made short work of the hyrax, and he set to feeding Snap one half-chewed mouthful after another. Soon, only small bones and a brown pelt remained of the animal.

"Do you want to sit up?" he asked.

She nodded, and he helped steady her against the stone back wall. Her legs were matted with dried blood, and he carefully kept his eyes elsewhere as he helped her move. Baby was still nursing, and now Ash could hear her swallow. Snap scratched her arm absently, and he winced at the peculiarly twisted hair and bald patches that covered both her forearms.

She waved away his concerned look. "Thank you. I'm . . . fine. Sorry to . . . cause trouble." Her eyes searched for a distraction and found an enormous lump, bisected by a partly healed slash, on his right forearm. "What happened to your arm?"

"The bone was broken, but it was well tended. It's healing

straight, and doesn't hurt much anymore." He showed her the purple swelling fading to yellow and green, the wound already healing into a jagged scar.

"How did it happen?"

"You first. Tell me what happened to you."

"Yes. A little more water, first."

Ash took all the water bags to the spring and rinsed them well in the clear, cold water. Snap seemed to be slowly coming to herself, but he didn't understand what had happened—why was she here, why was she ill and so strangely confused? Was this whole situation caused by this baby? How could he bring back the Snap he knew?

Ash carried the water bags up to the shelter, and then opened his pack and offered her a choice of dried antelope or smoked catfish. Her face lit up at the smell of the fish, and for the first time since he had entered the shelter, he recognized something of the old Snap. She held Baby in one arm and talked with the other hand while Ash fed her deboned morsels of fish.

Her words were slow, formed with a hand that seemed stiff, or unfamiliar with its task. Beginning in the spring when Ash had left Kura, she described the summer and Jackal's demise, the fall and Bapoto's vision, the permanent bonding. When Ash learned how she was forced to accept Burrow, he began to grind his teeth. Eyes on her own feet, she admitted taking charity from the Panda Ya Mto and from Hum, barely mentioned the four Fukizo visitors, and only hinted at the birth. Finally, her hand fell like an injured bird and she stared blankly at the top of Baby's head. Baby had fallen asleep, and milk drooled over the crook of Snap's arm. She tucked Baby into the sleeping hide on the floor beside her and then went on.

"I was hungry, and tired, and so confused. I . . . saw things. The fire went out, and I didn't know what to do." She used the smallest signs he had ever seen. "I asked the Great One to send you, and then I fell asleep." She looked at Ash again.

He shook his head uncertainly. "You asked the Great One? How?"

"I . . . I stood on a rock, and made Bapoto's whistle. I wished for you." The idea of Snap making wishes like children splitting the collarbone of a bird made Ash feel like either laughing or crying, but he just patted her foot.

"Well, I'm here now." He knelt before her and began to make formal fall greeting signs. Snap laughed out loud.

"You find me lying in my own blood, without food or fire, and address me as if I were the Mother? I have nothing to offer you, and I must look like something even the hyenas wouldn't eat. All I can do is beg for your help." She struggled to her knees and touched her head to the floor in front of Ash.

This was too much. Memories of Snap had driven him here— her laugh, the bossy hoots she used to direct her schemes, her hysterical mating squeals—and now she had become someone else. He didn't know what to do with this new Snap. Was the old one still in there?

He took her by the elbow and helped her sit up. "You must be the Mother now." He waved at Baby, and her face twisted into a wry smile.

"It's your turn. Tell me what happened to you."

"Last spring, I set out to find out why the Fukizo attacked the Kura. The hunters had met them far to the east, and traders whom I asked thought Fukizo lay that way as well, so I headed east. Someone directed me over a mountain range, and finally,

I met four Fukizo men: Granite, Falcon, Dika, and Agama." Ash made the strange, toothy smile she had seen on Dika. "Dika was born in the Fukizo, and has lived with the bachelors since leaving his mother's ukoo. Those four have been friends for many springs, and I liked them. Anyway, they told me how Bapoto had nearly destroyed the Fukizo a few springs ago, and everyone had thought him dead. Dika's sister is the Mother now, and he and his friends care very much about that ukoo. Once we had figured out the Fukizo hunting party had attacked the Kura only because of Bapoto, we thought we might be able to help them agree to stop fighting."

She snorted. "Handing Bapoto over to the Fukizo would calm everybody down, I bet."

"Hmm. At any rate, we wanted to do what we could to settle things down. The others couldn't leave right away because they were harvesting nuts, so they planned to meet me at the first full moon of fall. I gave them directions to find the men's shelter near Kura, and I set off immediately.

"More than a moon ago, a long way from Kura, I met a hunter—a huge man. He carried an antelope over his shoulders as if it weighed no more than an extra hide. I recognized his hoot as Fukizo, so I used the Kilima hoot of my mother's tribe. His name was Flint, and we shared a meal and exchanged stories. I told him several tales, including one very much like the story of Bapoto and the Fukizo, but with altered names. When he realized that I knew the history of his ukoo, he told me an intriguing story. Last winter, hunting was very poor near Fukizo. A group of men who were bonded there left the village early in the spring in search of game and traveled far to the northeast, where they met Bapoto, hunting with a group of Kura men.

He had cut off his hair and they didn't recognize him at first, but when they did, they tried to kill him. In the melee, Gorge and Cascade were injured accidentally. The Fukizo carried the injured men to their camp and took care of them until they were able to hunt. During that time, the two Kura men and the Fukizo learned about Bapoto from one another. When they left the Fukizo camp, Gorge and Cascade didn't want to take sides and returned to Jiti for the Bonding this fall. Some of the Fukizo men returned to their old region in the fall, but most of them felt that Bapoto must be found and dealt with before they could honorably return. I trusted Flint and went with him to meet the rest of the Fukizo. They shared their food, attended to my story, and seemed like reasonable men."

"Did the Fukizo say anything about Jackal, and what they did to Kura during the summer?" Snap asked.

"No. It sounded as though they had never been there. They apparently tried to find Bapoto all summer, but never caught up to him. It was clear he was the only one of the Kura to whom they had an objection, but when I suggested they make peace, one of them decided I was trying to protect Bapoto and threw a huge rock at me. I put my arm up to protect myself, and the rock broke it. Fortunately, the others thought I was only mistaken, not evil. They dragged off my attacker and tended my arm. It hurt." He pushed away the memory of Flint straightening his arm, of vomiting in agony while three men held him still.

"Someone hollowed out a piece of split tree trunk, and Flint tied my arm to it. They wouldn't let me move it at all. I couldn't hunt, couldn't even carry water. I'd have starved without them. They must have felt responsible, or felt sorry for me, anyway.

"One day, they left me alone at their camp with a supply of

food and water while they went to attack Bapoto. There was no way for me to warn anyone, and I was terrified you'd get hurt. When they returned two days later, Flint told me that the Kura were alerted by a watcher before they got near the village, and they had been forced to abandon their plan, so I thought you were probably all right.

"After more than a moon, my arm still hurt, but it no longer made that horrible grating noise, so Flint took off the splint and helped me pack my bundle. I went straight to Kura, and you were gone. Whistle ignored me, and everyone else followed her lead. Only Hum was willing to look at me, and she just cried and ran into her shelter."

Snap shook her head. "Then what?"

"I went on to the men's shelter near the Kijito where I planned to meet the peacemakers. A few men were staying there, and they told me about Jackal. The four Fukizo bachelors were there, and they told me about meeting you—it's a good thing only Kura are named after sounds, and they don't reuse the name of a living person." Her mouth fell open and he grinned. "Asili, huh? A good name for this place. So when I told my four friends where the Fukizo camp was, they went to try to convince the Fukizo to return home before winter keeps them from traveling. I told them I would be here."

Snap nodded. She looked around the pitiful shelter, made especially dreary by the setting sun. "I have nothing, I'm afraid. It will be cold tonight."

"I will go to borrow a fire from someone tomorrow. Tonight we will wrap up warm."

Snap wanted to clean the blood from her legs. Ash offered to watch the sleeping Baby while she made her way down to the spring, leaning on a stout stick and hanging on to bushes. While she was gone, he collected the bits of food scattered over the floor of the shelter, unpacked his dragger, and stored everything in the alcove. Although he couldn't burn it, he collected as much firewood as he could left-handed and piled it inside the shelter. Now and then, he looked at Baby, who seemed thinner than either of his baby sisters had ever been, and glanced down at the spring, but didn't interrupt Snap's painfully slow progress. Finally, she shuffled back up, exhausted, unkempt hair flying, and wearing a large leather diaper.

He eyed the diaper and Snap narrowed her eyes. "I'm sore, I'm tired, and I'm cold. Let's go to sleep."

"I have a few things for you." Ash waved at the things he had unpacked. Stiffly, she lowered herself to her knees at the empty fire ring. The collection of new tools, a new container of salt, five hides—each gift evoked profuse thanks. When he displayed several dozen smoked fish, Snap's hands shook with emotion as she expressed her gratitude, and the dried meat—nearly a whole antelope—made tears leak from the corners of her eyes. The last offering was an oval box about the size of her open hand. As he held it out, she realized the box was made of two beautifully patterned turtle shell carapaces. Both were exactly the same size, shaped and smoothed on the edges so the two shells joined perfectly, and bound together with a strip of zebra hide.

Snap gasped. "Wonderful! Did you make this?"

Ash nodded. "The matching shells were a matter of luck. I just happened on a pond with dozens of these turtles, all nearly the same size. I ate well that day. Open it."

She unfastened the zebra-hide tie and separated the two halves. Inside, in a bed of dry grass, lay a curiously shaped piece

of wood. It was no tool she had ever seen, not a food she recognized. Her brows knit as she stared at the object, and then
warmth spread from the middle of her chest to her fingers and
toes as she looked up. "It's me."

He gave her a huge Fukizo toothy smile.

As the day faded into blackness and rain began to hammer
on the shelter roof, Baby woke up and nursed again. Snap and
Ash ate a few more bites of smoked catfish, checked the shelter's
seams and drainage trenches, and curled up in the sleeping hides.
She was asleep in a moment. Ash had wrapped his broken arm in
a stiff hide to prevent him moving it while asleep, but it was still
aching, and he lay awake for a long time, nostrils filled with the
domestic smells of Snap and Baby, his mind uneasy.

By morning, the rain only whispered on the roof as if leaves instead of water were falling. The faintest of gray daylight crept in
around the edges of the door flap, and Ash woke to find a furry,
brown-and-white face so close to his own he could barely focus
on it. The mother hyrax skittered for the door as soon as he
opened his eyes, and two smaller gray-brown blurs darted from
the storage alcove and followed her. He forced himself to crawl
from the warm sleeping hides and opened the flap. A blast of cold
air and a few raindrops made Snap stir, but she just pulled the
hides tighter over her face. He made sure there was enough water
for several days, found Snap's fire-carrier, and promised her to
return as soon as possible.

Without his enormous pack, Ash made good time and reached
the men's shelter at the Kijito junction well before dark. The
bachelors occupied a natural cave that comprised several irregular

rooms on various levels and a small central space where a fire burned. The two older men and one around Ash's age who had established themselves there each had a separate cache of food and firewood and seemed to be avoiding one another as much as possible, but they all slept around the same fire. They were willing to let Ash stay for one night, provided he took a turn watching and left as soon as possible with his recharged fire-carrier. None of them offered the others food.

Ash slept very little. As soon as it was light enough to walk, he packed hot embers and warm ashes into the stone fire-carrier and started off. Although rain threatened, he reached Asili without extinguishing his coals. He found Snap with Baby in a front sling, skinning a hyrax. A tent of dry tinder lay ready in the fire ring. As he entered the shelter, Snap straightened up and gave him a half smile.

"It worked again!"

With a quizzical look, Ash squealed a greeting and then knelt at the fire ring. The embers glowed when he blew on them, and the grass and pinecones that Snap had arranged burst into flames. Small kindling, then larger pieces, sputtered and ignited. Finally, Ash built a framework of split firewood around the flames and rocked back on his heels. Snap squatted across from him with her arms wrapped around the sling. Ash raised his eyebrows at her.

"What worked?"

"The Great One brought you back. I did the ritual this morning, and here you are."

Ash looked at her, mystified. Was she joking? "I took the fire-carrier, and I told you I would come back. You can't be surprised to see me."

An annoyed squawk came from the sling. Snap stood up and began to swing her hips and croon softly. The sling fell silent.

The next day, Ash's arm was stiff and sore, his legs ached, and he had to drag himself out of his sleeping hide. He forced himself to do the necessary: check the snares, bring water from the stream, forage for firewood. Snap was willing to drink water he carried up from the spring and eat the smoked catfish he offered her, but she didn't seem interested in anything else and lay curled in her sleeping hide. Baby nursed and slept alternately, but after midday, Baby was no longer sleepy nor hungry, and she fussed until Ash picked her up and put her in the sling. She seemed more alert than she had before, but still too thin. For quite some time, she stared openmouthed at the sky, Ash's face, and anything that moved. He followed her eyes. "How does the sky look to you?" he asked her. "What do you see in my face?" Finally, she fell asleep again, but Ash didn't put her down.

Some days, Snap seemed more like herself; she got up, collected wood, carried water, prepared food, and responded to his attempts at conversation. On the mornings when she was most animated, he would invite her to mate, but she waved him away without explanation. More often, she moved only when absolutely necessary, used no signs, and made few sounds. Occasionally, when she thought Ash wasn't around, she climbed onto the uwanda rock, raised her arms, and made a strange whistle, not quite Bapoto's whistle, but somehow like it. It seemed to Ash that she was a little more lively after these episodes, so he didn't mention them. She continued to wear the leather diaper, and Ash began to wonder if it was permanent.

Baby changed every day. When she wasn't sleeping or eating, Ash carried her around and showed her things he thought might be interesting: water sparkling in the little stream, a herd of gazelles grazing, a smooth, pink rock. Her favorite object seemed to be his own face. She copied his smile, laughed at his funny faces, tried to touch his eyes, and pulled his beard, and Ash was sure she preferred his face to her mother's, although he didn't mention it to Snap.

Had returning been a mistake? This Snap was so unlike the old one, so uninterested in everything she had once loved, and apparently convinced that she had caused him to return by sending messages to the Great One. Snap, after her long and determined resistance to Bapoto's ideas, had been persuaded by something that happened during his absence. Was there any hope of returning to the unspoken understanding they had shared? Was there even hope of mating again?

These thoughts were occupying Ash one morning when Baby unexpectedly discovered that her hands belonged to her, and she babbled something that looked like "Ash" to him. He was quite pleased and decided that Snap was probably recovering from an illness and would return to herself in time. In the meantime, Baby needed someone to talk to.

One windy day, a cold sun escaped scudding clouds and made the damp landscape steam as the previous night's rain evaporated. Ash and Snap had collected all the dry downed wood and standing dead wood in the immediate vicinity, but every day was colder and the wood supply was nowhere near adequate. Ash thought that his arm was strong enough now to use the large stone axe, and so he prodded Snap into a wood-cutting expedition. By midday, they had returned to Asili several times, pulling a log or two, and the woodpile looked healthier than it had.

Satisfied with the morning's work, they collapsed in front

of the shelter door and tucked into one of the larger smoked catfish. Snap laughed at Baby's babbling and spontaneously recognized her "Ash" sign. When the fish had become a pile of clean, white bones and Baby had fallen asleep in the sling, Snap finally abandoned her diaper. Ash raised his eyebrows, along with other parts of his anatomy. Was it, at long last, an invitation? She gave a buzz he hadn't heard since the previous spring. When he squatted against the large rock in the uwanda and opened his arms, a powerful memory of their first Bonding flooded over him. She picked me! A grown woman, the most beautiful, the most powerful! The *first*! She cautiously backed up to him, careful not to disturb the sling. Both of them were a little tentative, even circumspect, but he soon found that she could still make the same hysterical squeals that pleased him so much. When he slumped back against the big rock and Snap laid her cheek against his chest, he thought whatever it was that had afflicted her, she was getting over it. Baby slept through it in her sling.

He was watching Snap drift off to sleep in a patch of intermittent sun when he heard a distant hoot. He prodded her with his toe, and she raised her head to listen as well. In a moment, the sound came again, and he had no trouble recognizing the unusual hoot—Fukizo. They both stood up and saw four figures hurrying along the base of the ridge, nearly at the place where the path started up to the shelter.

"Dika and company, I think," he signed.

"Definitely."

She hooted back, and the four looked up at them and waved. She waved back, and soon, Dika, Granite, Agama, and Falcon crowded into the uwanda. They signed formal greetings as if they were strangers, and Snap laughed. "I hope you're not looking for the Asili Bonding feast," she signed. "It's a bit late."

All four of them hooted with laughter and slapped one another on the backs.

"Lovely baby." Falcon waved at the baby sleeping in Snap's sling, and the others nodded.

Snap signed her thanks and invited them to share the uwanda fire. Ash added a log, and she located a basket of scabrous marula nuts and a water bag to pass around.

"Your arm looks much better," Agama noted as Ash lifted the log with two hands. "Whatever exercise you are getting here must agree with you." The men hooted again.

Ash looked at Snap. "Yes, indeed. This place agrees with me. Did you find the other Fukizo? What happened?"

Dika cracked a nut with his teeth. "Every one of them blames Bapoto for the loss of someone close to them. After they were driven off from Kura, they debated whether they should try again or return to Fukizo, and the decision was unanimous; every one of them wants to kill Bapoto, personally. We told them you would surely tell the Kura his history, but they expected the Kura would only drive him off. That wasn't enough."

"What about what happened at midsummer?" she asked. "Why did they kill Jackal?"

Dika chewed for a moment and looked thoughtful. "I told them what the women found when they returned to Kura at midsummer, and they seemed horrified. They could be lying, I suppose. They may have been ashamed afterward, and decided to pretend not to know about it, but I don't think so. I know these men, and they are honorable. Every one of them would kill Bapoto if he could, and they might kill someone who was trying to protect him, but they wouldn't kill someone just to frighten a bunch of women and children. At least, I don't think so."

Her brow protruded even farther than usual. "Who else would have done it?"

A puzzled silence reverberated around the uwanda, punctuated by the sound of cracking nuts.

CHAPTER 17

H aving visitors pulled Snap out of her lethargy. They treated her as the Mother of Asili, and somehow, from under the smothering, mind-numbing apathy, she dredged up the role of Mother for which she had prepared since birth and assumed it automatically. Life's normal occupations conspired to make her feel normal; the more she behaved like herself, the more she felt like herself again. Carrying firewood, checking the snares, mating with Ash, tending to Baby—ventures that had seemed insurmountably difficult gradually became possible.

Ash seemed pleased to have visitors too, and the change in

his disposition made Snap realize how much her unhappy state had tested his usual good temper. She welcomed them to set up their men's shelter in the neighborhood, and Ash helped them pick out a spot—a shallow cave within hooting distance of the shelter, but farther from the spring. Having neighbors, even unrelated, male neighbors, made Asili feel a little less hostile, a little more familiar. With other people around, Snap avoided thoughts more complicated than those required by the tasks at hand, but during her watch, Baby stirring in her sleep inspired other notions. My daughter has no ukoo, and it is my fault. No companions for her childhood, no women to share the harvest, no Bonding to bring her a mate. Kinswomen—our blood—endure all disasters; who are ours? Baby sucked momentarily on her thumb and fell back to sleep.

One morning not long after the men's shelter was built, Snap climbed to the ridgetop to check the hyrax snares. Out of sight of her shelter, she climbed onto a rock, closed her eyes, raised her arms, and made a soft warbling whistle, as she had done every morning since Ash's return. In her mind, she thanked the Great One for Ash and Baby, for their food and health, for their new neighbors. When she opened her eyes, she found Granite standing nearby, mouth agape.

Snap had wondered if Granite was a bit slow; he rarely signed, and his wide-spaced eyes gave no hint of deeper thoughts. She squealed a greeting and jumped down from the rock.

"You are greeting the Great One?" he asked. "We understood from Ash that both of you oppose Bapoto and his ideas."

Snap flapped her hands in confusion. "How do you know . . . I mean . . . you don't follow his . . ."

Granite smiled. "Most of the Fukizo and many in the ukoos

nearby follow the Great One, although they don't agree about Bapoto. I've been known to join a hunting ritual now and then, and I make the morning greetings if I have a special request to make—you never know what might be useful. Falcon joins me sometimes, but the older ones just hoot at us if they see us doing it."

"I see." Snap seemed interested in an eagle on the horizon, but she signed in Granite's direction. "Well, Ash thinks Bapoto uses these ideas to control people, and might not even believe them himself. I have to agree with the first part, but I'm not sure what I believe. When Baby was born, we were alone and hungry. The fire went out, and I asked the Great One to send Ash. When I woke up, he was here."

Granite nodded. "There are stories of things like that."

"Yes, but Ash says that the Great One never sent him here. If I mention the Great One, he rolls his eyes. If he catches me making the morning greetings, he snorts and walks away."

"Dika and Agama might do the same, so best not to mention the Great One to them. But I say, it never hurts to watch all the burrow holes. Who can say what might help?"

On a clear, cold morning soon after, the men set out to hunt gazelle, except for Falcon, who remained with Snap to make floor mats for the men's shelter. The men had admired her floor mats and wanted to have some of their own, but none of them knew how to weave, so she was teaching Falcon. So far, the two of them had covered about half of the men's shelter floor. She had come to understand Dika and Agama were mates, as were Granite and Falcon. She wasn't entirely clear about how that worked, as they didn't mate in public like everyone else, but they seemed satisfied with their arrangements. A fire blazed in the men's shelter, and Baby lay unwrapped on a leopard hide next to Snap, almost, but not quite, able to turn herself over. The little diaper was no longer necessary; Snap was so well attuned to her daughter's habits, she could carry her outside just in time to prevent indoor messes.

A distant Panda Ya Mto hoot resonated over the crackling of the fire. Falcon put down his weaving and stepped out into the uwanda, while Snap worked on. She had completed another row when the flap opened and Falcon ducked back in, followed by Rabbit, the mate of Dew's sister whom Snap had met in Panda Ya Mto. She stowed her weaving in its basket and knelt up to receive Rabbit's greetings.

"Welcome, Rabbit. This fire is Falcon's, but I'm sure you are welcome to share it."

Falcon smiled and gestured Rabbit to the fireside. Rabbit gave Falcon and his fire bemused looks and then squatted opposite Snap and stretched his hands to the flames. Falcon rummaged in the storage alcove for a moment and then produced a platter of winter greens strewn with fragments of smoked chenga, which he offered first to Snap and then to Rabbit.

"I'm looking for Lightning, the son of our Mother," signed Rabbit. "He left the village to collect grubs yesterday and didn't return. All the Panda Ya Mto men are out searching. Have you seen anything?"

Both Snap and Falcon shook their heads. "No one found any sign of him near Panda Ya Mto?" asked Snap.

"Prints of a cave hyena were found near our stream, along with the boy's prints. I'll be very surprised if any of us find anything, but our Mother is so distressed, we wanted to make an effort, just in case." Rabbit chewed a handful of greens and smacked appreciatively.

Snap shook her head. "I met him. A strong, healthy-looking boy. I'm sorry."

Rabbit nodded and chewed thoughtfully. "Your Baby is getting strong, too. Look, she's almost turned over."

Falcon squatted next to Rabbit and addressed him. "Snap told me about a Panda Ya Mto man who saw Jackal with another man early last summer. Was that you?"

"That's right."

"You don't have any idea who the other man could have been?"

"He wasn't known to me. I couldn't even tell what ukoo he was from, because he had almost no hair on his head at all."

Falcon hissed and shot Snap a look. "Bapoto? He wouldn't . . ." As he spoke, Baby swung her leg over her body. With a tremendous effort, she flopped onto her stomach and squeaked in surprise.

Rabbit snapped his fingers for Baby enthusiastically. "Good Baby! Now, I need to get moving if I want to get back to Panda Ya Mto by dark. Thanks for the food and fire." He stood up, addressed respectful farewells to Snap and, somewhat uncertainly, to Falcon, and then ducked under the door flap.

❧

Falcon offered her the last bits of chenga, licked the platter himself, and then addressed Snap. "Someone from Kura might be interested in knowing a few things about Bapoto."

"If Whistle were convinced the Fukizo are only dangerous to Bapoto . . ."

He patted her knee. "Then you could go home?"

She swallowed and shook her head. "No, never. Whistle didn't protect me. She did what she thought best for Kura, but I can't trust her to do what's best for Baby and me."

Falcon picked up his weaving again and watched as Baby managed to roll over once more. Her right hand stretched toward the wall of the cave. A heartbeat later, she screamed. Snap scooped her up; a red lump was forming on the back of the baby's hand, and a black scorpion the size of Snap's hand was trying to squeeze itself back into a crack at the base of the wall. Falcon killed it with a big stone scraper and dumped it onto the midden heap.

Baby continued to scream, and soon Snap was sobbing with her. Nothing comforted her, and the lump grew and grew. Her brown eyes dilated into black pits, her arms and legs began to twitch wildly, and still she cried. Foam oozed from her mouth and nose. Snap tried wrapping the tiny fist in a soft hide, dipping it into the cold stream, holding it tightly under her own arm, but nothing helped and still Baby screamed. Snap rocked her and crooned through her own sobs. Falcon hovered, offering water, food, and help. He fed the fire and watched for the return of the hunters. The hand grew larger and darker, Baby's screams became painful wheezes, and the foam at her mouth turned pink. Finally, the sun neared the horizon. The hunters had not returned.

Snap climbed onto the rock in the uwanda of the men's shelter, closed her eyes, raised the twitching baby above her head, and warbled a strange, choking intonation. Save Baby. As loud in her mind as Baby's screams had been, she repeated it to herself. Save Baby. Surely the Great One can hear me. Save Baby.

As she stood on the rock, the wheezing faded and the twitching slowed. Snap lowered her arms and stared at Baby's open eyes. Her arms and legs were at peace now, limp and lifeless. Her breathing muscles no longer strained.

Snap howled, and in the distance, a wolf answered.

The hunters returned in darkness. They had taken a zebra and tied the carcass to poles they carried on their shoulders. A half-moon gave enough light for them to shuffle back to Asili, but it was too dark, and the zebra too heavy, for them to run. Falcon heard their hoots and scrambled down the path to meet them. In the men's shelter, curled around Baby's body, Snap heard Ash's wail like a stone knife driven into her chest.

That night, she lay with Baby in the place where the scorpion had struck, awake, silent. All five men squatted or sat around the fire. They kept the fire burning low, shared a little food, and tried to fill unfamiliar spaces usually occupied by tradition and by decisions of the Mother. The cave of the dead that the Kura used was too far from Asili. Ash knew of another cave not far to the southwest that was near an often-occupied hyena den; Snap agreed to take Baby there. Ash offered to take Baby in her place, but her look of incomprehension and the other men's shock needed no response. In the morning, Ash assembled a small dragger, and the men accompanied her in a phalanx, Ash in front.

Snap took much longer to reach the cave than the men would have alone; she was not yet strong enough to move fast pulling a dragger, even a lightly laden one. The cave, when they reached it, was small and suitable. After a chorus of keening and a short rest, they started back, Snap crying silently.

At first, Snap felt almost as she did before Ash had found her—as if she weighed as much as an elephant, with the strength of a bird. She moved only to drink and to go to the latrine pit. The men butchered the zebra and offered her a perfectly grilled slice of liver, but she waved it away. Ash carried water and wood, and unobtrusively left food where Snap might find it, but then left her alone. On the second day, she ate a few bites of the antelope meat, and on the third day, she got up and did her morning chores.

"Not the same," she explained to Ash. "Never the same. But here we are, and there is work to be done."

Her morning rituals disappeared. Before Baby's death, she had made no great effort to hide them from Ash, but now he no longer heard warbles in the distance, or saw her outlined against the sky at the top of ridge, arms upraised. Early one morning, she met Granite near the spot where he had found her greeting the Great One, and he offered to join her in the morning ritual. She snorted. "You go ahead."

Granite shook his head. "Why would the Great One cause such a thing? Is she not able to keep babies safe? Or doesn't she want to?"

Snap looked west, at the formless clouds not yet lit by the morning sun. She had thought the Great One lived far to the west, on a high mountaintop, or in a great cave, but those thoughts had moved to a place of memories, along with the ideas that Chirp would always be the Mother, and Whistle would always keep her safe.

"Maybe 'why' is not the right question." Snap made a sign of leave-taking, patted Granite on the arm, and walked on to her next snare.

Snap forgot Rabbit's visit, but Falcon didn't. A few days after the scorpion attack, he told the others Rabbit's story about seeing a short-haired man like Bapoto with Jackal shortly before his death. Ash volunteered to hunt near Kura in hopes of meeting someone who would attend to the story of how Bapoto nearly destroyed the Fukizo and how he might know the circumstances of Jackal's death. Whenever the weather permitted, Ash made forays in that direction, but the Kura men seemed to be hunting only in large groups that always included Bapoto. A moon passed, and Ash had met only a few alone, none of whom were willing to acknowledge him.

After eight days of storms kept the Asili men from hunting, the men set out one morning after antelope. By dark, they hadn't returned. Snap was not surprised—hunting expeditions often lasted more than a day—but she slept badly. The morning chores were done and a couple of lizards roasting over the uwanda fire when Snap heard distant hoots she didn't recognize. From a large rock, she could see five familiar figures at the base of the ridge, two holding the ends of a pole from which hung a large male antelope. She waved and tried to copy the odd hoot she had just heard.

When they reached her uwanda, the fire was blazing up and the butchering tools laid ready on the large rock. She greeted them enthusiastically.

"Good hunting! What's the new hoot?"

Ash lowered his end of the pole. "Asili hoot. We worked on it last night. Falcon has an idea for hair twists as well. What do you think?"

Privately, she thought it was just the kind of thing men did when left to their own devices, but she signed, "It's great. I think we should use it. Did you meet anybody?"

"This one led us on a long run, and we were near Kura when we finally took him." As Ash told the story, the other men and Snap began to butcher the antelope, but paid attention to him as well. "It was after sunset, and we didn't want to walk in the dark with the sinkholes all filled with water from the storms, so we bivouacked in a little cave. We were so close to Kura, it seemed like a perfect opportunity to let someone know about Bapoto, so I crept up to the village from the west and found Rustle and another boy watching. He recognized me and let me pass without an alarm.

"Hum's shelter is a little distance from the others, so I reached it without meeting anyone else. I'm afraid I startled her a bit, but she didn't raise an alarm either. She attended to my whole story without a sign. I don't know if she believed me, but she did help me avoid Bapoto on my way out."

Snap pursed her lips at the hoof she was removing. "By now, everyone knows you were there. I hope Hum is all right."

The next day was stormy, and the next. When the sun finally appeared, the men trotted toward the Kijito with seines in hand, while Snap rushed out to check her snares and drag home as much firewood as she could before the next downpour. High above her shelter, she reset the last snare and stood up. A bent female figure was approaching from the east along the base of the ridge. Snap climbed down to her own uwanda, and recognized the figure—Whistle. The older woman turned up the path to the spring, looked up at Snap, and hooted. Snap responded with the new Asili hoot.

Jaws clenched, Whistle reached the little uwanda and looked around—the sodden wood pile, the ragged shelter, the cold fire ring—and then at her daughter, who stood in front of the door flap. The older woman was obviously pregnant, and Snap thought she had aged years since the Bonding. Whistle stood unmoving, as if unsure what greeting to use.

"Welcome to Asili, Whistle." Snap used formal gestures to wave her mother inside. "Please share my fire."

Still wordless, Whistle followed her into the shelter and squatted at the fire while Snap stirred it up and added wood.

"Why do you leave your ukoo, Whistle? It's cold and dangerous."

Whistle looked around the inside of the shelter and then signed with stiff, slow hands. "Hum said—I don't believe her, of course, but—your Baby?"

"A scorpion sting. Hum is telling the truth."

"Please come home, Snap. You were born to be Mother of Kura. This Asisha or whatever you call it is not meant for you, and not for your daughters." A tiny squeak escaped from Whistle, and Snap thought she had started to keen and then stopped herself.

"Bapoto has received another vision. It is time for reconciliation. You and Ash shall return; Bapoto will say nothing of your disobedience and rumormongering, and you will not repeat lies about him. We will live in peace and be safe from the Fukizo." Whistle's hands fell to her thighs as if exhausted, and she rocked shakily.

Snap reached out to steady her mother. "Ash did not lie to

Hum. The Fukizo have told us the truth; Bapoto nearly destroyed their ukoo with his visions and desire for authority, and he was seen with Jackal just before Jackal's death. You must expel him from Kura, or he will bring more evil to you."

"The Fukizo! You deal with the Fukizo? What are you thinking?"

Snap shook her head. "They are just people who are terribly angry at Bapoto because of the nightmare he has inflicted on them. Please believe me."

Whistle shifted her weight to her knees and stared at the fire. "Please come back. Everything will be as it was. Please."

Snap looked at her mother with eyes that had been where Whistle would never go, and saw a woman she didn't know. Who was this Whistle? Where was the calm leader, the great judge, the patient midwife? Snap shook her head. "It is impossible. Bapoto is wrong about how the world works. I can't be Mother to people who believe him."

Tears rolled down Whistle's cheeks. "I am no longer young. Another baby is coming, maybe before spring. Things can happen, and Swish is too young to be Mother. Peep is smart, but crippled. Warble is well liked, but silly. What will happen to the Kura if this birth goes badly?"

"Things can happen, yes, but you've had five babies and helped with dozens more; you're an expert. Everything will be fine." Snap patted her mother's shoulder and offered her the water gourd. "Have a drink and I'll get you some jerky."

Whistle accepted a slice of jerky and a gourd of water, and then rose to her feet, looking more composed. "Thank you for your hospitality." She used formal signs, but Snap answered one-handed.

"Bye. Be careful on the path; it's starting to rain again."

She watched Whistle go out of sight, shaking her head. Snap's mental fog had cleared, and she knew two things: Whistle must never be responsible for her and Baby's safety, and she could never be Mother to Bapoto and his allies. Nevertheless, she hoped her reassuring words to Whistle wouldn't prove false. With a frown, she ducked into the shelter.

CHAPTER 18

The shortest days passed and gradually the sun began to rise a bit earlier each day, but the winter grew fouler. Thunder, lightning, and wind joined the frequent rain. It was too cold to hunt, but maintaining drainage trenches and repairing wind-damaged shelters had to be done no matter what the temperature. Snap and Ash slept as much as possible, but even so, the stored food disappeared rapidly. Fortunately, the hyrax population seemed unaffected by the weather, and the snares were still beyond their understanding.

After a storm during which high winds had forced Snap

and Ash to sit on the stakes that held down the shelter, she woke one morning to find she could produce white clouds inside the shelter with her breath. She desperately wanted to stay in the warm sleeping hides until Ash got up and stirred up the fire, but she had to visit the latrine pit or get wet. Snap scooted out of her sleeping hide and tried to keep the warmer air inside as she ducked under the door flap.

Just outside the door, her feet shot out from under her and she landed hard on her backside. The ground was covered with something shiny, cold, and extremely slippery. Bushes, rocks, even the puddles all had a hard, transparent covering of the same stuff. Looking through a piece of the odd stuff distorted the world into strange shapes, and she enjoyed the smooth, wet, chill feeling of it on her tongue. She wondered if the solid water had appeared at Kura, wondered if Swish was playing with it, too. Before long, she remembered why she was up and made her way down the path to the latrine pit, sliding part of the way on her bottom.

A cold rain began around midday. Ash made the fire blaze up until it threatened to set the roof aflame, and then laid out his tools and began to shape a new piece of wood. Snap worked on a hide at the hearth.

"Ash! Do you hear something?" Through the noise of the rain and wind, she imagined a Kura hoot. He turned his head, listening. The sound came again, clearer. Snap pulled the hide she was working on over their heads and they stepped out into the downpour. A stooped figure had already climbed past the spring and was nearing the uwanda. Ash gave a booming Asili hoot, and the figure looked up and waved—Hum. The path was treacherous, and it took the older woman some time to climb up to the uwanda. All three of them were drenched and shivering by the time they squeezed into the shelter and shook themselves. The fire hissed and spat.

"Welcome, Hum." Snap squealed greetings and dug in the alcove for something to eat.

"Thank you. I . . . we need help."

Snap turned and took a good look at the wet visitor. She had a cut above her left eye and held her right arm at an odd angle.

"Of course. What do you need?" Ash helped Hum kneel at the fire and draped a dry sleeping hide around her, while Snap found her a handful of nuts.

"Wart and I—we told Bubble your news."

Snap and Ash exchanged a look.

"It didn't take long for everyone to learn it. Bubble was glad you were alive, and upset about your baby. Bubble's mate, Hawk, is Rabbit's brother. Hawk already knew Rabbit's story about seeing Jackal last spring, and he agreed that the other man was probably Bapoto. There were rumors that Whistle and Bapoto had some loud discussions about it, and that Whistle came to visit you."

Snap nodded. "She asked me to make peace with Bapoto and come back to Kura. I refused."

Hum was still shivering, but managed a smile. "After that, Whistle declared that everyone should shun us. Wart, me, Bubble, and Hawk. No one else believed us, or at least, no one else admitted it. Bubble and Hawk were all right; Peep didn't address them, but she let them stay in her shelter. Since Wart and I were no longer Kura, Bapoto declared that my shelter was unoccupied and came with his thugs to send us away. Wart fought them, and he's hurt—he can hardly walk. I packed up as many of my possessions as I could, and took him as far from Kura as he could go, but that wasn't far. Bubble and Hawk came after us, and I left him with them, but we have no fire, and we can't carry Wart."

Snap didn't mention Hum's injuries, but she suspected that Wart hadn't fought alone. "We'll come now. We can bring a dragger for Wart—there's still plenty of daylight."

Ash looked at Snap. "This storm isn't over. What if the wind comes up again? You should stay here, keep the fire going, keep the shelter from blowing away, and I'll get the other men to come along and help Wart."

Snap agreed. "But you have to send Bubble and the babies as fast as she can go. The little ones will freeze."

While Snap rigged a large dragger, Ash dashed up the ridge to ask for help. They chose Falcon to watch over their shelter and fire, and the other three trudged off into the rain with Ash and two large draggers. After they were gone, Snap gave Hum some water and dried zebra and looked after her injuries. The cut over her eye had bled down her neck and over her chest. Snap washed it out well and couldn't see any bone at the bottom. Hum's arm had been twisted behind her back and the elbow was swollen and sore, but it didn't bend anywhere that it shouldn't.

"I think both of these will heal if you get some rest." Hum thanked her, curled up next to the fire, and fell asleep.

Snap propped up the door flap so that she could see across the uwanda and down the ridge, and watched through the rain until darkness made her give up and fasten the shelter flaps. She curled up next to Hum, but every gust of wind, every change in the sound of the rain, troubled her sleep. Vague gray light finally reappeared, and she resumed her vigil at the door, her attention divided between the rain and a partly finished floor mat. Hum arose like a newborn giraffe unfolding unfamiliar limbs. Snap shared with her some barely edible dika nuts, and they started to work on a gazelle hide that needed scraping and stretching. Neither mentioned those they were expecting, but both glanced into the rain often as they worked.

When the gray sky had become as bright as it was likely to get, Snap heard a Kura hoot not far away. She stepped under the door flap and saw Bapoto climbing the path with a small bundle on his bent back. The rain was giving them a brief respite, but he was soaking wet, and a cloud of steam rose from his body as he climbed. She dropped the door flap behind her and waited silently for him to approach, arms folded across her chest.

Although he was as tall and muscular as he had ever been, he moved like an older man than the one in Snap's memory, and stood stooped as if his small bundle weighed much more than it possibly could have. His matted hair was plastered to his body, and his breathing sounded labored. As he reached the uwanda, he began another hoot, but cut off the sound as he caught sight of Snap standing in front of the shelter. When he recognized her, he squealed briefly in greeting and began to sign a formal salutation, but she responded with a low growl deep in her throat. The door flap flew up and Hum appeared with a short spear in her left hand. Bapoto squatted in front of the two women and signed with his eyes on the ground in front of him.

"Please don't attack. Whistle is dying."

Snap's growl ceased. She made a formal sign of welcome and motioned him into the shelter. Water dripped from Bapoto's short hair onto his shoulders and the floor mats as he squatted at the fire. Snap and Hum faced him across the flames, arms folded. Snap raised her arms questioningly.

"Well?"

"Whistle has been ill since shortly after her visit here. Her feet and face are swollen, she won't eat or drink, she feels hot, her urine is dark, and there is little of it. This morning, she didn't know where she was and asked for you over and over. I finally had to promise her that I would bring you." Bapoto's hands fell to his knees. He swallowed hard several times and hid his face.

His obvious emotion moved Snap. She couldn't feel sympathy for him, but he had taken a dangerous trip in a storm for Whistle's sake, and Whistle was still her mother. A sudden blast of wind roared around the shelter, shook loose one of the roof's anchor ties, and showered all of them with droplets of rain through a small, newly created gap. Snap jumped up and retied the anchors. By the time the shelter was whole again, Bapoto had collected himself. Snap folded her arms again and looked down at Bapoto. "I will go to Kura."

Hum shook her head, rumbling to herself.

Bapoto signaled his thanks and stood up. "Whistle will be grateful."

Snap rummaged in the alcove for a sling to hold her water bag and a little dried meat, and tied it over her shoulders. Hum hovered near the door and flicked her eyes from Snap to Bapoto. "I'll come, too."

"I need you to stay here. Keep the fire going, and keep the shelter from blowing away. Tell Falcon where I've gone."

Hum nodded and lifted the door flap for them. As she followed Bapoto carefully down the path, she stopped at the first turn to give Hum a Fukizo smile and an Asili hoot. She hooted back from the edge of the uwanda and watched them out of sight. Soon after they turned north at the end of the ridge, it began to rain again and the wind blasted into their faces. The rain intensified and Snap's vision was limited to Bapoto's back. She could make out her footing only just in time for each step, and thunder rumbled behind them.

Bapoto turned back and grinned unpleasantly. "Good thing we're not up on that ridge now. Probably get struck by lightning." She gritted her teeth and turned her attention to climbing over a large, loose rock.

Because she could see very little, it seemed to her they were making no progress at all. She could think only of Whistle, and wondered if she would be able to recognize her when they arrived, or if she would perhaps be dead. She was soaking wet and shivering, although the effort of scrambling over wet, irregular rocks kept her warmer than she might have been. Finally, she began to feel she ought to start recognizing landmarks near Kura, but none appeared. Her steps dragged. When she fell behind, she hooted at Bapoto's back to make him turn around. "I think we've gotten turned a bit in the storm. I think we need to go more to the right." She waved in the direction she thought Kura should be, but the visibility was still so poor she really wasn't sure.

"We're on the right track; we're just moving slowly because the footing is so bad. But we can turn a bit to the right." Bapoto seemed fairly sure of their location, so Snap followed him as closely as she safely could and tried to stay on his leeward side. The wind moved slowly around to their left, so she found herself walking to Bapoto's right, rather than following him.

Bapoto appeared to stumble and stepped directly in front of her; she sidestepped him and slipped on a loose rock. As she teetered on one foot, Bapoto shoved her hard, and she tumbled down a short, steep incline and fell through a partly concealed hole into thin air. Her scream ended abruptly as she landed on her hands and knees on a pile of debris, slid downhill a few feet, and splashed into a pool of cold water. She yowled an alarm to attract Bapoto's attention to the hole into which she had fallen, and his face appeared immediately in the center of the circle of light far above her.

Snap could see his words clearly; he stood in the gray light and signed with both arms. "You ignore the power of the Great One. The Great One healed your arm, and you showed no gratitude. The Great One brought us plentiful game and an abundant harvest, and you showed no gratitude. The Great One instructed us to take permanent mates, and you displayed your disrespect in front of the entire ukoo. The Great One asked you to return to Kura, and you disobeyed her. You have been guided with patience and understanding, and you continue to flout the authority of the Great One. She is angry, and the vision I received yesterday ordered that you should be punished, so that the power of the Great One will be glorified."

"Bapoto! Please help me!" she signed as clearly as possible with both arms, but Bapoto ignored her.

"This is the cave of the unbelievers, Snap. You can join Meerkat and Jackal in your plots against the Great One. You refused to accept the rituals, and now you know where unbelievers end. Good-bye." Bapoto disappeared, and she could see only the gray circle of sky through the cave mouth with large raindrops falling through it.

She took stock of her injuries. Her palms and knees were scraped and bleeding, but nothing seemed to be broken. The cave was roughly circular and the width of a short spear throw. The roof of the cave was more than the height of three tall men, with the opening in the roof near one wall. The width of the opening was the distance from her nose to the end of her outstretched fingers. The detritus of many years had fallen through the hole and a debris mound had accumulated with its highest point centered on the cave opening. The opposite side of the room was filled with water.

As her eyes adjusted to the darkness, the details of the room became easier to see, and she noticed the debris heap was composed of rocks of varying sizes, pieces of rotting wood and other plant refuse, a few small animal bones, and surprisingly enough, a well-made wooden spear. She picked up the spear and examined it. The shaft had been shaped to fit someone's hand, and a curious mark was carved into the shaft. Snap turned the spear and held it up so the maximum amount of light struck it, and she felt a lump rise into her throat as she recognized the tiny meerkat scratched into the spear.

Snap held on to the spear and continued to investigate her cave. Near the bottom of the mound, close to the water's edge, she found a collection of larger bones, human bones. They had been disturbed by animals, but she guessed the person must have been tall, probably a man. One of the large femurs was broken in two, and Snap shivered, grateful she had not been injured by her fall. She didn't see any obvious way out of her predicament, but she had barely begun to explore the possibilities and wasn't ready to give up yet.

She squatted at the water's edge, away from the steady stream of rain falling into the cave opening, and noticed the water level was rising. There couldn't be that much rain falling into the opening, she thought. There must be a spring or an underground river as well. The limestone karst in the area of Kura was riddled with sinkholes and underground streams, and she guessed she had landed in one of these. She ate a bit of her dried meat, which was no longer very dry, and drank from her bag. As the water around her rose, she moved slowly up the debris heap. The gray light at the opening above was beginning to fade by the time she reached the highest point of the debris mound. Snap clutched her small bundle to her chest and shivered violently.

When the water reached her knees, she thought she felt an occasional fish brush against her legs and kicked out in alarm, but when the rising water neared her waist, she could no longer feel her legs and the fish ceased to bother her. The rain stopped, and the gray circle above her began to get darker. As feeble light faded into inky blackness, the sounds of dripping water and soft plash of fish drifted away as well. The world disappeared; only shivering remained. Night fell.

CHAPTER 19

Hum's description of where she had left Wart, Bubble, and Hawk had seemed clear to Ash, but familiar landmarks became less familiar in the storm, and he finally admitted to himself that he was not quite sure where he was or where he was going. The rain obscured the view from every high point, trails were obliterated, and even the direction of the sun was uncertain. Fortunately, Agama had paid close attention to Hum, and had already become fairly familiar with the district. As Ash tried to survey the landscape from a low rise, Agama tapped him on the arm, pointed at an acacia with an unusual double trunk, and headed in that direction. Relieved, Ash followed.

It was almost completely dark when they reached the huge baobab tree that Hum had described. Sometime in the past, a lightning strike had split the tree down one side. Eventually, the interior of the tree had worn away, leaving an alcove as large as Snap's shelter. At Ash's hoot, Hawk emerged and waved at the four men to follow him inside.

Wart lay curled in a corner, moaning softly. Bubble sat cross-legged by the door with a baby tucked under each arm, nursing both at once. The contents of two large draggers had been jammed inside, leaving just enough space for the five men to squeeze in out of the rain. Dika knelt near Wart and put a hand on Wart's arm until he opened his eyes.

"I am Dika, of Asili. How are you hurt?"

Wart rolled over and pointed, and all the men winced. Dika opened his pack and made a poultice of fine red dust mixed with chewed tree bark. Wart's moans turned to a sigh of relief, and he fell asleep.

Hawk wedged himself in next to Bubble. Boy Baby finished eating and Bubble passed him to Hawk, who let him sit in his lap and pull at his beard without protest. Hawk had to lean forward to sign around the infant. "I thank you for coming. Wart couldn't walk any farther, and Bubble can't move very fast with the babies. I couldn't leave Wart and the women here alone. Thank you."

Ash waved his thanks away. "It's nothing. We will get you all to Asili in the morning. Soon you'll be warm and dry." A clap of thunder shook the tree and both babies started to cry.

The night was long and uncomfortable, as no one could lie down except Wart, but there were enough sleeping hides to go around and enough food and water to quiet their stomachs. During a lull in the storm, Ash fell asleep propped against Agama's shoulder, and woke much later when Wart roared in pain because someone bumped into him. Gray early morning light showed him seven grumpy adults and two oblivious babies stirring and finding their ways out into the cold morning.

Bubble held Girl Baby out the door just in time. "Don't step in the mess," she signed.

It took a long time to figure out how they would travel. The baobab tree was southeast of Kura, a good morning's trot from Asili, but a long slog in bad weather. Ash and Agama decided that the best route was straight west until they were nearly due south of the white Kura ridge, south to the east end of the Asili ridge, and then west along the southern edge of the ridge to the Asili spring. Bubble started off as soon as she could, carrying both babies, with Hawk pulling their dragger and Agama for navigation. Dika, Granite, and Ash proposed to take turns pulling two draggers, one holding Hum's possessions and one holding Wart, but Wart found the bumping worse than trying to walk. He gave up the idea of riding and shuffled along as fast as he could manage, with the other three men keeping him company and pulling Hum's dragger.

The rain began again. Poor visibility made it hard to keep together, so Dika pulled a light rope from his pack and each man grabbed it. Traveling in a straight line was just as difficult as it had been the previous day, and Ash stopped often to get his bearings and allow Wart to rest. The Kura ridge was hidden in mist, and Ash had to guess at the right place to turn south. Although the sky was as flat and gray as slate and gave no hint of the time, they inched along until Ash supposed it was around midday, and then stopped under a rock overhang to rest and eat.

Wart found a relatively flat spot and curled up on his side. The other men shook themselves and squatted to eat fragments of dried fruit and jerky from their packs. The sound of something large scrabbling up the slope below them brought the three to their feet, spears in hand. A figure struggled up the slippery path in the mist, clutched a branch for support, scrambled on hands and knees, and pulled himself up. He neared the overhang, and Ash recognized Bapoto. Blood dripped from his hair and filled the scar that stretched from the corner of his mouth to his ear, so it appeared to be painted on.

Bapoto looked up and saw the three men standing above him with spears. He fell to his knees, eyes on their feet, and showed them his palms. "I am unarmed, and injured."

Dika glanced at Wart. "Shall we kill him?"

Wart pulled himself to his knees and looked at Bapoto. "I'm too weak to do it, and you've no reason, but I'm glad someone has made a start. What happened to you, dung beetle?"

"It's Whistle, all for Whistle. She's sick, dying, she wants Snap, she asks over and over, she wants Snap. I went to get her, but we were attacked, attacked by Fukizo."

Ash stepped forward into the rain and grabbed Bapoto by the arm. "Snap? She left Asili with *you*?"

"Please! Whistle is dying; she wants Snap." Bapoto didn't resist Ash. He stayed on his knees, eyes down, and Ash released him.

"They ambushed us, six or eight of them, huge men, a war party probably, about to attack Kura. Snap was beaten, probably killed. They hit me in the head, I was knocked out. When I woke up, they were gone. I need to get to Kura. We need to get ready, organize the warriors."

Granite rumbled in disbelief and Ash turned to look at him. At that moment, Bapoto leapt to his feet and crashed headlong back down the slope he had just climbed up. The men started, took a few steps after him, and then returned to the overhang. Wart spat after Bapoto, and the other men growled and bared their teeth.

Dika shook his head. "That man is a liar. Why would the Fukizo attack Snap? Why would they leave Bapoto alive? If Snap *is* dead, he probably did it. I bet Snap gave him that knock on the head herself."

"I don't think he would lie about Snap being dead," signed Granite. "If she turns up alive, everyone knows he's a liar."

Ash turned away from the others and stared into the rain. She couldn't be dead, he thought. I'd know it, I'd feel it. "Let's get back to Asili. If she got away, she probably went back home." Dika and Granite nodded and picked up their bundles, and Wart pulled himself to his feet with a grunt.

When the four men rounded the east end of the Asili ridge and started west along its base, the clouds lifted enough to show columns of smoke rising from both shelters. Ash's heart beat faster, but he forced himself to walk at Wart's pace. Dika boomed an Asili hoot. In a moment, Falcon came sliding down the path.

"Can you walk, Wart? Mother's blood! Come up to the men's shelter—the others are already there, and I've got something cooking." Ash caught Falcon's eye and raised his eyebrows. Falcon let the others pass and then turned to Ash. "Snap's not here."

"I know. We met Bapoto." He related their encounter with Bapoto, and Falcon shook his head.

"She hasn't come back."

When they had all squeezed into the men's shelter, Agama poked at the fire, deep in thought. "Bapoto's going to stir up the Kura against the Fukizo, and they probably have no idea what's happening."

Dika frowned. "I don't know what to make of it. The Fukizo attacking Bapoto would be understandable, but then what happened to Snap? If Bapoto is lying, what is he trying to do? There must be an easier way to push the Kura to go after the Fukizo."

"The Kura men will attack out of the blue," signed Falcon, "and probably slaughter them. There are only ten Fukizo, and at least forty Kura men."

Hawk leaned forward into the firelight. "It only seems fair to warn the Fukizo." Boy Baby, propped between Hawk's knees, crowed and tried to pull himself up by one of Hawk's ears.

"In fact, it only seems fair to try to help them," Agama added. "I'm not saying we should return to Fukizo with them; there is no place for us there. But I do think we should stand with them when Bapoto and the Kura attack."

Ash nodded. "I agree. I will stand with the Fukizo as well, but I also have to do what I can to find out what happened to Snap." A small choking sound escaped him, and he turned away from the fire.

Bubble hiccuped and dripped tears onto Girl Baby. "Surely she would have come back by now if she could."

The men agreed to set out to look for Snap as soon as it was light in the morning. Bubble and Hum were afraid to stay at Asili;

Hum was sure Bapoto would return with evil intentions, but only Wart was willing to miss the action.

"And we'll probably have to protect him," signed Hum with a upward jerk of her chin.

With his spear, Agama marked lines in the floor and described to each man which part of the area between Asili and Kura he would search. He didn't forget the Fukizo.

"When you find her, bring her back to Asili and send the Asili hoot along to the next man. That will be the sign for the rest of us to assemble *here*." He scratched a crude depiction of fig trees signifying the Fukizo camp. When the plans were complete, Hum and Wart went with Ash to sleep in Snap's shelter, while Bubble and Hawk stayed with the men.

While Hum tended Wart's injury with another poultice, Ash climbed to the ridgetop and surveyed the prospect. The rain had drizzled itself out, and a narrow band of orange appeared between the western horizon and the lower edge of the clouds. To the north, the only sign of Kura was the white ridgetop, picked out by the horizontal rays of the setting sun. The long shadow of Asili's ridge stretched east, touching the horizon, empty and black.

The travels of last summer, and the summer before, stretched out before him, long and hot and dusty. Always looking for something, he thought. This time it's Snap. Ash's eyes burned, and a gust of wind made him shiver. As he turned away and started down the path, a brown-and-white hyrax chittered her offspring back into a burrow.

Ash slept badly and awakened to a nearby hoot. He came out of the shelter with his bundle and his two best spears, blinked at the brilliance of the first rays of the sun, and found Dika, Falcon, Granite, and Agama waiting for him in the uwanda, similarly equipped. Hum and Wart followed him out of the shelter, and a puffy-eyed Bubble came down the path with both babies. Ash squealed a greeting and asked, "Where is Hawk?"

Bubble shook her head. "He packed a bundle and some spears and left as soon as it was gray light. He told me he will meet you, and he wishes you success finding Snap." Her hands wavered uncertainly.

Ash nodded, and the men headed east along the base of the ridge. At the end of the ridge, they fanned out over the rough terrain, all going more or less north, but by different routes. The ground was still wet, and the air chilly, but the storm had generated no new sinkholes or landslides. His eyes swept the ground, searching for broken branches, a spot of blood, any sign of Snap, but he saw nothing out of the ordinary.

She had to have come this way if she was going to Kura, he thought. There has to be something. Ash widened his sweeps and caught glimpses of Agama to the east and Dika to the west, but still no footprints at all, nothing. By midmorning, he was nearing Kura, and he circled the entire village looking for anything suggestive of an injured person, but again in vain. The sun still held its own and the Fukizo camp was no more than a half-day run, so Ash covered his assigned area once more, back and forth across the savanna, all the way to Asili, and then to Kura again. Finally, he turned west and angled northwest toward the Fukizo camp.

The stunningly clear day held. Steam rose into the sparkling air from Ash's sodden hair and left it standing on end in a strange parody of the style into which Snap had attempted to train it; he bristled into a fierce warrior of indeterminate ukoo.

The Fukizo had not moved their camp from the grove of fig trees where it had been on Ash's prior visit. When he neared the grove shortly after midday, he heard an Asili hoot and stopped to scan the vicinity. Dika appeared from a thicket of scrubby cork bush and approached Ash at a trot.

"Find anything?" asked Ash.

"Nothing. You?"

"Mud and standing water. How did the Fukizo greet you?"

"Well, they know nothing about any attack on Bapoto and Snap. None of them have been out of camp for days because of the storm, not even to hunt. At first, they assumed we were here because we wanted to return with them to Fukizo. Then, when we told them about Bapoto, a few were angry and wanted to go after him right away, but the others stopped them when we pointed out that all of the Kura men were probably about to attack them. They haven't decided what to do next. I came out to watch for you, so you wouldn't be attacked accidentally when you arrived."

"Thank you," Ash signed. "I think they will remember me, after they took care of my arm for all that time, but why don't you carry my spears, just in case?"

Dika grinned and took the spears.

Small shelters were scattered through the grove of trees, but it appeared to Ash the only fire was the one blazing in the center of the camp, around which Granite, Wart, Falcon, and Agama were squatting with the Fukizo men. A tall, fierce-looking Fukizo man, whom Ash recognized as Flint, was signing with two arms. As they approached, Dika hooted softly.

Flint stopped and waved them toward the fire. "Welcome, Ash. I am sorry you have lost your mate. I don't know what happened, but I'm sure it's Bapoto's fault. How is your arm?"

"Greetings, Flint. My arm is as good as new." Ash held up his right arm, and Flint inspected it.

"Excellent. Are you here to fight with us?"

"Yes. Whatever happened to Snap, it is Bapoto's fault. I will fight with you, for her sake."

Ash and Dika were offered water and food and found places in the circle of men. The debate that had been interrupted by Ash's arrival then continued. Flint and four others argued that the Fukizo should try to prepare some kind of fortification against the expected Kura attack, three were in favor of a preemptive attack on Kura, and one, seemingly the oldest of the men present, suggested that since the Kura men would outnumber them tremendously, they should return to Fukizo as soon as possible. The Asili men didn't express their opinions. Finally, by the time it was quite dark, all had agreed on a plan. The Fukizo invited the visitors to share their shelters. Ash was exhausted, but once again slept little.

The next morning was overcast, but fortunately, the rain held off all day. The Asili men helped Flint and the others dismantle their shelters, pack their goods and stored food, and move everything about ten long spear throws to a place where an irregular valley between two of the ubiquitous limestone ridges narrowed to a blind end, the steep slopes strewn with boulders that were each large enough to hide several men. Ash and Flint were designated scouts, and set out in the direction of Kura as silently and as invisibly as they could, while the rest of the men erected two shelters near the narrow end of the blind canyon, and hid their goods and the rest of the shelters in several small caves.

The scouts returned at sunset as the first large drops began to fall. The men had moved fires from the old camp to the shelters.

"The Kura men have left the village," Ash reported. "They are spread out, as if hunting on their own, but they are all traveling roughly northwest. It will soon be dark, and there will be no moon or stars tonight. Attacking in the dark, in the rain, seems too foolhardy even for Bapoto. I think they will bivouac and attack at dawn."

Flint nodded. "We will bivouac as well. Two men will tend the fires in the shelters, and the rest of us will take our places for the attack."

Granite and one of the Fukizo volunteered to stay in the shelters and make them appear occupied. They kept the fires burning vigorously and did their best to imitate the snores of a much larger group of men, while the rest of the men hid above them on the steep, boulder-strewn sides of the canyon and slept little. Near morning, the rain stopped and a few stars appeared. Ash and his allies made a hearty breakfast of some dried zebra before the slightest hint of gray had appeared in the sky.

As soon as it was light enough for an accurate spear shot, Ash heard the sound of an owl, the signal from the Fukizo watchers. The Kura were coming. Ash made sure his stone hand axe was strapped to his chest, held his best spear at the ready in his right hand and the second best in his left, ready to transfer for a second shot. Soon, Ash heard soft running footsteps, and he tensed as he waited for Flint's signal, an out-of-season cricket. When it came, Ash leapt to his feet and searched for Bapoto among the pack of thirty or so men running silently up the canyon floor twenty-five feet away. There he was! In the center of the pack, head down and choppers in both hands, he was easy to pick out by his cropped hair. Spurred by Ash's adrenaline, the spear flew fast and true and hit the man in the neck. He tripped several of the others as he fell, but as he did, Ash saw his face clearly and realized it was not Bapoto, but someone unfamiliar. In a heartbeat, Ash transferred his second spear to his right hand and searched for another short-haired head.

There! Another cropped head was among those still running, now only a long spear throw from the shelters. Ash took aim and threw, and the spear whistled through the chill air, passed cleanly behind Bapoto, and struck someone else in the foot. Another pileup occurred. The Fukizo spears had disturbed the organization of the Kura attack, and only a few men were still running toward the shelters. Bapoto slowed and fell back, helped some of those who had fallen to their feet, and waved his arms incoherently as he tried to organize a counterattack on the men above them.

Now, Ash saw spears fly from the open flaps of the shelters, and the two men closest to the shelters fell, one hit in the upper arm and the other in the leg. The men followed the butts of their spears out of the shelters, dashed up the slopes, and joined the rest of the Fukizo. The Kura men began to collect usable spears from the ground, but seemed confused about their next move. Bapoto, near the center of the mob, tried to divide them into two units, apparently with the intention of sending one up each canyon slope, but with little success. Ash thought the Kura men didn't seem to realize the Fukizo were focused only on Bapoto.

If the Fukizo had taken advantage of the Kura confusion to disable as many of the Kura men as they could, they might have overcome their numerical disadvantage, but their attack wasn't fueled by hatred of the Kura. A single purpose united them, and all but one of the Kura attackers were merely in the way. Ash joined the other men on his side of the valley as they clustered above Bapoto, ready to charge down the slope at their target. Another group formed on the opposite slope, and at another signal from Flint, both groups hurtled downward in tight alignment directed at Bapoto.

The two Fukizo units splintered the Kura formations. As Ash reached the bottom of the slope, he lost sight of Bapoto, but his momentum carried him through the bulk of the Kura men as he shouldered most of them aside. He swung his chopper at random, occasionally connecting with something or someone, but he paid no attention to anything except locating Bapoto. Kura, Fukizo, and Asili hair were everywhere, but Ash saw no one with Bapoto's cropped hair, and then he burst through the other side of the fray and found himself blasting up the opposite slope, alone. He turned again, high enough to see what was happening, and his heart sank.

The valley was filled with swinging fists, some holding weapons and some without, and most of the Fukizo were fighting at least two Kura each. Several of the Fukizo had fallen, which allowed the Kura to redouble their attack on the Fukizo still standing. Roars, screams, thuds, and snarls deafened Ash. He glanced down the valley and saw, below the main battle, five or six Kura men trotting downhill. Bapoto was apparently in the lead. Roaring, Ash leapt after them. His roar attracted the attention of Dika and several of the Fukizo, who shook off the Kura men they had been fighting and ran after Ash.

Shortly, Bapoto and the group of Kura men neared the place where the walls of the narrow canyon flared out into a wider valley. Ash and the other Fukizo were still well behind them, followed by several of the Kura who had given chase. Ash thought he and the others would have trouble catching Bapoto once he was able to run flat out in the open; nor would their attack be effective if they caught him after a sprint. However, just as Bapoto and his band reached the mouth of the canyon, two groups of seven or eight men each charged from the tumbled karst, one from each side of the valley. Ash recognized Panda Ya Mto hair, and he realized where Hawk had gone. The men around Bapoto scattered and allowed Ash, Dika, and several other Fukizo to catch up.

In the pandemonium, Ash once again lost sight of Bapoto. He fought his way out of the fracas and climbed a rock for a view of the battle. Up the valley, the remaining Kura men had finally realized their leader had departed and left the site of the initial attack to follow him down the valley. The Kura men who had been retreating with Bapoto were in full rout; some struggled to escape the Panda Ya Mto attackers, and some ran pell-mell toward Kura. They were in such disarray it was difficult for Ash to identify any individuals, much less pick out Bapoto, but soon it was clear that all the Kura men had left the valley to the Panda Ya Mto, Fukizo, and Asili.

Ash climbed down from his rock and tried to help those nearest him. He saw Dika not far away, his face covered with blood, apparently trying to find Agama. Hawk and Falcon were tending to a Panda Ya Mto man who was unable to walk. As Ash moved up the canyon toward the Fukizo shelters, he found that although nearly everyone was injured, most of the injuries didn't appear serious. Flint, who looked unhurt, located a supply of rabbit hides among the Fukizo stores and divided them with Ash to distribute to those who were bleeding the most. Ash found he had a gash behind his left ear that had bled over most of his back; he felt rather foolish as he tied one of the rabbit hides around his head, but decided he would rather look odd than bleed unnecessarily.

As Ash handed out hides, he came upon the body of Cascade, who had been injured and then nursed back to health by the Fukizo. Cascade's cousin Gorge sat nearby, keening, and from him, Ash learned how they had come to be in the battle. In the fall, Cascade and Gorge had found mates at Jiti. While hunting, they had met the Panda Ya Mto men en route to join the Fukizo defense and had joined them. Cascade had been struck in the back of the head with a large stone axe, and his body lay on the ground in the occasional sun. His eyes stared up at the broken clouds, and his body already felt cold in the morning chill. Ash helped Gorge wrap the body in a large hide borrowed from the Fukizo so Gorge could drag it to the cave of death.

The short-haired Kura man that Ash had hit in the neck with his first spear lay alone where he had fallen. As Ash recovered his spear, he felt pity for the man who had clearly been so taken by Bapoto's ideas that he had copied his strange hairstyle. A few inquiries led him to a relatively uninjured Panda Ya Mto man who had been distantly related to the dead Kura, and he kindly agreed to take the body of the short-haired man to the cave of death after he had finished attending to his friends.

Near the Fukizo shelters, Dika and Agama were bent over Granite, who lay on his back and took shallow, rapid, excruciating breaths. He didn't appear injured, except for a few nicks on his arms, but pointed to his lowest rib on his left and grimaced with pain. He accepted a little water from Agama and then they tried to help him sit up, but he lost consciousness. Ash borrowed a hide from the Fukizo, cut two strong saplings, and the three of them fashioned a stretcher for Granite, who awakened screaming as they moved him onto it. It was just past midday when Ash, Dika, Falcon, Hawk, and Agama started home with Granite once again unconscious on his stretcher.

CHAPTER 20

At *first* she thought the slightly less black patch of darkness above her head was imaginary; her desperate desire for warmth and light was finally causing her to invent morning inside her head. Another eternity passed, and the patch above Snap was definitely leaden gray. Slowly, it lightened to slate, then silver, and finally brilliant, dazzling sapphire. Intermittent sprinkles had fallen through the cave opening during the night, but by morning, not a cloud appeared in the tiny circle of sky she could see. Her feet were completely numb, and pain stabbed her legs as they began to warm up. Hoots of an owl and the distant whoop of a hyena had arrived wrapped in the inky blackness of the coldest part of the night, along with the cresting of the water level and its slow retreat, but by the time sunlight filled the circle overhead, the water had receded to one side of the cave floor and the hyena had been silent for a long time.

The water bag was empty, so Snap drank a little of the brown water, chewed on one of her two remaining pieces of damp dried meat, and stamped around until her legs were warmer and less painful and her feet had begun to burn as the feeling returned to them. She was trapped and hungry, but there was water. Her feet hurt, but she was still alive, and there might be some way to get out. While she judged the potential of every piece of rubbish in the cave, she made a tiny bit of meat last as long as possible by chewing it into paste.

The debris mound under the cave opening was unstable; it shifted as she climbed over it. Carefully chosen fragments of wood and rock made it steadier and able to support larger rocks. Moving the biggest pieces of debris required inclines, which she made from soil deposited in the lower parts of the cave by the occasional stream. The work was exhausting; her fingernails were soon torn and bleeding and her back and arms ached. As the day went on, a bit of direct sun came into the opening above her and shone down on the pyramid that was growing there. The water receded from the cave floor until only a small stream passed through it along one wall. The slightly sulfurous water nauseated Snap, but she was thirsty enough to drink it anyway. By the time the cave opening had begun to grow dark for the second time, the top of the mound under it was several feet higher, and she was shivering with exhaustion. When it was too dark to work on the pyramid, she wedged herself into a niche in one wall with a piece of damp, rotting wood to sit on. She made the last fragment of dried meat last until she fell asleep.

She woke in cold, damp darkness, so black she pressed her hands to her face to make sure nothing shrouded her eyes. Something small skittered across the floor—a rat? Something hard rolled down the embankment above the cave, crunched onto her pyramid, bounced, and chattered across the floor. A hyena whooped nearby, a hunting scream, then something sniffed at the edge of the cave opening. Still as a stone, she breathed so shallowly she couldn't even hear herself. Where had she left Meerkat's spear? Was it near enough to reach without making a sound? The night crawled on; the hyena seemed to depart. She may have slept. When a faint circle of dim light appeared at the top of the cave again, every muscle was stiff, and it was some time before she could loosen the cramps in her legs.

The day was overcast, and the cave remained dank and chilly. Snap worked steadily fitting rocks and broken wood into the pyramid. Soon, she had used all the loose debris and started to dig up imbedded pieces of limestone and partly buried logs. This was slow work. She had avoided using the human bones at first, but it soon became clear to her that the arm and leg bones would stabilize the structure, and she incorporated them as well.

The pyramid grew. As the apex rose, it required a wider and wider base, and needed more and more material. She dug everywhere with the strongest stick she could find, and added every rock, every animal bone, and every bit of wood to the mound. The cave floor was riddled with her excavations, and finally there was no more debris to be found. Everywhere she dug, she found only a thin layer of soil and then solid limestone. Her pyramid was as big as it was going to get.

The light of the third day in the cave waned. Snap stood on the top of her handiwork and felt the roof of the cave and the smooth walls of the cave opening with her hands. Without handholds in the limestone, and the top of the opening two feet beyond her reach, she couldn't pull herself up. Hungry and frustrated, she began to cry. As the last light faded from the cave, she wedged herself back into the niche, spear in hand. Hunger burned inside her and somewhere, water began to drip . . . drip . . . drip.

This night, like the others, seemed interminable, but it was not filled with rats' footsteps and hyenas' breathing. The darkness closed in, thick and impenetrable. No fish, no scuffling rodents, no whooping hyenas—nothing alive made a sound. Only the steady drip . . . drip . . . drip filled the darkness, filled her ears and her mind and her consciousness. Nothing else existed, no mound of debris and rock, no spear with the tiny meerkat etched into it, no sulfurous brown water, only the drip . . . drip . . . drip.

I am alive, she thought. I pinch my arm, it hurts. I am alive. The cave floor is cold, the air smells of ancient fish and rotting leaves. I am alive. But there was nothing to fill the endless wait for the next drip, the wait . . . and . . . the . . . drip.

She began to scream. She screamed and screamed; her throat was raw, surely it was bleeding, and the drip . . . drip . . . drip . . . went on and on and on. The screams wore out, and sobs replaced them, somebody else's sobs, who was it? Somebody was wailing, wailing, wailing.

Light. She must have slept—it was daylight. Snap climbed to the top of the mound again and stared at the two vertical feet that imprisoned her. She had not put Meerkat's spear in the mound;

in her mind, it kept the rats and hyena at bay. Now, she took the spear to the top of the mound and jabbed experimentally at the side of the cave opening. A tiny dent in the limestone appeared. Could this work?

Snap stabbed feverishly with the spear—a handhold appeared. The sharp wooden point wore down to nothing. She found a fist-size rock that seemed harder than the limestone, wedged it into a sturdy branch, and gouged several more handholds in the limestone. She couldn't reach any higher, so all were near the lower edge of the opening, but they were a start. Around midday, the sun made an appearance at the opening, and Snap decided it was time to try. Without food, she knew she would not get any stronger than she was, so she drank from the stream and planned her assault.

First, she climbed to the top of the pyramid and threw out the things she wanted to take with her: Meerkat's spear, her water bag, and the empty sling. Snap knew her arms were strong; she could dig kinanas faster than any woman in Kura. She wedged her fingers into two of the newly gouged handholds and lifted herself into the cave opening. She tried to shift one hand to the next highest handhold, but her fingers slipped from the first one, and she fell onto the summit of the pyramid and rolled partway down the mound.

She rested and tried again. A handhold for the right hand, another for the left, pull up, curl until the feet touch the opposite side—almost there. Swing again—almost there! Finally, she got her feet wedged against one side of the opening, her back jammed into the other. A sharp rock tore into her back, but she pushed hard with her feet and moved one hand higher, then the other. Press with the arms, move the back up, press again, move one foot. Like a caterpillar, she scooted upward, one limb at a time. Finally, she reached the upper edge of the hole with one hand and one foot. With a tremendous effort, she pushed off with the other two limbs and pulled herself over the edge, where she lay, facedown, gasping for breath.

She felt a few drops of rain hit her back; the sun that had encouraged her earlier was gone. Shortly, she raised her head and looked around. There was the sling, the water bag, the spear. In an instant, the pain in her fingers and arms and back vanished and Snap leapt to her feet, whooping and hooting. She swept up her things and climbed the nearest rocky outcrop to get her bearings. No longer hidden by foggy downpour, an oddly shaped tree growing on a distinctive ridge told her immediately that she was far to the east of the route from Asili to Kura.

Her brow furrowed and she chewed on a torn fingernail. Which way now? Does Whistle need me? Is she dying, or dead? Has Ash gotten Bubble and the others to Asili? Is he waiting there, or out looking for me? Where is Bapoto? A cold breeze whispered in a thicket, and she cast around nervously for possible hiding places.

Raindrops struck her face. Without a conscious decision, she found herself loping southeastward toward Asili. Was there food for Bubble and the other visitors? Firewood? Pain in her battered muscles and torn hands and feet pushed her on, a vision of food and a fire lay in front of her, and suspicious sounds seemed to follow behind. She tightened her hold on the blunted spear. Bapoto probably lied about Whistle, she told herself. She probably knows nothing about this. Eventually, the sun made a brief appearance in the gap between the clouds and the horizon and Snap sped up.

She began hooting well before anyone could possibly have heard her. When she reached the spring below her shelter, Hum ducked under the door flap, hooted, and waved her left arm incoherently. Snap's hands and feet scrabbled for purchase on the steep path to the shelter, her muscles screamed, her breath came in agonizing gasps. At the edge of the uwanda, she fell onto Hum's neck and sobbed. Hum patted Snap's back with her good arm and then backed up enough to sign to her.

"Mother's blood, you look terrible! Drink, and come inside. I have a couple of hyraxes on the fire."

Snap's hands wavered in the air; words seemed beyond them. Hum put her arm around her and led her into the shelter. Snap fell to her knees. The floor mat was warm and dry—she pressed her face against it, filled her nostrils with dry grass, Ash's sweat, Baby's accidents. She rolled over and stared at the smoke hole— wisps swirled around it and through it and disappeared into the overcast. Another smell—the meat roasting—made her drool down her front.

Hum offered her a handful of dried marulas. "The hyrax is almost ready; that'll hold you until it's done. I want to know what became of you, but it can wait until you're up to it. I'm going to get Bubble and the babies. Wart's not very well, but he can tell you what's been happening." She waved at the back of the shelter where an unhappy-looking Wart crouched on hands and knees, covered with sleeping hides.

Snap crammed all the fruit into her mouth. "Where is Ash?"

"The other men have gone to the Fukizo camp. It's a long story, and I'll tell it when I get back."

Snap lay by the fire, eyes closed, warmth soaking into her muscles. Presently, she sat up and drank from her water bag. Wart shifted from one uncomfortable-looking position to another. "Bapoto told us you were dead."

"Pretty close. He tried to kill me. How are you, Wart?"

He shrugged and tried another position. Hum and Bubble ducked into the shelter, each carrying one of the babies. Both of the women gurgled relief and Bubble put down a stone crock that smelled of dried wildebeest, fermented amaranth, and honey. Bubble's babies were both awake; they were happy to be put down on a sleeping hide where they prodded each other, squealed, and tried to get up on their hands and knees.

A water gourd was passed around while Snap told Hum and Bubble what had happened when she and Bapoto left Asili in the storm. When she repeated Bapoto's words as he stood over the cave mouth, Wart growled and spat. "Murderer. Not a very good one, but a murderer all the same."

The onlookers clicked their interest and barked astonishment at Snap's story as if they were watching a fireside tale, and by the time she was finished, her ordeal already seemed less real, more distant, like the adventure of a long-ago Mother. At the end, she looked around the shelter at the others.

"Bapoto said that Whistle was dying. He's a lying snake, but when she was here, she was worried about this birth going wrong. She might really be ill. I need to go to Kura, and I'd rather not go alone. When will Ash and the other men be back? What's been happening?"

Bubble knelt up and started in. "Well, Hawk, Agama, and I got back here with the babies not long after you had left with Bapoto. I'm surprised we didn't meet you, but the storm was terrible. The others did meet Bapoto. He had a cut on his head and told them you two had been attacked by the Fukizo. He told them you were dead."

Hum jumped to her knees as well. "We didn't believe it, of course."

"It sounded like Bapoto was raising a war party to go after the Fukizo, so the other men went off to warn them, and maybe to help them."

Snap looked at Hum's swollen cut and at Wart, who twisted uncomfortably under the sleeping hide. Her jaw clenched, and her scrapes and aches throbbed. Ash gone to help the Fukizo fight the Kura? Snap shook her head.

"That meat looks done," she signed. "What do you think, Hum?"

Hum wiggled one of the tiny legs to see if it felt loose, and then removed the two roasted hyraxes from the fire. She divided the meat and Bubble's concoction, offering Snap more than her share. She accepted with a guilty glance at Bubble and her babies.

Wart pulled himself into a sort of half-crouch and shoveled in his food as fast as he could swallow. Snap could see that one of his testicles was black and swollen to the size of two fists. She felt sick and kept her eyes elsewhere until he finished eating and lowered himself carefully on one side, covered again with the sleeping hide.

Wart turned to Snap. "We don't know anything about Whistle, but you can't go to Kura alone, and none of us is in any shape to go along in case Bapoto attacks again."

She shook her head. "What's happening to the others? When will they be back?"

Bubble freed a hand to answer. "This morning, a big band of Panda Ya Mto passed by, and Hawk was with them. He climbed up here and told us the Panda Ya Mto were going to help the Fukizo as well."

Snap raised her eyebrows. "Was Thump there?"

"I couldn't tell."

The fire burned low. Dusk filled the corners of the shelter, and Snap shivered. Bubble got ready to return to the other shelter, and Hum offered to carry one of the babies. By the time she returned, Snap had rolled herself up in her sleeping hide and was snoring softly. She felt she had barely dropped off when a distant Asili hoot woke her again. Hum was already ducking under the door flap as Snap disentangled herself from her hide. Outside, the rising full moon shone on several figures climbing the path. Three carried a heavy-looking, makeshift stretcher, and two more trailed some distance behind. She returned the hoot and directed another up the ridge to Bubble. As she followed Hum down the path, she recognized Ash, Hawk, and Falcon carrying Granite's stretcher. Some distance behind, Dika helped Agama as he struggled to climb the path.

Ash had one of the front poles. When he recognized Snap, he gurgled relief that she could hear two spear throws away, and squealed fervent greetings. Her own exhaustion vanished as she scrambled down to meet them, seized Ash briefly but enthusiastically around the middle, and then took the fourth stretcher pole from Hawk, who had been carrying two. Unable to sign, they carried the stretcher up to the men's shelter and lowered it gently to the floor. Ash and Snap knelt next to Granite's feet, but neither looked at the injured man.

"Bapoto said you were dead."

"Nearly right, if he'd had his way."

She took Ash's hand and held it to her face; dust, and blood, and Ash filled her nostrils, and a sound somewhere between a gasp and sob escaped her. He pressed his cheek into her hair and she heard a deep indrawn breath. Then they turned back to Granite. Bubble had arranged a mat and sleeping hide next to the fire, and the others moved Granite off the stretcher. He grunted and winced, but seemed unaware that he was home. The women offered the men the remains of their dinner, and while they ate, Snap and Bubble carried water to the men's shelter. As they were returning with their last load, Girl Baby woke up, and then Boy Baby. Bubble turned to Snap.

"Can I take them to your shelter to get out of the way?"

Snap nodded and gestured her out the door. Bubble carried the babies, and Hawk went along with arms full of hides and other necessaries. When they were gone, the others attended to the injuries. Granite lay on his back, eyes closed, his breathing raspy and irregular. Falcon and Snap cleaned the wounds on Granite's arms, but they were minor and clearly not causing his agony.

"There's something wrong inside," he signed woodenly to Snap. "It hurts him there." Falcon pointed at Granite's left side. After Granite's arms were tended, Falcon sat nearby with a piece of an old, soft mat soaked in water. Occasionally, he held the wet mat to Granite's cracked lips, and he sucked at it.

Agama had a messy laceration on the front of his thigh. Hum and Dika settled him on his sleeping hide and started to clean him up, but he pushed Hum's hands away. "Just Dika, please." Hum nodded sympathetically and moved around to work on Dika's head while he worked on Agama.

Snap unwrapped Ash's head and looked at his injury. "Tell me what happened."

"It's nothing. I didn't even feel it when it happened," he signed, but then went on to give her a brief account of the last three days while Snap washed the blood from his hair with water from a large gourd and cleaned the wound with her tongue. He growled a bit when she pulled the wound together and wrapped it in a clean, soft rabbit hide.

She watched his words with interest, hummed her approval of their decision to help the Fukizo, and frowned her disappointment at Bapoto's escape.

"Did you see my brother?" she asked. "Was Thump there?"

"I don't think I've ever met him."

"And Whistle? Have you heard any news of her? Is she really dying?"

He shrugged and turned up empty palms as if to display his lack of information. "Now, tell me what happened to you."

Snap repeated the story she had told Hum, Wart, and Bubble. This time was a bit more distant from the reality, a little easier than the first retelling. Ash was a good listener. He stroked her foot while she signed, growled at Bapoto's parting words, keened when she found Meerkat's spear, hummed at her ingenuity, and gave a final gurgle at her clever escape. At the end, she went back to Granite's side and squatted next to Falcon. She touched Granite's hand and crooned as if to calm a colicky baby. Granite's face relaxed.

"Can we help him?" asked Ash.

Falcon shook his head. "I don't think there's anything to do except give him water and wait."

Dika finished cleaning Agama's leg and tied a clean rabbit hide around it.

"I can't squat properly with this thing," Agama signed. "I'm going to have to sit on my poor behind until it heals."

Dika chuckled. "Good thing you have plenty of behind to spare." Agama threw a small piece of dried baobab at Dika. It bounced off his nose, and he gave Agama a rather bleak smile.

A rain shower passed sometime during the night. Granite's breathing grew louder, more raspy, and he sucked at the wet mat. A mouse investigated the door flap. His breathing became softer. An owl hooted; another answered. The fire burned down, and Snap stirred it up again. The raspy breathing stopped—Snap held her own breath—it started again, fast and shallow. Ash brought in wood. Falcon held the wet mat to Granite's lips, but he didn't respond. Now the rasping was gone; Falcon held his ear to Granite's face—still breathing. A thin, gray light began to seep in around the door flap, and Snap went out to get water.

Halfway back from the spring, she heard Falcon roar like the white rhinoceros that had charged her. She pushed against the door flap and stepped in. Falcon lay over Granite, and the roof hides vibrated with his grief. His body shook as the bellow became a convulsive sob. Dika and Agama sat together near the rear wall, arms around each other, silent. Snap thought they were both biting their tongues, as if they were afraid any sound would become a howl like Falcon's.

Without a word, she put down the water and began to keen softly. While Ash knelt next to Falcon and patted his back, Snap touched the hands of Falcon, Dika, and Agama in turn. She caught Ash's glance, gave a brief nod toward the door, and they shuffled out. The sharp dawn breeze stung her eyes, and she realized how little she had slept in the five nights since Hum had arrived at Asili. Careful not to wake Bubble's babies, they crept into Snap's shelter, crawled into sleeping hides, and slept. Around midday, Snap woke to find Bubble's family had arisen and departed. Dika was at the door flap, and wanted Ash to help take Granite's body to the new death cave.

The body was tied into Granite's sleeping hide and fastened to a long pole, in the fashion of the Fukizo. As Falcon, Ash, Hawk, and Dika hoisted the pole and started down the path to the new death cave, Snap found herself wondering which end of the hide held Granite's sturdy shoulders and wide brown eyes. She pressed her fingers to the inner corners of her eyes and focused instead on Bubble's oblivious babies, who were tied front and back to their mother and trying to reach around her. When the men returned with the pole and empty hide, Snap lay curled on her shelter mat, her eyes on the fire. Ash said nothing about Baby's body, and she didn't ask.

By the next morning, Snap's aches were familiar and dull, her exhaustion almost ordinary. Without a word, she carried water, collected wood, and helped the injured tend their wounds. The others were just as taut and preoccupied, and only Hum remarked on the weather, pointed out signs of animals, and tried to entertain the babies. A few meals had not yet filled Snap's empty belly, and hunger drove her to make an impressive bed of coals and assemble ingredients for Dew's winter stew. By evening, the smell in her shelter had attracted all the others. They exchanged only a few words as they squatted in a circle, smacking their lips.

Absent their usual raucous mischief, Dika and Agama occupied a corner, grooming each other solemnly. Falcon chewed on his knuckles, eyes unfocused and almost as empty as Granite's had been when they tied the hide over his face. Bubble and Hawk each tried to distract a cranky baby, and Hum helped Wart make a poultice for his wound.

Bubble caught Snap's eye. "Tell us the story of the cave again. Some of us haven't heard the details."

Snap shook her head, but the others nodded and Ash put on a wide-eyed, pleading look that made her smile and begin at once. Soon, a storytelling atmosphere crept into the shelter, and the audience responded to her tale with tongue clicking, finger snapping, and hissing at the appropriate times. When she told of returning to Asili after escaping the cave, she frowned and paused before going on.

"What of Whistle? Bapoto is a liar, but he may use the truth for his own purposes. Whistle was worried about the next birth when she visited here, and she didn't look as strong as she usually does. She may be dead or dying, as he said."

Bubble snorted. "Let Bapoto look after her."

Snap frowned. "She has betrayed me, but she is the Mother of Kura, and she has to know what Bapoto has done. How can she lead her people properly?" She waved at Dika. "You know what he did to your mother's ukoo. I know what he did to Meerkat, and what he tried to do to me. He could destroy the Kura as well."

Ash shook his head. "He has tried to kill you already. I don't think Whistle could stop him, even if he did it in front of the whole ukoo."

"I can outrun every man in Kura, Ash. Whistle may not believe what I have to tell her, but she has to have the truth from me. I need to go."

Agama growled softly, Dika clenched his jaw, and even Falcon looked worried. Hum patted Snap's knee. "If Whistle is dead or dying, there is nothing you can say that will make her better. We are all tired, hungry, and hurt. We must do what we can here, for Asili."

Snap nodded miserably. "For Asili." The coals over the winter stew had burned down. She opened a corner of the packet and tasted a bit of meat. "Time to eat."

As soon as the stew was eaten, contagious yawns passed from person to person. Agama invited Bubble and Hawk to sleep in their shelter, and Hum and Wart settled down in Snap's. All was quiet when Snap made a last visit to the latrine pit. Partway back, she met Falcon, who had apparently been looking for her.

"I will come with you to Kura. They didn't believe Hum when she told them what Bapoto did to the Fukizo, but I saw him do it. They must believe me." Falcon's empty eyes now had a spark of life in them. Snap shook her head.

"No. I can't let you do that. They won't make a distinction between Fukizo and Asili; they would kill you on sight."

"Not if I'm with you. You may be exiled, but you are the first daughter of their Mother. They have respected you and heeded you too long to attack your companion without warning." Snap wasn't at all sure he was right about that, but the idea of bringing someone who could testify to Bapoto's history seemed likely to bolster her story in Whistle's eyes.

In the end, she agreed. "All right. But Ash will plant himself in my way like a stubborn water buffalo if he knows. Can you meet me here after everyone is asleep? The moon will be up soon, and it's still nearly full; we can get to Kura well before dawn. We'll find Whistle when the sun rises."

Jaw set, Falcon nodded and turned back up the path to the men's shelter.

The moon was rising above the mungomu trees to the east when Snap returned carrying a sling, a water bag, and Meerkat's spear. Falcon was waiting. With a fierce grimace, he thrust his spear into the air and signed, "Let's go."

She was jittery, and every scuffling rodent, every bat moving through her peripheral vision startled her. Would Whistle listen to them? Would she protect Falcon? Would she protect her daughter? Was she even alive? Snap's feet found the path to Kura without conscious direction, but her thoughts wandered far afield; disconnected memories and fears crowded her brain. Her ragged, loved-to-death rabbit hide. Sitting on the stream bank with Whistle, remembering Meerkat. Bapoto's foot on her neck. Whistle's tears spilling down her pregnant belly.

Speechless, Falcon plodded on with his hands balled into fists. Snap caught a glimpse of him as she walked and tried to compare his life and his losses with hers, but couldn't. Was losing a mate like losing a baby? Was separation from one's ukoo because of believing differently better or worse than separation because of mating differently? She had no idea. The night was cool but clear, and a brisk walk kept Snap warm enough. The moon was well past the zenith when they reached a grove of mpingo trees not far from Kura and crawled into a thicket to wait for the dawn.

When it was light, Snap led Falcon to the place where the Kura stream widened and slowed, where she had once sat with Whistle and remembered Meerkat. She didn't want to confront a watcher, and she knew Whistle liked to visit the stream often when she was pregnant to rinse the dust from her hands and hair and cool her swollen feet in the water, so she proposed they wait in a clump of bushes for Whistle or anyone who might be willing to fetch her. Soon they had hidden themselves where they could see the path and the stream, but were nearly invisible themselves.

A few people came to the stream for water, but none Snap trusted to take a message to Whistle. Near midmorning, she saw a clearly pregnant figure approaching the stream. When she was convinced the figure was Whistle, she signed to Falcon to remain hidden and went forward to meet her.

Whistle was startled, but she recognized Snap and gurgled relief. With her swollen feet and large belly, she moved slowly, but she wrapped her arms around Snap as if she had last seen her the previous day. Snap breathed in her mother's smell, and she knew, for an instant, that Whistle would heed her. The older woman stared into her daughter's face and signed, "Bapoto said the Fukizo killed you."

"He was mistaken. *Bapoto* tried to kill me, but he didn't manage it."

"What!" Whistle used a rude sign Snap had never seen her make. "What do you mean?"

"Look, that's why I'm here. I want to tell you what happened to me. Come and sit down, put your feet in the water, and I'll tell you everything." Snap led Whistle to the water and helped lower her unsteadily to the bank. She told her mother her story, from leaving Kura to Baby's birth, Ash's return with the four Fukizo men, Baby's death, and Bapoto's lie about Whistle's illness. She repeated Bapoto's words when he pushed her into the cave, and described finding Meerkat's bones and spear. Whistle took the spear from her daughter and examined it. The tiny meerkat scratched into the shaft was still clearly visible, although the point was badly blunted. Her face crumpled, and she keened briefly.

"I know this one. It was his best spear that last fall."

Snap went on, making her escape from the cave sound considerably easier than it had been. Finally, she stroked Whistle's hand and decided to trust her with Falcon. "I brought someone else with me, a man named Falcon. He has a story that you should see as well. He was a Fukizo, but lives now in the men's shelter at Asili. Bapoto was bonded in the Fukizo tribe before he came to Kura, and Falcon knows how he came to leave them. Please attend to him. He means no harm to you or to any of the Kura."

Whistle stiffened and examined her daughter's face for several long moments before she replied. "I will see Falcon, if you vouch for him." At that, Snap waved at Falcon, who had been able to see most of their conversation from the bush. He stood up and made his way out of the thicket in which they had waited. Snap was so used to his appearance that she no longer noticed it, but now she saw him as Whistle would, tall and strikingly handsome, with his hair groomed carefully into the style they had invented for Asili. She heard Whistle's intake of breath, and realized that her mother imagined Snap had bonded with Falcon. She nearly laughed.

"I am still bonded with Ash. Falcon is with me today because he knows firsthand of Bapoto's previous dealings with the Fukizo."

Whistle nodded and stood to welcome Falcon. He greeted her ceremoniously, and then Whistle sat back down and put her feet into the water again. "We needn't be formal, Falcon. Please tell me your story."

Falcon plunged into the tale of Bapoto and the Fukizo. Whistle watched politely at first, and then with growing anger and distress. By the time he had finished with the story of the recent battle, from the point of view of the Asili rather than the Kura, Whistle looked as if she were ready to burst. She jumped to her feet and sprayed the others with water, as vigorous as the mother of Snap's childhood memories.

"Sorry about the water! Will both of you come with me now and tell your stories again? I will call everyone to the great uwanda now. The Kura must see this, and they must believe it."

Snap felt a surge of relief. She still might be attacked, but at least her mother believed her. At least her mother would no longer be taken in by Bapoto's lies. The entire village might attack them, she might never see Ash again, but Whistle's trust made it possible for her to master her fear, and she nodded. Falcon, now a bit pale around the lips, nodded as well. Whistle turned and charged up the slope toward the great uwanda, Snap and Falcon on her heels.

As Whistle reached the nearest shelters, she called the Kura with thunderous hoots, and people dropped their work and followed her, looking at Snap and Falcon with suspicion. Snap walked as erectly as possible and tried to keep her face calm and dignified. She pulled Falcon forward and placed him between herself and Whistle. "Keep your eyes open," she signed to him, and he nodded again.

By the time they reached the great uwanda, it was already filling with people. Snap looked over the crowd; Bapoto stood at the eastern edge of the uwanda, arms folded, a spear at the ready.

Peep and Warble were late, but herded their families right up to the front. Snap's other relatives and friends arranged themselves near Peep and Warble. When it seemed most people had found places in the uwanda, Whistle climbed onto the large flat rock and began signing with two-armed signs.

"My people! See the words of Falcon, an honorable man of Asili. He is under my protection, and no one will harm him while he is a guest of Kura." Whistle jumped down and held her hand out to Falcon to help him climb up. He looked still more pale now, thought Snap, but his back was straight and his gaze steady as he looked over the people of Kura.

Snap had never seen Falcon addressing anyone other than their small group, but she soon discovered he had a great talent for public discourse. He signed slowly and clearly and chose words all would understand, but with emotional depth even Chirp would have been hard-pressed to match. He drew his viewers into his tale in the way of the best storytellers, and soon, most of the Kura were engrossed in the faraway difficulties of an ukoo they had known only as foreign killers. Falcon held the gaze of one person at a time, pulled them in, and made them care about his people as he cared for them.

When he began to describe how the schism had nearly destroyed the Fukizo five springs ago, Bapoto growled, paced back and forth, and began to sign with both arms. "This man is a liar! He is one of the Fukizo killers, and he has made up this story for his own ends. He wants to trick you into accepting him so he can murder you in your sleep! Don't look at his words!"

Falcon went on as if Bapoto were invisible. A few of the Kura began to glance at Bapoto, and some of the men looked nervously back and forth between Bapoto and Falcon and picked up their spears. At last Falcon finished and climbed down from the rock. Whistle embraced him as if he were her son and climbed onto the rock again.

"Now see the words of Snap, my daughter, Mother of Asili. Bapoto has told us he saw her killed by the Fukizo. You know this woman as well as you know your own daughter. She may not believe as we do, but you know she is honest and trustworthy." Snap replaced her mother on the rock. With a stern expression, Whistle stood between Falcon and the main part of the crowd, and she glared at any of the men who seemed too threatening. None of them was brave enough, or stupid enough, to point a spear at the Mother of Kura.

Snap told them how the people at Asili had came to live there. She told them how Bapoto had asked her to come to Kura in the storm because Whistle was dying. Bapoto growled again and insulted Snap. He shook spears with both hands and tried to induce people to look at him instead of at Snap, but with little success. By the time she repeated the words that Bapoto had signed as he stood over the cave opening, he had begun to edge toward the eastern path that led away from the uwanda. Snap held up Meerkat's spear, which several people recognized, and some of the men growled. When she told how she had scrabbled out of the cave, people began to snap their fingers and click their tongues, and a few hooted loudly and rhythmically, as if they were watching a story at a festival. Some of the younger people in a corner under a tree started to dance.

Snap's story ended. With a bloodcurdling scream, Bapoto heaved one of his spears at Snap. She saw it out of the corner of her eye and dodged. Even so, it struck the side of her face and tore a gash from her left ear to the corner of her mouth. Although he had no weapon, Falcon leapt onto the speaking stone in front of Snap just as Bapoto launched his second spear. The blackwood weapon passed through Falcon's neck, leaving an arm's length of wood protruding from the point of entry and a hand's width from the exit. The bloody tip nearly touched Snap's cheek. For a moment he stared blankly, arms wide, and then fell sideways into Warble's lap.

There was bedlam. Women grabbed children and pulled them toward the edges of the uwanda. A thicket of spears shook in the air, and one or two flew in apparently random directions. Anger and fear rose from the crowd like a volcanic eruption. Snap clutched her face. Blood was pouring down her neck and chest, but the wound didn't feel deep. She stanched the flow with her hand and jumped from the speaking stone. Warble had pulled the spear from Falcon's neck and held him propped in her arms to ease his labored breathing. Snap swept up the discarded spear, dove into the jumble of elbows, screeches, and randomly aimed weapons, and pushed through to the east where she had last seen Bapoto.

People were spilling out of the uwanda down every path. Snap reached the edge of the clearing and leapt onto a battered stump, a sometime workbench for feasts. The crown of Bapoto's gray head was obvious among the scattering brown ones around him. She vaulted after him, dodging around howling children and avoiding a carelessly swung hammer, until she was clear of the crowd. Bapoto was fleeing east, out of spear range for Snap, but she readied the spear on her shoulder and sprinted downhill after him. Her breath came in great gasps, a cramp tore into her side, but she pushed her feet against the crumbling limestone with all the effort she could muster.

Bapoto was strong, but no match for Snap's young muscles. By the time he reached level ground and turned slightly south toward the Kijito, Snap had gained enough ground that she felt sure the spear would reach him. With a roar like a lioness, she drew back the spear and let fly at Bapoto's broad back. Her speed and the strength of her arm gave the weapon enough momentum to reach its target, but its encounter with Falcon had blunted it. It struck Bapoto between the shoulder blades and fell to the ground. He shuddered and broke stride as the spear struck, but recovered immediately and ran on.

Snap fell to her knees and covered her face with her hands. In a few moments, she had regained her breath. She pulled herself to her feet and trudged back to Kura, tears of frustration and grief tracking through the blood on her face. By the time she returned to the great uwanda, the chaos had resolved itself into a milling crowd of confused people. The women squatted among clusters of children, calming the ones who were crying, while the men stood watchfully near their mates, weapons in hand. As she neared the speaking stone, she saw Falcon's body lying next to Warble and her family, eyes closed, lifeless and still. Snap knelt on his other side and took one of the still-warm hands. Her tears dripped onto his arm and she wiped them off, one by one.

Whistle touched her shoulder gently. "Bapoto?"

Snap shook her head. "Gone."

Whistle climbed back onto the speaking stone and hooted for the crowd's attention.

"People of Kura! The ways of our mothers show us how to face trouble. When the herds move, when the weather changes, when the harvest doesn't come when it should, we remember the words of our mothers, repeated in our stories, and we survive.

Our traditions are the tree trunk of Kura, and they keep us strong and growing." Everyone was attending to Whistle now, and even Snap looked up.

"Soon, it will be time for the Naming, and we will celebrate as we have always done. Our men will hunt and trade, as they always do in the summer. Our women will harvest and prepare for another winter, as they always do. Kura will go on, according to the traditions of our mothers. If any of us choose to meet for hunt rituals, or healing, or funerals, there is no harm in that, but none of us will ever again claim to have special knowledge or privileges that allow him or her to destroy our traditions. Anyone who wishes to go with Bapoto may leave now, and good luck to you. We will not hunt you, nor will we hunt Bapoto, but neither he nor any who leave with him will be welcome here again, not ever."

One of the taller men who had been shaking his spear while Falcon spoke turned and strode out of the uwanda. A woman wailed and began to rock back and forth, but she didn't follow him. Snap patted Whistle's foot and indicated she wanted to climb up again. Whistle waved Snap onto the rock, and slid down herself. Snap stood up as straight as possible and ignored the tears that continued to streak her face.

"I am a daughter of Kura, but my path has led away from here, to a place as near as the Kijito, but as distant as the Great Water. I hold no ill will against you for your shunning last fall, but I'm not able to join you in your beliefs. Asili is my home, as it was Falcon's. My daughter was born there in my own shelter, and I belong to that place just as all of you belong here. Any of you are welcome to visit Asili, or to join us permanently if you feel more comfortable in the company of our beliefs. Kura will always be in my heart, and I hope I will be welcome to visit here."

A loud hum of approval rose into the air as Whistle helped Snap climb down from the stone.

The Kura dispersed with a good deal of conversation and many glances at Snap, who was squatting next to Falcon's body. Rustle and Swish joined their sister, and she put an arm around each and pulled them close. Swish wriggled around to face Snap and began to clean up the gash on her face, while Whistle went off to find a dragger. When she returned, Snap's siblings helped her tie Falcon's body into it and drag it to Whistle's uwanda.

Whistle had little dried fruit or meat left in her alcove, but spring greens had already become plentiful. While Swish finished cleaning Snap's wound, their mother collected a large platter of tiny amaranth seedlings pulled up by the roots. The four of them huddled together and ate while Snap told them what she knew of Falcon's life—his birth in Fukizo, how he came to Asili, the death of his mate. The listeners listened and ate and cast thoughtful glances at the long thin dragger. Whistle offered Snap a handful of nuts for her trip back to Asili, but Snap had seen the barren alcove, and she declined. Whistle made no mention of Snap's staying at Kura.

Snap decided to take the body to the Kura death cave, since it was nearer. She departed at midday, pulling Falcon's dragger along the easiest route, while Whistle, Rustle, and Swish boomed Kura hoots after her until she was out of sight. Snap's lack of sleep once again caught up with her, and she plodded like a browsing aardvark. In a daze, she was almost surprised when she reached the cave. It was just as it had been the last time—musty and quite empty. The body was stiff now, and she untied the hide and left him facing the rear wall. Snap's tears were exhausted, but she sat for a few moments keening outside the cave opening before she rolled up the dragger and trudged southward toward Asili.

She had not gone far when she saw Ash and Dika approaching from the direction of Kura. Her hoot made the two men break into a run, and in no time Ash scooped her into his arms and held on as if she might try to run away. When she pulled away to speak, he blinked furiously and seemed to have something in his eye, but Dika was able to tell her how they found her.

When Ash had woken that morning and found Snap missing, he had guessed where she had gone. He learned that Falcon was gone as well, and he and Dika set out for Kura. They arrived just after she had left. Whistle received them graciously and told them the story of Falcon's death and Bapoto's escape from Whistle. After a rest, they had followed her.

The three of them keened together for a few moments and then turned south with no further words. As the Asili ridge appeared in the distance, Snap noticed a morojwa tree on the eastern end of the ridge outlined against the gray sky, its leafless branches dead-looking and unmoving. The tree remained in sight for a long time, and as they neared the end of the ridge where they would turn west, she realized that the apparently dead branches of the tree were covered with tiny yellow flowers, just beginning to open. On one of the branches a rat investigated the buds and stuffed the most promising into his cheeks. She shivered slightly and sped up.

Ash and Dika hooted as they neared Asili. Hum appeared from Snap's shelter and returned the hoot. Bubble, carrying both babies in slings, Hawk, and Agama came out of the men's shelter and down the path to the smaller uwanda. Wart dragged himself through the door flap and knelt awkwardly near the fire ring. When she reached the small uwanda, Snap greeted each of them in turn. Somberly, she embraced Hum and Bubble and touched the fingertips of Wart, Hawk, Agama, and Dika. Finally, she nuzzled Ash and then climbed onto the low, flat-topped rock she used as a work surface. The others squatted around her, and she signed with two arms as if addressing a large crowd.

"Welcome home, people of Asili!"

AUTHOR'S NOTE

Daughter of Kura is set in southeastern Africa about a half million years ago. Its characters are human in the sense of being ancestors of modern humans but are another species—either *Homo erectus* or *Homo ergaster,* depending on which naming system one uses. Snap's world is based partly on the work of scientists—paleoanthropologists, evolutionary biologists, and evolutionary psychologists—and partly on speculation. The geologic features, technologies, and social system that form the structure of Snap's life are constructed from a combination of reasonably secure scientific facts, plausible theories, and wild (but not provably wrong) speculation.

Some of the technology used by the characters of *Daughter of Kura* is supported by archaeological finds, and some is speculative. Stone choppers, axes, hammers, and grinding stones have been dated from this time, but not stone-tipped spears or arrowheads. The remains of ancient hearths, where fires burned repeatedly in the same location over a long period of time, prove that people could control fire and that they stayed in one place for extended periods, but don't tell us when people learned to start fires. Thus, Snap's people must keep their fires burning or obtain fire from a lightning strike or another person. Making containers was an extremely important technological advance, because it made the collection and storage of food for later consumption practicable and because the ability to carry water made more distant travel possible. Unfortunately, wood, leather, and woven containers of that age have left no archaeological record, but their existence seems plausible, because the level of skill required to make the known stone tools is so advanced that those artisans must have been capable of making containers as well.

Details of the social structure of Snap's people have been constructed from those of several species, especially modern hunter-gatherer societies, baboons, and hyenas. Big, dangerous animals have to be either fairly solitary (orangutans) or have a complicated social structure to avoid killing one another regularly. Social structures don't fossilize, but since there are large animal bones from this time that seem to have been hunted and butchered by groups of people, most likely people were not solitary. Thus, Snap lives in a matriarchal, status-conscious society that is in some ways like modern nonagricultural groups, in other ways like baboons and hyenas, and in yet others distinctive.

Spotted hyenas inspired several aspects of Snap's society. Hyenas live in clans of about fifty and have a rigid, hereditary ranking system. Offspring acquire their rank from their mothers. Female offspring stay with their birth clan, and males are expelled at puberty. The expelled males must join other clans to find mates and are ranked lowest on joining the new group. Choosing mates is mostly controlled by the female hyenas. The males don't participate in raising the cubs. The related females in the clan keep their cubs together in a den, all nursing the brood fairly indiscriminately.

Snap's people are similar to the spotted hyenas in a number of ways. The Kura are more or less related, and very status-conscious, women. Children acquire their rank from their mothers. By puberty, children have acquired the necessary knowledge and skills needed by adults and assume an adult role at that time with no period of adolescence, like most animal and preagricultural human societies. Young men leave home at manhood to find a mate in another clan. Choosing a mate is mostly determined by the woman, and the man acquires her rank. The related women of each clan live closely together throughout the year, sharing child raising to some extent, while the men stay with the clan only for the winter and then spend transient summers hunting and trading.

The development of spoken language is difficult to pin down to a particular time. The human voice box is cartilage and doesn't fossilize, so it is impossible to say for sure whether Snap would have used a spoken language, a signed language, or only simple vocalizations like many other species. *Homo erectus* could control fire, manufacture complicated tools, and trade goods over great distances, and thus it is possible that humans have been capable of quite complex ideas for a very long time. Complex ideas probably lead to the development of language. As a result, Snap's people have a signed language not requiring a modern sort of voice box so as to fit whatever fossil evidence turns up.

The capabilities, appearance, and lifestyle of human ancestors are largely uncertain, so *Daughter of Kura* makes assumptions that are consistent with available information and fit the story best. Primeval religion, the earliest hint of art, each trait that makes us human started somewhere, and we can't help but wonder how. Imagine visiting the past in a floating time bubble. Here, one of your ancestors soothes her baby; she could be your sister. Over there, another captures a lizard and eats it; inconceivable. In the distance, two strangers greet each other and negotiate peace between their families; they could be two packs of wild dogs, or Germany and France. We have always been just the same, and unimaginably different.

ACKNOWLEDGMENTS

Thanks to my family and friends for tolerating my obsessions, to Ann Rittenberg for mining her slush pile, and to Trish Grader for gambling on an oddball. Comments from Mary Jones, Elaine Tietjen, and Karen Levin were crucial. Special thanks to the paleoanthropologist Thomas Plummer, without whom this book would never have been. To all unmentioned helpers, apologies and gratitude.

GLOSSARY

AGAMA: type of lizard

AMARANTH: edible green plant

ANNONA: fruit tree

ASILI (Swahili): home, origin, or ancestor

ASISHA (Swahili): to incite rebellion

BAMBARA: edible legume (grows underground)

BAOBAB: large tree with edible leaves and fruit

CARISSA: fruit tree

CHENGA: type of fish

DIKA: edible nut

EGUSI: edible seeds of a type of gourd

FUKIZO (Swahili): smoke, steam, vapor

FUU (Swahili): type of berry

GWARU: type of small edible bean

HIPPARION: extinct horse

HYRAX: short-tailed herbivorous mammal the size of a large rabbit

IMBE: type of fruit

JITI (Swahili): large tree

KAO (Swahili): dwelling

KIJITO (Swahili): small river

KILIMA (Swahili): hill

KINANA (Swahili): yam

KUNAZI (Swahili): type of fruit

KURA (Swahili): destiny, chance

MARULA: type of tree with edible fruit and nuts

MAVUE (Swahili): tall grass

MCHI (Swahili): pestle

MEDLAR: type of fruit tree

MOROJWA: type of fruit tree

MPINGO: flowering tree (also known as African blackwood)

MUNGOMU: type of nut tree

NERINA: South African flower

PANDA YA MTO (Swahili): river fork

SERVAL: medium-size African wildcat

SHAZIA (Swahili): large needle for mat making

UKOO (Swahili): clan

UNANASI (Swahili): plant fiber

UWANDA (Swahili): open area, village square